COOL
RUNNINGS

ALSO BY RICHARD HOYT

Decoys
30 For a Harry
The Manna Enzyme
Trotsky's Run
The Siskiyou Two-Step

COOL RUNNINGS

RICHARD HOYT

THE VIKING PRESS   NEW YORK

LIBRARY OF CONGRESS CATALOGING IN PUBLICATION DATA
Hoyt, Richard, 1941–
  Cool runnings.
  I. Title.
PS3558.O975C6 1984   813'.54   83-40228
ISBN 0-670-24050-8

Grateful acknowledgment is made to Hallnote Music for
permission to reprint lyrics from "Faster Horses," written by
Tom T. Hall. Copyright © 1975 by Hallnote Music.
International copyright secured. All rights reserved.
Used by permission.

Printed in the United States of America
Set in Aster

This book is for my mother, Nellie Allen Hoyt,
of Umatilla, Oregon.

The antinuclear group in this story, the Vrienden, is an invention of the author's imagination. *Vrienden* is the Dutch word for friends. It is pronounced "freenden." One friend is a Vriend. The Vrienden should not be confused with the American Friends Service Committee, the Friends of the Earth, or any other group with friend as part of its title.

TRAVELERS

1. *They called him Mad Marty Spivak. He was*

the pride of the Big Apple. He was the American record holder at both five thousand and ten thousand meters. He had beaten Kenyans; he had beaten much-fancied Englishmen; his all-white running shoes had put space between himself and masochistic Russians, between himself and determined Finns. Olympic gold, it was said, would be his.

Marty Spivak ran for the Big Apple Track Club. New Yorkers loved him—all five foot two inches of him, the whole one hundred and three pounds. There were those who said if Mad Marty shaved his arms and legs, he'd lose ten pounds. They had a point. Spivak was one of the hairiest human beings imaginable. He had black hair down his back and across his ribs. He apparently had hair all over his body except for his forehead and around his eyes. But it wasn't like he was a swimmer; the hair didn't make any difference running the five thousand.

Marty had been an abandoned baby. A city bureaucrat assigned him the surname Spivak out of the Manhattan telephone directory. No adoptive couples wanted such a hairy child, so he grew up in a series of foster homes. He went to City College. He lived in the Village and trained on pizza and beer. He was a city boy. Everybody claimed him. Jewish folks said, Well, he's circumcised, isn't he? He's Jewish and spider monkey. The Irish said he couldn't be Jewish; if he were Jewish, he'd spend all day in the library. The Italians said he couldn't be Irish; if he were Irish, he'd spend all day in a bar instead of training. So it went. The Puerto Ricans had their claim. Mad Marty was everyman's runner.

Spivak's training routine, much reported by the New York press, made him a city-wide curiosity. He trained in the streets. If he felt like it, he cruised north all the way to Harlem and the Bronx, his running shoes going pad, pad, pad on the cement. Stories of violence in Harlem didn't bother him. Mad Marty said he'd turn on the afterburners. Sometimes he ran east through Queens and on out onto Long Island.

Mad Marty liked to run Broadway from Wall Street to Central Park. He ran Broadway flat out, darting between yellow taxicabs like a Jets halfback. The police asked him several times to knock it off, but he ignored them. Tourists went home to recall how waiting in line for Broadway tickets at a Times Square vendor, they saw this hairy little figure sprinting through traffic and hubbub, grinning at bond salesmen and banking executives. One midtown Irish bar ran a pool to guess the month Mad Marty would be flattened.

On his return from his daily runs, Spivak cruised Greenwich Village because of all the crazy-looking women on the streets, and because he was a folk hero and knew it. Marty liked being a legend.

Of course, nobody as original as Marty Spivak was allowed to run in peace. The television people all wanted Marty on their morning talk shows so the folks in Grand Rapids and Gainesville could see what he looked like. NBC had in mind a slot between the Vice-President, who wanted to talk about his love of baseball, and a woman who exercised her pectorals to help American housewives have more impressive bosoms. Spivak wasn't interested. He was a runner, not a freak in a sideshow. If people wanted to see what he looked like, they could go to New York and hang out in the Village.

This curious attitude made him all the more desirable. A visiting Arab sheik, ensconced in the fabled Dakota apartment building on Seventy-second Street, let it be known one day that he would like to see Spivak cruising up Central Park West. He would pay, he said, for the privilege. Money was no problem.

Spivak replied in language so coarse as to be unprintable in a family newspaper, not even the *New York Post*. A reporter for the *News* deleted the expletives, but the message was clear.

The next morning folks gathered on Fifth Avenue on the opposite side of the park and waited. Spivak cruised up Fifth, grinning, fist clenched, thumb up in recognition of the applause. He was a New Yorker, Jewish maybe, maybe not. In any event, he told the *Village Voice* what the sheik could do with himself. The *Voice* let the expletives stand.

2.

The rise of the European environmental parties in the early 1980s was inspired by the success of the West German Greens. The Green party won its first seats in Hamburg municipal elections in 1982. By the spring of 1983, they had elected twenty-seven members to the West German parliament in Bonn.

The Greens were mostly young, born well after the Second World War. They didn't worry about the Soviets to the East; they wanted American missiles and nuclear warheads off European soil. They didn't worry about the Arabs and sources of energy for German industry; they wanted a halt to the spread of nuclear reactors. They wanted clean air and clear water.

Although the Greens were far outnumbered by the Social Democrats and the Christian Democrats, they were an inspiration to other Europeans. Soon there were Austrian Greens, and the environmental movement spread quickly throughout Europe and Scandinavia. Those seeking the greening of Europe had one thing in common. Lacking the deutsche marks, the francs, or the kroner necessary to win seats and influence policy, their members found new and ingenious ways of calling attention to environmental problems.

The Greens were not admitted to the back rooms of power where governments are negotiated and policy is made. First, the Greens knew, they had to get supporters. *Then* they would be admitted to the back rooms. The way to acquire supporters without a treasury was to get the word out—to be filmed, taped, written about.

It was a humbling experience for the Germans when the best idea, a stroke of inspiration for protesting the spread of nuclear power, came from Holland. The idea was that of Wim van der Elst, informal leader of the Vrienden, a group of Dutch pacifists based in Amsterdam.

When they weren't living on their canal boat, or *woonboot*, the Vrienden traveled Europe in a double-decker bus protesting missile installations and nuclear power plants. Unfortunately, van der Elst's idea was expensive—at least to the Vrienden. The Greens pledged every kind of support except money and waited to see what would happen. The Greens were the vanguard, the mother party. An outright grab would have been impolitic.

The Vrienden would have turned the project over to the Greens too, had it not been for a Vassar-educated Spanish woman, a widow who owned the Football Club Sevilla. Pilar Aguirre heard about the proposal from her daughter, María, who studied art at the Rijksmuseum in Amsterdam.

María Aguirre was at the Melkyweg that night because it was Wednesday and her boyfriend wanted to jam with his trumpet. It was the custom at the Melkyweg for aspiring performers to wait their turn at stage left. A musician's thirty minutes on stage with the band were measured by a large hourglass that hung from the ceiling on a rope. The spectators could tell by the hourglass how much more they had to endure or enjoy.

While María's boyfriend was on stage playing his trumpet—along with six frenzied bongo players, five saxophonists, three possessed drummers, and a young man in knee-high turquoise boots who rattled a tambourine—Maria overheard her neighbors discussing the Vrienden's startling proposal.

When a break came, she found out more.

All that was needed, she was told, was money.

The next day María wrote her mother a letter.

Pilar Aguirre was an intelligent, passionate woman. She read the letter once, twice, three times through. She concluded that the Virgin Mary had somehow intervened to cause her daughter to study art at the Rijksmuseum, and so be in a position to learn about this clever idea. She decided to drive to Amsterdam.

It was a lovely spring morning in Andalusia when Señora Aguirre got into her silver Porsche and headed up the Río Guadalquivir for Córdoba, Madrid, and points north. She was a fast driver. As she passed groves of olive trees and Spanish vineyards, she became angrier and angrier at the competition between the Soviets and the Americans that threatened all of Europe with nuclear terror.

Señora Aguirre was surprised at how long and narrow the *woonboot* was. She was welcomed into the tiny cabin with a big hug from María, who introduced her to a young Dutchman with long blond hair that flopped down over his eyes. The Dutchman wiped the hair back with his fingers and adjusted his rimless spectacles as María introduced each of the Vrienden.

"Mama, this is Wim van der Elst."

"I'm very pleased," Wim said. He bowed politely and shook Señora Aguirre's hand.

Señora Aguirre smiled. In Spain she would have gotten a kiss on both cheeks, a more satisfactory custom.

"María has told you about the idea?" Wim asked.

"Yes, she has."

"There is no danger, I assure you. It will be empty."

Pilar considered that.

"There have been plans published in American magazines. It can be done. The German Greens will help us."

"How large would it be?"

Van der Elst held his hands out in front of him. "About so big. The size of a fat baby or a big dog. It would have fins like a pub dart."

"That's not large at all!" Pilar was surprised.

"Somewhere between twelve and fifteen kilos if it were loaded, señora. It would need about five kilos of plutonium."

"For what strength?"

Wim cleaned the lens of his glasses with a soft cloth. "About the size of Nagasaki."

"An educational replica, this would be."

"Exactly, señora. No plutonium. We were thinking of covering it with tiny decals of the flags of all the nations of the world. And we want to have a transparent plastic duplicate so people can see inside."

"I can't give you the money unless I'm assured there is no danger."

"It's empty—harmless. There's no way we could arm it even if we wanted to. Where would we get the plutonium, señora? Where would we get the equipment to load it? It's safe, I assure you."

"I see," said Pilar.

"You could maybe steal it from a nuclear plant, but how? You'd have to be a professional—an insider, or somebody with access to construction plans."

Pilar closed her eyes and thought about the project. "How much do you need?"

"A lot of money, señora—as much as ten thousand U.S. dollars."

Pilar Aguirre handed her car keys to her daughter. "There is a valise in the trunk of my car, María, *por favor.*"

When María Aguirre returned with a valise bulging with money earned by the skills of Spanish soccer players, her mother rose and hugged each of the Vrienden, who had sat listening in awe to the conversation. She kissed them each on the forehead. "Be careful. Please be careful," she said.

Pilar Aguirre zoomed away. The Michelins of her Porsche went bu-bump, bu-bump, bu-bump on the brick street. The engine went uuu-dn, uuu-dn, uuu-dn as she shifted down for a stop sign.

3.

The last Japanese pilot of World War II was born in 1960 and didn't know how to fly an airplane. His name was Hideo Yasuda. He was the only son of Masahiro Yasuda, an executive of the Mitsubishi Corporation.

Masahiro was a devout man, a follower of Shinto. On a wall in the Yasuda home there was a small shrine to Masahiro's ancestors. There were pictures of Masahiro's parents, grandparents, and even his great-grandparents. The photograph of the latter was small and brown with age. There were trinkets and mementos on the shelf to remind Masahiro of his past, of the legacy of his ancestors. When guests came, Masahiro showed the male visitors the tiny pictures of his ancestors. He told a little story about each of them, their children, their accomplishments and honors.

On his fifth birthday, Hideo's father hoisted him up so he could see the shrine. His father explained the pictures to him. Hideo was too young to understand, but not too young to be impressed. Two of the figures in the picture, Hideo's grandparents, had died an awful death; he had come to know that much from eavesdropping on his father's conversations. When Masahiro explained his parents' death, his guests always looked solemnly at the tatami mat. As Hideo grew older and learned more about the world, bits and pieces of information, snatches of conversations, came to make sense. One day he understood.

Hideo was a homosexual. There was no curious or exotic reason for this; apparently it was in his genes. This was never discussed by the family, but it was understood. When he was fifteen, his mother found muscle-building magazines stashed under the tatami. She thought nothing of it. Hideo was interested in muscle building and had his own barbells. But when she found gay magazines from San Francisco, she knew the truth.

Yasuda read the novels of Yukio Mishima, who had also

been homosexual, and regretted that he had been too young to be part of Mishima's private army. He felt a great pride when Mishima committed seppuku and was then beheaded by a follower according to custom. Yasuda made a private shrine to Mishima. He framed a small photograph of Mishima and put it on a tiny shelf, just as his ancestors were on a slightly larger shelf in the next room.

Yasuda often thought about how it would be to commit seppuku. It was an honorable way to die. When he was a teenager, he often sat cross-legged, holding an imaginary knife poised at his body. He could do it, he knew. In his fantasies, he sat on a tatami, dressed in a handsome kimono, and plunged a neat, thin knife into his abdomen just below the sternum. In these dreams, he ripped down and out. His belly followed. If he had followers, they beheaded him as Mishima's followers had. If he was alone, he remained erect, his head up, a solitary figure.

Like Mishima, Yasuda wanted to return to the traditions of the samurai. He believed in the samurai ideals of beauty and loyalty. Yasuda was passionate by nature, a romantic. He dreamed of committing a magnificent act of honor.

Hideo told his father he wanted to travel. He wanted to study in the United States. The truth was, he wanted to find out for himself just why it was that the Americans had done what they did on August 9, 1945. He could understand what the Americans did on August 6, at Hiroshima. They had to make their point. But why the second bomb? Why? Yasuda had originally learned English so he could read the memoirs of Harry Truman and the other men who participated in the decision. He couldn't find an answer. As a matter of fact, the Nagasaki bomb was dropped on the authority of a commander in the Pacific, independent of Truman.

Yasuda wanted to find out about Nagasaki. His father wanted him to study at Harvard, but on his way to Cambridge he spent a weekend in New York. As nearly all visitors do, he went to Greenwich Village, and walked into a gay bar near the Oscar Wilde Memorial Bookstore at Christopher and Gay streets.

When Yasuda told his father that instead of going to Harvard he wanted to study business administration at New

York University, his father was supportive. He would have preferred Harvard for his son, but NYU was impressive too, and equally American. It was in New York. A degree from NYU would be respected in Japan.

Yasuda lived in the Village and took a liking to pasty-skinned round eyes. He walked into a gay bar wearing a leather jacket he had bought in Manila, and looked around with his hard black eyes. He had a moose-muscled neck. He didn't look much fun. Frail young men just went all aflutter.

Yasuda despised them. Standing straight up, their pathetic, anemic little pricks were hardly larger than cigarillos. Still, he violated them savagely, fucked them in the asshole. To Yasuda the American national leaders were, in a figurative sense, very much like the village gay boys: they debased their country with compliant, liberal gestures. Jimmy Carter had been among the worst—not blowing the Iranians off the map when they took over the American embassy in Teheran, allowing Fidel Castro to dump criminals and homosexuals on the United States. The Americans smiled benignly when the Japanese flooded the rich American market with their goods and effectively shielded their own market from American products. Even President Robert Lyle went along with that. The position of rump-up was as natural and congenial for Lyle as it had been for his predecessors.

In the end, Yasuda decided there ought to be some form of accounting, some retribution for years of accumulated American perversity. It seemed to Yasuda perfectly outrageous that any country could be allowed to go on being so stupid forever. The United States had gotten out of hand.

The question was, how to get his revenge? His father died when he was a senior and Hideo, having inherited a fortune, stayed on for graduate school.

Of course, the chemistry had gone wrong in Yasuda's brain. He made no attempt to hide his opinions, and eventually came to the attention of the New York City Police Department. His eccentricities were deemed sufficient to warrant his inclusion on the New York City "loon list." The loon list was the unofficial, cynical title of a register of psychopaths and screwballs maintained jointly by the FBI and NYPD.

When the President or a VIP visited Manhattan, the where-abouts and activities of the folks on the loon list were routinely checked in the interest of security. But Yasuda's presence on the list wasn't enough to justify taking him off the streets or deporting him.

This seeming snafu was one of the prices of democracy.

4.

When the British Secret Service became interested in the services of Alistair Jones, MI5 was duly alerted. For years MI5 had been rather an embarrassment among world intelligence services for its apparent incompetence in deciding which British citizens to trust. Their predictions of human behavior somehow always seemed to lag behind their technical advances. The British designed the Harrier jet and made the best washing machines in the world, but had an awful list of exposed Soviet agents who had been happily dispatching British secrets to Moscow Center. One of them had even been art adviser to the Queen, and had to be stripped of his knighthood.

So MI5, smarting from the allegations of ineptitude, was careful in the extreme. When Jones's dossier came up for review, the people at MI5 said no, no, no. Wait just one minute. We have to make sure Alistair Jones is still trust-worthy, that his LIDMC is still good. LIDMC—pronounced Lid-Mac by the MI5 chaps—stood for loyalty, integrity, discretion, morals, and character. These were the qualities required for an Englishman to possess top-secret information. Investigators greeted one another with, "How's your Lid-Mac today?" If an investigator caught his mate eyeing a woman at lunch, he'd tell him to watch his Lid-Mac.

The British suspected, probably correctly, that their American cousins had unearthed their moles as well, but had done a better job of keeping them secret. In America, scholars began applying computers to the study of human behavior. This made them scientists. They talked the way scientists ought to talk and wore their lab smocks to lunch.

The British followed suit, and scholars plugged away in Europe and America, trying to understand what it is that makes an individual do what he does.

Dings, or warts, on one's LIDMC included alcoholism, use of drugs, homosexuality, chronic adultery, indebtedness, craziness, or being an agent of the Soviet Union. Realizing that if the standards were too rigorously applied hardly anybody could be trusted, the boards that ruled on such matters made some allowances for indiscretion. This was a matter of common sense.

MI5 found Jones to be a straight, highly conscientious security inspector. He was just fine by MI5.

Five department chiefs from MI6, covert operations, met to choose from a list of possible recruits. The officers read the dossiers with care and met at teatime in a lovely room. A comforting artificial fire was burning bluish in the fireplace. The decision was made to the accompaniment of an occasional civilized clink of cup to saucer. Men like these had been making decisions like this since before the Empire.

The chairman was Sir Geoffrey Ward, the man in charge of the powerful and much fancied covert operations group. Sir Geoffrey had the sniffles, an affliction that had gripped him for weeks. He put extra sugar in his tea. He cleared his throat, a signal that it was time to get to the business at hand. "For my money, it's Alistair Jones," he said. He took a sip of sweet tea.

Sir Geoffrey knew how to carry a grudge. For him to begin a meeting that way meant that he'd already made up his mind. Anyone who opposed him would have to sleep with his eyes open, in the manner of an Apache pursued by John Wayne. Come budget time, Sir Geoffrey watched his flanks like a ragged old lion. On a routine appointment, he had his way.

Sir Geoffrey hoped his cousin Alice would reward him with a big package of rum balls come Christmas. Alice had the rum sent from America, where you could buy something stronger than seventy proof. Alice had produced charts showing how Sir Geoffrey and Alistair were distant cousins. She said Jones was a super chap.

Certainly none of the other committee members would oppose him. That would be pointless. Turning a nuclear security inspector into a British agent didn't have anything to do with power. MI5 seemed to have covered everything in its investigation. Everything looked fine.

"Oh, yes," said the first member of the committee. "Jones it is."

"He's our man," the second added. He wanted to go home and take a nap.

"Solid in every way. First-rate training. Experience." The third man had never voted on the losing side in forty years of service to His/Her Majesty's governments.

"A good chap as well." The last committee member didn't give a bloody squat.

It was unanimous.

Sir Geoffrey sniffled. "Damnable nose," he said.

Thus it was that Alistair Jones hit the road for MI6. He was placed under the control of MI6 officer Thomas Cunningham, known as Op Four.

Jim Quint was in Amsterdam when he got the call from the managing editor of *Rolling Stone* magazine. Quint had written for Grigsby several times before, but had met him just once. Grigsby was a slender, thoughtful man in his mid-forties. He had a good-looking gray mustache and smoked a pipe. He looked as though he belonged in the editorial offices of *Forbes,* say, or *Fortune.* He was a professional.

"Jim, my friend, Grigsby here."

"Grigsby!" Quint said. All right! A job, Quint thought.

"Lucky we got you in Holland."

Probably saved you a couple of bucks, Quint thought. "Good hearing from you, Jeff."

"Saved us a few dollars." Grigsby laughed. "Leo Tull told us where we could find you."

Leo Tull was Quint's agent. Good man, Leo! Quint thought. He said, "Leo's my main man."

"My oldest kid drug home one of your Humper Staab paperbacks the other day. Those are yours, aren't they? The author's name was Nicholas Orr."

"Good old Humper. Did you like it?"

"I think you're a helluva magazine writer, Jim. That's why I'm calling. Have you been paying any attention to stories about the Vrienden? The folks with the bomb. An anomaly, the State Department calls it."

"There was an article in yesterday's *Guardian* and one in *Der Spiegel*, but I can't read German. They always have fabulous women on the cover but no skin on the inside."

"We want a story of our own, Jim, a good one, not a quickie." Grigsby's voice sounded distant and tinny beneath the hiss of the long-distance connection. "We want you to get on the bus. Put your readers on the bus. Take 'em on a little trip."

"I can't say as I know a whole lot about nukes," Quint said.

"We liked the piece you did for us on the PLO camp last year. All that detail. We want a story in human terms. Maybe you could do a little set piece on the bomb itself—tell us what it looks like and feels like. Get a little fancy, if you want. The old Quint magic. We'll find some space if you need it."

"You say you want me on the bus?"

"On the bus, that's right. Our readers like their stories with the rubber off, a little more warmth that way. We'll pay your expenses, as before."

"Every magazine in Europe is trying to get somebody on that bus. Did you ever stop to think of that?"

"You'll find a way," Grigsby said. Getting on the bus might be a problem for Quint. Grigsby and his colleagues had discussed that.

"How much for the story? You're talking a lot of work here. There's no telling what I'll have to do to scrounge my way aboard."

Money was an ugly, vulgar topic. No editor wanted to part with money. Grigsby made an odd sound, as though a bone had suddenly gotten stuck in his throat. He coughed twice. "Sure, we're willing to pay, Jim. We were thinking the same as for the PLO piece. I really went to the mat for you on that one. Not bad money."

Quint thought it wasn't especially good, either. "A thousand more," he said. If Grigsby'd had a good word for Humper Staab, Quint wouldn't have started as high. He could imagine the ordinarily calm Grigsby suddenly puffing his pipe furiously, passionately, the smoke rising in a haze. Were editors this way with their wives and mistresses, squeezing each coin, weighing it like Scrooge, biting it like Dracula?

"Okay, Jim, five hundred more. You know I support my writers. Only this time we want you to keep better records of your expenses. There's no telling how many massage bills you had tucked in there last time. Our accountant just raised hell."

Quint laughed. "A man on the road has needs, Grigsby. A *seven-fifty* raise plus expenses. You'd be getting a bargain at twice the price."

The sound started in Grigsby's throat again but he choked it off manfully, his pride intact. "I'll send you a letter."

"I'm worth it," Quint said cheerfully. Quint didn't mind haggling with Grigsby. It was Grigsby's job to be a cheapskate. He had to know where to put commas and how to make a profit. He was an editor. Editors were also born to be blamed. Later, Quint would say everything that happened to him was Grigsby's fault.

So the American officials were calling the Vrienden bomb an anomaly. It was a useful word for bureaucrats, Quint thought. When a congressman gets caught inside his secretary on the back seat of his Mercedes, he calls in an anomaly—something inconsistent with his normal behavior. When two submarines collide in the middle of the Pacific, the navy calls it an anomaly—a deviation from the usual form. Quint once read a story in the London *Times* about a Hindu student who was using kerosene as a remedy for hemorrhoids and blew himself up. The coroner ruled it death by misadventure.

An anomaly, he said.

Then there was the case of Korean Air Lines flight 007 from Anchorage, Alaska, to Seoul, Korea. The Boeing 747, flying in the early-morning darkness, strayed two hundred miles north of its scheduled route and crossed Soviet-owned Sakhalin Island—site of some Red army bases. The Soviets didn't think this was a mere error, an anomaly; it couldn't be. Thinking the jumbo jet was another disingenuous American ploy—a spy plane—they shot it down, killing all 269 people on board.

Jim Quint was an incorrigible Montanan. He believed in the honest and straightforward term "fuck-up." The truth was that both the Korean and Russian pilots had fucked up; the resulting tragedy was redeemed only by the fact that World War III did not ensue. There were so many anomalies reported in the newspapers every day—so many fuck-ups—that Quint wondered just what it was that could be considered standard or usual.

5.

A Vienna-based agency of the United Nations was charged with inspecting nuclear facilities in all those countries that signed the Nuclear Non-Proliferation Treaty of 1968. This made it the target of environmentalists and malcontents all over Europe. The volatile Portuguese in charge, Senhor Emilio Gutierrez, seemed to bring out the worst in the anti-nuclear people. After several cloistered meetings, marked by passionate murmuring, Gutierrez was transferred to a United Nations post in a country where people ate garlic. The UN looked to the glacial North for help.

What was needed was someone nimble enough to dodge bricks, yet bland enough to be poor newspaper copy. Scandinavians were good at that. A Norwegian named Bernt Walther was placed in charge. He was a proven anonymity. He was competent. He had a history of enduring, with apparent grace, the antics of clowns from all over the world.

It didn't take Walther long to discover the most obvious omission among the many shortcomings of Senhor Gutierrez's tenure. Walther knew that with the emergence of the

Greens in Germany and other antinuclear groups in Europe, his agency was going to come under increasing criticism for supporting the spread of nuclear energy. What was needed was one exemplary inspection team prepared to handle those delicate cases where a country might be suspected of skimming plutonium for weapons. This team would also be used in Europe when demonstrations were anticipated from people like the Greens and the Vrienden.

Walther assumed he would need the support of the major powers on this, and consulted privately with the Americans, the British, and the Soviet Union. The Americans suggested Harold Woods, a native of Baltimore, Maryland. The British suggested Alistair Jones, an Englishman whose employment as a UN inspector was in furtherance of his career as a British security expert. The Soviets suggested Leonoor Lund, a clearly superior inspector from Budapest.

The Soviets informed Walther that either the team leader or two out of the three members would have to be from a Communist country. No other combination was acceptable.

Walther finally had his ninety inspectors rate their colleagues on a lengthy, complicated, and anonymous chart. He reviewed all ninety dossiers and finally made his choices: Harold Woods, Alistair Jones, and Leonoor Lund. Mrs. Lund would be the inspector in charge.

Mrs. Lund was handsome and smart, a spirited woman. She was the wife of a Budapest labor official. When she wasn't on the road, she played the harp for the Budapest Symphony Orchestra. Her integrity was unimpeachable. No bureaucrat could resist her charm.

Leonoor Lund turned out to be a superb team leader. If there was a sensitive inspection due, it was her group that went. Nobody argued with the care and thoroughness of a Lund report. A smart move on Walther's part, people said. Brilliant, was the word used in Vienna. That is why Harold Woods, Alistair Jones, and Leonoor Lund were assigned to Norgent-sur-Seine. All chance has a cause.

It was easy enough to trace the chain of events that led to the necessity of assigning Mrs. Lund's team to the Norgent-

sur-Seine inspection. In the late 1970s the French government had built a nuclear power station there, just thirty
miles upstream from Paris.

A lot of soreheads didn't want a plant at Norgent-sur-
Seine. An accident, they said, would pollute drinking water
downstream. One French official, a W. C. Fields fan, asked
what difference did it make? Parisians don't drink water:
fish fuck in water.

The soreheads nevertheless complained, with Gallic enthusiasm.

French officials ignored the complaints with Gallic stub-
bornness. They went ahead and built the plant. This was
the way the French handled soreheads.

The soreheads, provoked, accepted the challenge. They
refused to go away. They used any excuse to picket the
plant—ennui, the urge to joust, whatever.

When the UN notified Norgent-sur-Seine that it was time
once again for reinspection, French officials despaired. Inspections were routine at other plants; there had never been
a routine examination of Norgent-sur-Seine. Someone on
the inside always tipped off the environmentalists.

The resourceful French sent an emissary from the foreign
minister's office to have a chat with Bernt Walther at the
UN complex in Vienna.

. "Please, Monsieur Walther," the Frenchman said. "Let us
do the intelligent thing for once. We know the demonstrators
will appear. They always have. Let them. Send us your best
inspection team. We'll schedule our own inspection of the
reactor at the same time. We'll make a production of it."

"You want them to see how careful you are." Walther
thought this was naive, but did not say so.

"Precisely. How safe. We'll give tours. Bring out a band.
The mayor, charming little man, can make a speech."

Walther sighed. He didn't want to do it. The agency did
well to stay low, he felt—less chance of shrapnel. Walther's
experience with the French was that he needed plenty of
IOUs to keep them from pushing him around. He found it
hard to resist an IOU of this magnitude. "You'd be wanting
Mrs. Lund's team. No problem at all. I understand what
you're trying to do."

The Vrienden read newspapers along with everybody else. At Norgent-sur-Seine, they piled out of their old bus, laughing, and set their unloaded atomic bomb up for display.

Alistair Jones was assigned the task of mingling among the people gathered to view the French nuclear power displays at Norgent-sur-Seine. His French host encouraged him to move about. "Mingle, monsieur, mingle, mingle. Answer their questions." Jones's French wasn't bad by foreign standards, but his escort winced. Harold Woods was in another part of the same hall, mingling as well. Woods talked with his hands moving constantly, gesturing. A French official at his side struggled to translate. Woods's American English had him baffled.

Leonoor Lund took questions from members of the press and leaders of antinuclear organizations.

Jones, cup of coffee in hand, suddenly found himself face to face with a young blond woman with a figure that was all elbows and angles. She had blue eyes and a quick, active face. She was a flirt, that was obvious, a charmer. She read his name tag. "So tell me, Mr. Alistair Jones, Great Britain, do you really believe all that stuff you're telling everybody?"

Hard A's. She was an American. "I beg your pardon?"

"The risks don't bother you? You haven't thought about what we're going to do with the waste?"

Jones smiled. "The French have an industrial economy. They have factories and cities to run. All that takes power."

"Really?" she asked. "There's no other way? Have you looked into it? Really studied it, I mean?"

"Believe me, we have elaborate security precautions to ensure that nuclear fuel is used for energy, not for weapons."

"That's not what I asked!" She wasn't going to let him off easy.

Jones liked her spirit. "There's a finite supply of fossil fuels. Only so much oil, so much coal. Solar power sounds good, I know, but the truth is it may be decades before it's worth much."

"And the waste? You didn't answer about the waste."

Jones's French host began to guide him by the elbow, attempting to rescue him from the American girl. Jones didn't want to go. "Are you with one of these groups?" he asked.

"I'm a Vriend. I'm with the Vrienden."

"The people with the bomb?"

"Yes." She laughed. "It's a beauty. You should come over and take a look at it. I can be your guide if you want." She winked.

Jones laughed. "I'll pass, I think."

"It's impressive. It really is."

"I'll bet," Jones said. The girl was charming. He thought about his wife Debra's lips.

"Are you married?" she asked suddenly. "I'm not looking for a husband or anything. I'm just curious."

Jones didn't wear a wedding ring. "Why, no," he lied. It was the first time he had ever done that. "Well, yes, I guess I am too," he added. He felt foolish.

6.

Georgie Farr couldn't sleep. His mind raced at high speed, driven by the amphetamine of doubt. There were no sedatives in the house; Farr lay in bed considering the options and possibilities as his wife, Ruth, slept with one leg flopped over his. He turned the problem over and over in his head.

The British proposal was weak, he felt, because there was too much that could go wrong. Just what could go wrong, he wasn't certain. But under the circumstances, it was hard to argue with Thomas Cunningham. The business of the Vrienden carrying an empty atomic bomb around, inviting theft, was one of the most perplexing anomalies to confront the Europeans in years.

Cunningham said the Europeans just couldn't continue to shrug the bus off as some kind of gypsy sideshow without taking some precautions. Somebody had to do something. If they confiscated the bomb or sent professionals in to steal it, Cunningham said, then they would be in effect admitting it was genuine. Do that, and every radical with an arc welder and a garage would be building bombs. Who in the bloody hell would be able to monitor all those things? Cunningham wanted to know.

Cunningham said it was imperative that everybody deny the authenticity of the bomb. When the furor dies, he said, the public will conclude that the bomb's a fake. *Then* you steal it. Maybe blame it on an intramural squabble: Greens vs. Vrienden.

In the meantime you need someone on the inside to keep an eye on it.

Up to this point, Farr agreed. What Cunningham said was logical. Farr suggested that a young agent penetrate the Vrienden. The problem was that there was an enormous waiting list of would-be Vrienden bus riders.

The waiting list was a barrier.

In order to get around the barrier, Cunningham said, what you do is offer the Vrienden somebody they can't refuse to accept, say, a nuclear security inspector for the United Nations. The environmentalists lay great store in propaganda coups, he said. They love newspaper headlines.

Whereupon Thomas Cunningham suggested the Alistair Jones gambit: a getting-older, goes-nuts routine. Jones was perfect for it, perfect, Cunningham said. He was the right age. He was a proper chap, but a sport. He looked a bit like Prince Charles. A good-looking beak there, a grin.

What you do, Cunningham said, was tip off the Vrienden in advance of the Lund inspections. Encourage the inspectors to mingle with potential adversaries—good for the UN image. Be sociable. In a couple of months Jones could go. Be a bit of a holiday for him.

Cunningham said Alistair Jones's "defection" would be embarrassing to the British, but the embarrassment had to be real and public for the ploy to work. The chaps in the British secret service would just have to keep a stiff upper lip and try to ignore the popular press. The Vrienden had to believe Jones was genuinely smitten by the young woman, that he was theirs in spirit, if the ploy were to work. The dangers involved in not watching the bomb were sufficient to justify the move, he said; it was bad enough that the nuclear powers had allowed themselves to become mutual hostages, but the idea of freelancers having an atomic bomb—loaded or not—was flat-out unacceptable.

Later, he said, when the press grew tired of writing about the bomb and printing British and French denials that the bomb was workable, why then a British commando could nip off with the bloody thing. Cunningham said there would be a bit of a fuss and more charges by the Vrienden, but everything would die down eventually. Everything would return to normal. Let them demonstrate, he said. That was fine.

Cunningham said Alistair Jones could go home to his wife later on.

Farr got up extra early, much to Ruth's annoyance. He wanted to shampoo and blow-dry his hair; the dandruff was coming back. Ruth, a high school chemistry teacher in Reston, Virginia, would ordinarily have made his breakfast. She liked to make his breakfast.

This morning Georgie said no. He wanted to fix his own breakfast. He needed time to think. Why did the Brits need to get so damned fancy? Where the hell was James Bond? Georgie took his morning heart pill, made some toast and a pot of tea, and scrambled himself two eggs. Georgie scrambled his eggs in low-cal margarine over low heat. He scrambled them loosely in the pan, stirring them flop, flop, flop with a fork. Nobody else could scramble eggs as well, not even Ruth. Georgie had an instinct for that divine, sweet moment when scrambled eggs are done just right—overcook them, and they taste like rubber.

Georgie listened to the weather and the news while he ate. The Redskins quarterback, Joe Theismann, had broken his thumb trying to unstick a garbage disposal with a broom handle. The sportscaster said this freak accident could destroy the Skins' season.

Harold Woods was regarded—or rather, regarded himself—as the team expert on the habits and psychology of people

like the Greens and the Vrienden. Woods was a veteran of
the Berkeley Free Speech Movement in 1964. He never let
Mrs. Lund or Jones forget that he had been a conscientious
objector during the Vietnam War. It was as though he had
passed some kind of test, like the Bataan Death March, that
others had been denied. This made his opinions more val-
uable than others'. What did other people know?

During a cocktail party at Antwerp, Woods—sloshed on
ten percent Belgian beer—mumbled something about having been arrested once. He let words drop about another
incident involving the steps of Sproul Hall, tear gas, and the
California National Guard. He said the gas masks on the
guardsmen made them look like giant bugs out of a Japanese
movie.

Woods said he had been a good friend of Mario Savio in
those first, fabulous days of freaking out for the six-o'clock
news. This was street theater, he said; Mario Savio and
Harold Woods had invented a new form of street theater.

When the television people got bored taping people burning draft cards, Woods said, well then, he and Savio'd throw
in a naked girl. When one naked girl wasn't enough, they'd
throw in three or four naked girls—Chinese girls, black girls,
whatever—all painted up with flowers and peace symbols.
He said they even thought of having a naked girl ride a
donkey along with a straw dummy of Lyndon Johnson. They
found a woman on San Francisco's North Shore who was
willing to do the trick, but Savio didn't think she'd come
off well in the interviews afterwards.

"She had these boobs, big numbers," Woods said. "We
were going to paint peace signs on them. Unfortunately, she
was one brick short of a full load."

They were delicious, fine memories for Woods. He was
like an old RAF pilot recalling how it had been at the Battle
of Britain—of being up there in a Spitfire with Messer-
schmitts buzzing like wasps at ten o'clock high. He was the
grizzled leatherneck who had been there on the beach at
Iwo Jima, the sun over his shoulder, dirty lemon-colored
rats up ahead.

When it wasn't Woods's Berkeley stories, Leonoor Lund
had to put up with Jones's complaints about the scandalous

inadequacies of nuclear safeguards. Jones said it was madness, handing out nukes like candy. There were now hundreds
of sources of plutonium. Something would certainly happen
one day. Something would go wrong. He was obsessed by
what might happen. What if? What if? He told Mrs. Lund
and Woods detailed fantasies of how the apocalypse might
come about. In these fantasies, crazed groups operating under the banners of passionate causes stole plutonium for
bombs and flattened beautiful cities.

One day, as he was having breakfast with Harold and
Leonoor before inspecting a Czechoslovakian reactor, Jones
asked what would happen if some nut pinched some plutonium and matched it with the Vrienden's bomb. "Have
you ever stopped to think of that? Have you? It could happen, you know. What if it did?"

Mrs. Lund said, "Alistair, I think you have to remember
that you're a professional. You have inside information and
technical skills other people just don't have."

"Outsiders rob banks all the time," Jones said.

Woods said, "Alistair, an amateur would only wind up
with radiation poisoning and lung cancer. Who in his right
mind wants to walk around with no hair and six months to
live?"

"Harold, there are people in this world so obsessed with
one truth that no hair and six months would be nothing for
a shot at a bomb. You know that's so."

Some of Jones's schemes were clever, Leonoor and Harold
had to admit. Thriller stuff, Mrs. Lund said. She was a fan
of Eric Ambler and liked a good story. But Jones wasn't an
entertainer; he concentrated on arcane technical details. He
repeated himself—far more even than Harold Woods—and
fixated on gruesome what-ifs for days at a time.

This was all hard on Jones's colleagues. They both thought
on several occasions that Jones's paranoia went beyond being
merely boring. But this they kept to themselves. Neither
Mrs. Lund nor Woods wanted to go before Bernt Walther
and accuse Alistair Jones of being a fruitcake because he
took his work too seriously.

"We have a name for people like him in the United States,"
Woods said. "He's a red-hot. I remember in high school we

had this kid who worried all the time. Thirty seconds before math class was over, this kid's hand'd go up. Never failed. He'd ask if there was a homework assignment that night." Woods shook his head. "We should start calling Jones Plutonium Man."

7.

Jim Quint had done a little thinking about heroes and would-be heroes before he began writing Humper Staabs. He understood that in an age of disasters people have a need for heroes, and so he made Humper a can-do guy. Humper was unburdened by a past; he was just there in the middle of things, doing what had to be done, and in the nick of time.

Humper's surname was Staab (as in Saab), a cold, killer name. Quint gave Staab eyes that were sometimes icy blue, sometimes as cold as steel. Staab carried a throwing knife strapped to his wrist. He could split a thorax at fifty feet and had done so on several occasions—always with justification. Quint fixed it so his readers actually urged Staab on.

Staab's ladies were always beautiful. They had nipples as hard as diamonds, thighs as soft as velvet. Their pussies pouted. They begged Staab, please, please. The Humper rammed his throbbing member into their fiery cauldrons of love. They moaned in ecstasy. Staab was a cool guy; he once used a woman's anus for an ashtray while she cooed with pleasure.

Quint loved all this. There are perhaps limits on how beautiful a woman can be, but who cared? Quint himself went to bed with good-looking enough women. One of his wives, in fact, had been sensational. But he pushed the limits on behalf of Humper Staab. The beauty of Humper's women was metaphysical. They belonged in *Guinness* or in centerfolds. How hard can a woman's nipples be? Quint compared aroused female nipples to just about everything imaginable: granite, stainless steel, tungsten. But he always returned to diamonds.

Diamonds, Quint concluded, were still a girl's best friend. Quint had never in his life met a woman whose pussy pouted, but Humper Staab met them all the time. Breasts like melons. Nipples like diamonds. Pouting pussies.

Quint told his friends that if his character wasn't Humping somebody, he was Staabing them. Staab never just "said" anything—he barked, spat, hissed, and growled. This was so the reader would know Staab was in charge. Quint once sat at his typewriter, high on pot, and tried to bark and talk at the same time. He couldn't pull it off. He wondered how people like Staab did it. He had known people who could talk and belch at the same time, and even people who could talk and sound like Donald Duck. Those wouldn't do for Staab.

Humper Staab walked the meanest of mean streets. He was an educated, street-wise stud. An avenging angel.

Jim Quint didn't exactly have the makings of a hero. He was a blue-eyed, loose-jointed, grinning sort of American, a quintessential Westerner, born in Bison, Montana, a place so small as not to appear on most maps. He was given to blue jeans and tee shirts in the summer, blue jeans and tweed jackets in the winter. He wore hats—a panama in the summer, an Irish walking hat in the winter. He sat easily on a neighborhood bar stool but was uncomfortable in a cocktail lounge. Television, fashion, and discussions in the abstract all made him giggle.

Quint had learned about life from the cowboys who rode into town in pickup trucks and shed flakes of dried cow shit when they sat down for bacon and eggs at Miss Gloria's.

When he was a boy, Quint had listened to old men talk about hard winters and high-priced hay. They talked often with their heads hung down, stringing brown streams of snoose into brass spittoons. On the jukebox, deep-voiced men sang songs of loves lost. Quint's grandfather said their voices were deep because they had hair on their chest and their balls hung low.

The old boys had a lot of advice. Don't piss into a stiff wind, they told him. Don't eat yellow snow. Never trust a

left-handed banjo player. Stay away from long-backed mares.
Be polite to grizzlies. Quint never said anything. They were
good people and meant him well. He was told always to
take a leak after you've been with a hooker.

When Jim Quint was sixteen years old, a young lady named
Cecilia Dixon stole his cherry in an alfalfa field a half mile
out of Bison, and he was obsessed by women forever after.
He discovered Cecilia—or she him—as he was running from
a spotted goat in a neighbor's field. The goats were penned
in by a fence made out of lodgepole pine. It was sport to
poke a ram with a stick and sprint for the fence.

Cecilia was fifteen the day she first came to watch. She
was everything Jim Quint's heart could desire, and then
some. That first day, she sat on the limb of a mulberry tree
and watched the running of the goats with her knees tucked
up under her chin. When she jumped down, her front
bounced. Quint was certain he was in love.

Quint loved to tell the story. He said he was a pothead
writer who toiled in the most overworked and familiar ditch
of fiction. He received goats, which is what he deserved.
Ernest Hemingway got the bulls.

Marissa Stanley was standing in front of the main entrance
to the Biblis C atomic energy plant at Worms, in the Rhine
River Valley, and Quint briefly caught her eye as she strode
through the crowd that had gathered to see the Vrienden's
atomic bomb.

The media people were gathered at Worms with their cameras and notebooks. Collectively, if unintentionally, they had
given the bus the status of God's Special Chariot. They loaded
their stories with wistful, poignant, or outrageous quotes
and had some fun with officialdom. There wasn't much else
to write about. The Irish were unaccountably lethargic. The
Americans hadn't done anything stupid in weeks. Even Qad-
dafi was quiet.

Quint eased through these merchants of hype and the assembled spectators much as his grandfather had taught him
to stalk elk in the Bitterroots. He knew talking to other

writers wasn't going to get him on the bus. Quint needed a Vriend for a friend.

The woman at the entrance was in her late twenties or early thirties, Quint guessed. She had sleek, black hair, long legs, powerful hips, and a slender, almost breastless torso. Her long, good-humored face had, as its centerpiece, an over-sized nose. Her complexion was Mediterranean; her posture was pride and optimism. She had smart brown eyes. She wore boots with red wool socks that she pulled over the bottoms of her jeans.

She poured coffee for herself and a girlfriend. The girl-friend was shorter and had blond hair cut in a shag. She was quick and full of energy. The police liked to have people like that up front.

When the first of the three Mercedes limousines appeared at the gate, the Vrienden got ready for the press photogra-phers. They arranged to have their best signs and prettiest girls positioned so as to give the photographers the best possible light on them. The tall woman and her girlfriend put their coffee away and picked up their signs. Their pic-tures would probably be on the front page of the local news-paper the next day.

Quint couldn't keep his eyes off the taller one.

She turned suddenly, and looked in his direction.

Or had she? Quint couldn't be sure. She should have been paying attention to the arrival of the limousines. She held a sign with the others, but looked different, Quint thought.

After the inspectors disappeared inside, the long-legged girl went back to the bus, empty thermos in hand, walking with loose strides.

"Do you speak English?" Quint asked.

"Sure," she said. "I'm an American, Montana-born." She laughed. "My name's Marissa Stanley."

"Well, does a bear shit in the woods! Jim Quint, late of Bison, Montana." Quint shook her hand, thumb up.

Marissa looked amazed. "Bison! Nobody's from Bison."

"You've been there?"

"A bunch of times, but I can't tell you what it looks like. I always manage to blink on the way through."

Quint giggled. "You do know Bison. Where you from in Montana?"

Marissa, grinning, shook her head at the idea of meeting someone from Bison at Worms. "I'm a Lost Horse girl," she said.

It was Quint's turn to shake his head. "I bucked bales up Lost Horse way when I was a kid, lugged irrigation pipes."

"Which place was that?"

"Ted Garver's. He had a rocking S brand that he called the Slow Stud."

Marissa Stanley laughed. "Uncle Ted!"

"Uncle Ted?"

"You're looking at his niece, Jim. What are you doing here?"

"I've got an assignment from *Rolling Stone* to do a piece on the bus and your bomb."

"So you're the guy! They said there was a writer from *Rolling Stone* on the list. They wondered who he was. From Montana! You."

Quint fumbled at the throat of his sweatshirt. "Jeez, I forgot my necktie." He checked the fly of his jeans. They, she had said. Why did she use the third person?

"Have you talked to Wim?" she asked.

"Why would I do that?"

"I suppose even writers from Bison have to talk to people."

"Oh, I see," Quint said. "I will have to talk to him eventually, but if I mailed back the same old stuff, Grigsby'd yell at me. His readers don't want 'spokesman said' crap. They want to know what it's like to be you, but then again I don't suppose you're a Vriend."

"No, I'm not."

"But you do have a seat on the bus. You were standing up there with the rest of them."

Marissa grinned. "Oh, yes. I'm on the bus."

"I see," Quint said. It was obvious he didn't see at all.

"It's a long story."

"I'm patient," Quint said. He wanted to get on the bus too.

"My father owns a logging operation and a spread just up the road from Aunt Madeleine and Uncle Ted. When he was a young man he went East to find himself a lady a bit more refined than the local action."

"A regular Jay Gatsby."

"My old man. He got Mom, fresh out of Vassar College."

"I just bet you went to Vassar too."

"Oh, yes. So here I was, living in New York and studying at Columbia without the foggiest idea of what I was going to do for a dissertation when Mom, bless her, went to her twenty-fifth class reunion, where she met her old friend Pilar, a lady who lives in Sevilla."

"The woman who gave these people the money for their bomb."

"The very same. All of a sudden I had myself a research project and here I am, just like Margaret Mead."

Quint slapped his thigh in admiration. "All right!"

"Fame awaits, I'm sure of it. All I have to do is hold signs with the Vrienden and take a few notes."

"What a scam! What a scam! Say, I don't suppose it's possible for me to get a cup of that coffee so we can talk a little Montana? Maybe you could introduce me around."

"Just go ask them at the bus, big boy. They've got paper cups, and donations help the cause."

Quint bounded over to the Vrienden bus for his coffee. If Grigsby'd seen that demonstration of charm, he wouldn't complain about Quint's expenses. This was the first time in his life that being from Montana had been worth a damn. A Lost Horse lady. What a break!

When Jim Quint got back to the women, the first thing Marissa Stanley wanted to know was how he could prove he was with *Rolling Stone*. Quint gave her an envelope from his jacket pocket.

Marissa shared Grigsby's letter of agreement with her smaller friend, a blonde whom she introduced as Anita Hawkins. Marissa looked up when she'd finished. "They don't pay very well, do they?" She looked surprised. "I've seen your by-line before. I thought you'd get paid more than this."

Quint shrugged. "I tell myself the freedom's worth it." He paused and added, "As it stands now, I'm going to have to follow you people around Europe in a car. Gas here costs three or four bucks a gallon."

"Poor man," she said.

"You don't think I could hitch along on the bus for a couple of weeks, do you, Anita?"

"You and every other writer in Europe. You're on the list. We've got a list you just wouldn't believe."

Quint's shoulders slumped.

"Do you work for any other publications—besides *Rolling Stone*, that is? Anything would help," Anita said.

"I've done pieces for *Esquire, The New Yorker, The New York Times Sunday Magazine, Parade* magazine. Do you know about *Parade*?"

"Comes with the Sunday papers."

"That's it," Quint said. "I can do one version for *Rolling Stone* and one for *Parade*, maybe, although I can't guarantee it. Would that help?"

"It might," Anita said.

"Maybe you could put in a good word for me."

Marissa said, "If they ask what kind of person you are, what should I tell them, Mr. Quint?"

"Jim. Tell them I'm a fun-loving rascal, a Montanan. Mischievous is the word. I'm on a fabulous adventure. What about you?"

Marissa laughed. "I'm an earthy broad, a Montana woman, horny, a guffawer."

"My kind of woman exactly."

A chilling wind stirred. "I'll do my best," Anita said.

Later, before she got on the bus, Marissa turned and called, "Jim!"

"Yes?"

"We'll be at Gundremmigen two weeks from Wednesday, that's Gundremmigen B. Ask Wim then about being on the bus."

"That's in West Germany?"

"Yes, West Germany. Bring your toothbrush and razor blades."

Quint watched as the bus left for the ride to Amsterdam. Its riders, Marissa among them, waved handkerchiefs out of the windows.

8.

The Vrienden seemed surprised at what Jim Quint looked like when he joined them at Gundremmigen. They had voted for a reporter from *Rolling Stone* magazine on Marissa Stanley's recommendation. They thought, All right! *Rolling Stone.* Far out! They had in mind somebody in his late twenties, maybe, early thirties at the most.

One of the Vrienden said later she heard someone swallow audibly when the group first beheld Quint. Quint was suddenly standing before them at the front of the bus: blue-eyed, graying at the temples, grinning. He was a grown man, in his late thirties at least. He was an adventurer, as Marissa and Anita had reported. He wore faded blue jeans, Nike running shoes that had seen miles, and a San Francisco Forty-niners sweatshirt. He wore a flamboyant mustache suitable for an RAF pilot or Buffalo Bill. He wore a splendid aged panama with the front and back of the brim turned down. A madras band of lively reds, yellows, blues, and greens lay in uneven, soiled clumps around the hat, which had been rained on so often it was soft as flannel and mostly shapeless.

Wim van der Elst glanced quickly then back at the grinning man. "Meneer Quint?" he asked.

Quint sat his portable Olivetti on the floor. "Jim, they call me, originally of Bison, Montana." Quint caught Marissa's eye. He retrieved a joint from the band of his friendly old panama. Jim Quint had been retrieving joints from his hatband for years. He was a smoker, a traveler who lived for that sublime, exquisite moment at the typewriter when everything was working. "They were down to last year's beef when they pulled me out of the freezer. That's a fact."

Quint was an apparition to most of the Vrienden, and knew it. He was grateful for Marissa's help, but was nonetheless an enigma to her companions. He passed the joint. It was accepted, and he followed easily, giving five high ones to a black who watched him with a grin. "Jim Quint's my handle."

"Shee-it man, long time since I seen a white man with style. They call me Teets."

Quint laughed. "U. S. of A. I'll just bet five bucks you're not any kind of car dealer either."

Teets liked that. "You know how to spot a candy man. Used to sell these folks hash until a dude named Murrant started giving it to them."

"When I finish here, I'll see what you've got," Quint said.

Quint was exuberant, ebullient, asking who had what name and was from where. As he talked, he retrieved joints from the band of his panama and when the band was empty, he rolled more, talking all the while. "Well, what I want to know is when the frenzied sex starts? Where's the coke?" Quint's rattling prattle had charm. He was soon holding people by the shoulder, grinning broadly. "Well, how are you?" he asked. "Pleased to meet you. I wonder what's under there. Pleased to be here. My heavens! Quint as in Quintius."

Marissa watched in amusement as Quint, stoned, went through the introductions. He was wasted, red-eyed, leaning against a seat when he finally got a chance to talk to her.

"So?" she asked.

"Thank you for getting me a seat on the bus. I appreciate it."

"My pleasure. You did well. How old are you, by the way?"

"I'm thirty-nine years old and twice divorced."

"Twice!" She looked impressed.

"Everybody gets divorced once. I did it for the experience." Quint brushed his marriages away with a wave of his hand. "I travel alone, ma'am, seeking the company of strangers in bars or double-decker buses. I think I could use another joint, how about you?" Quint's hand sought the band of his panama.

"Well, Jim, the deal is this. The Dane who designed the interior of this thing fixed it so the bunks upstairs slide this way and that, on runners, sort of. You can latch two singles together—that's for if you have a friend."

"The Danes are clever."

"Now if you have a friend," Marissa said, "and you're reading a book and you come to a good part you want to share, why then, all you do is slide the curtain back."

"And you have a double bed." Quint took a toke, grinning. "I want to tell you, Marissa, I'm a reader. Richard S. Prather, Louis L'Amour—all the biggies."

"You can have your own little *Rolling Stone* bunk if you want, or..."

"I can swap paperbacks with you."

"If that's your druthers."

"I just love dirty books," Quint said. "When I was a kid I used to turn the pages back at the good parts. No sense wasting time with plot and dialogue and all that garbage. All us boys who read that book were Lady Chatterley's lovers."

Jim Quint thought the hashish smuggler, Gerald Murrant, was the most interesting of the hangers-on at the Vrienden bus. The affable Murrant had curly black hair that looked as if it belonged on a poodle. He wore designer jeans and an expensive leather jacket which was, Quint was told, the costume of choice for dope smugglers.

Murrant was a passionate supporter of the Vrienden cause. "Listen," he told Quint one night. "We don't have any choice but to support the Greens and people like the Vrienden. There's only so much air, so much water, so much oil. We're pissing in the stew."

Quint remembered bright stars and crisp Montana nights. "It'd be nice to keep it clean, I'll grant you that."

"I'd do anything for these kids, anything," Murrant said. The next night he was gone, to Morocco, the Vrienden said.

A week later Murrant was back, grinning, with a huge slab of hashish for the Vrienden. "My contribution, Jim. My support. You write about them in *Rolling Stone*, I give them hashish. We're both doing our bit, helping the best way we can." He grabbed Quint by the shoulder, brother to brother.

Quint, who was not given to causes, was uncertain how to respond.

One night, high, Gerald Murrant told Quint how he had come to be a European hashish smuggler.

"I used to fly pot into the United States, mostly ganja from Jamaica." Murrant remembered his past and sighed. "This is all a matter of public record, so why not? A couple of years ago there was this fireman in Fort Myers, Florida, and one day he responded to a call with his unit. He was going up these stairs when the staircase gave way."

"Oh, wow," Quint said.

"Oh, yes. He broke his spine in the fall. He was confined to a wheelchair and became a little despondent, you know."

Quint said, "I can imagine."

"So his brother, who owned a construction company, gave him an expensive camera outfit so he could shoot pictures out of his window. He had these huge lenses." Murrant demonstrated with his hands. "Pretty soon he was taking pictures of birds. These were published in the local paper and praised by a Fort Myers taxidermist."

"All right!" Quint said. "I like spirit."

Murrant sighed. "I just love this story, because it means I have to spend the rest of my life on the run."

Quint didn't know what to say.

"One day this fireman is looking for finches and hears a commotion. He turns his eight-hundred-millimeter lens—that's right, eight fucking hundred—and catches me wasting four United States marshals with a Soviet-made ARM automatic weapon."

"Whoa!"

"You got it, Batman. A common loon. My sister, Robin, was the lucky bird. She didn't appear in one frame, not one. So Robin, she gets to go home for Thanksgiving and eat roast turkey and some of Mom's cranberry and walnut salad. I gotta eat fried eggs and cheese in Amsterdam."

"Where's Robin now?"

"Ahhh," Murrant said. "Good kid. I gave her the contacts for my old pot run from Negril. The Americans don't have any reason to believe she had anything to do with the shootout, so everything's cool."

"Negril? Where's that?"

"Jamaica," Murrant said. "The western tip."

Once the inspection team was inside the Belgian plant at Antwerp, Wim van der Elst, looking for Anita and Marissa, eased through the gathering of demonstrators. Wim wore an old army fatigue jacket and patched blue jeans. His long blond hair flopped down over his eyes. His girlfriend, Catherine, trailed behind him, holding on to his hand. Catherine wore a World War II leather pilot's jacket and jeans as tight as the laws of physics would allow. Where Catherine walked, eyes followed. Wim lost Catherine's hand momentarily and stopped, holding his hand behind him for her to take.

Catherine was a special case among the Vrienden. She was interested in environmental issues, but they weren't her whole life. She got on the bus; she got off the bus. Because of Wim, the Vrienden were patient with her. Besides, she was fun and a kind of exotic they wouldn't ordinarily have met. If street education is worth anything, then Catherine had a Ph.D. She was a prostitute. When she wasn't traveling, she was one of Amsterdam's famous window ladies. She was tall, with blond hair and a slow smile. She was lovely. She could earn a lot of guilders in a good window. She liked it. She liked sitting on her chair in the window having men admire and appraise her. She didn't want to give it up. This passion was Wim's burden in life.

Wim found Marissa and Anita. "Ah, so how did it go?" he asked Anita.

"Everybody wants to get into my pants," she said. She whacked herself on the rump. "This here butt may not be the biggest, but they go for it—truck drivers, United Nations nuclear inspectors, doesn't make any difference. Isn't that right, Marissa?"

"The way she tells it, the boys all think she's fabulous. Hundreds of them. Can't control themselves."

Catherine said, "She'd make a fortune in a window, easy."

Wim was excited. "He'll do it, then. A UN inspector. Our bomb and a British peace defector. What a coup!"

Anita tried to look modest. "We're dealing with a man, of course, so you never know. But I'd say so, yes."

"Yes!" Wim said. "A UN nuclear inspector. I can't believe it!"

"He'll come," Catherine said. "I've been watching him give Anita the eye. Believe me, I know when a man will step inside and when he'll walk on down the street. First they come back to take a second look. Jones did that. Then they hang around trying to be cool, but still watching. He's been doing that. Everything builds up inside them. Then they break. They can't help it. They don't care about the consequences. Jones will come."

Wim said, "Really, Catherine? You think so?"

"You've got him, Anita, believe me."

"Boy, you know that Harold Woods is some kind of guy," Wim said. "He said he's been a fifth columnist for the peace movement for years. He gave us five hundred dollars. Five hundred American dollars, can you believe that? He says it's Milan Thursday after next."

Marissa said, "I love Italy. That food! Where's Jim? Jim'll love Italy."

Wim rolled himself a cigarette and drew Catherine close. "Woods says the people in Vienna are just going crazy over us following these people around. I wonder how he gets away with it. You have to hand it to him. With opinions like his, you'd think they'd be right on him, fire him or something."

A warm breeze stirred in the valley of the River Po. Jim Quint and Marissa Stanley could hear leaves stirring in the cottonwood branches above the bus. The leaves fluttered quickly, then died. They had just emerged from the buds and were small and pale green. Later on, in the heat of July, they would be broad and dark green. Spring leaves fluttered; summer leaves flapped.

There was an Italian farmhouse below them as close to the river as it could be without lying in the flood plain. There was a low barn where cows were milked. On the far side of the river, a vineyard rose to the horizon. The vineyard was interrupted by windbreaks of slender Lombardy poplars, cousins to the cottonwood beside the bus. It was a scene that might have been rendered by the dappled strokes of an Impressionist and later auctioned at Sotheby's. But Jim and Marissa chose to remember the Bitterroot River and the Sapphire Mountains. They had both used a yellow-bellied goofus to catch German Browns on the West Fork of the Bitterroot. They had both played five-card stud at Haigh's and the Signal Bar in Hamilton, had skied smoke on The Cliffs, powder ass-deep to a tall squaw—a run so steep the adrenaline squirted.

The Vrienden were on the bottom of the bus listening to Pink Floyd tapes, smoking Moroccan black, and telling ethnic jokes. The Dutch told Belgian jokes. The English told Spanish jokes—there was an uncomprehending waiter named Manuel on a popular British television comedy. The Americans told Polish jokes or Italian jokes.

There was a pause in the music while a new tape was selected. Jim and Marissa could hear Wim:

"Do you know how you tell a Belgian at the airport?"

Catherine said, "No. How do you tell?"

Wim's reply was drowned by a new tape—Steely Dan— then everybody laughed.

"If Alistair Jones grants me the interview in Milan tomorrow, I think I just might stay behind and write Grigsby's piece for him. Maybe I'll start another Humper, I can feel the juices."

Marissa rolled onto her back and put her hands behind her head. "Will you be back or will I read an article in the *International Herald* about you being caught down here buggering goats or something?"

"I'll stick with the woman from Lost Horse." Quint ran his finger down the ridge of her nose.

"A plowshare of a nose," she said.

"No, no. It's aristocratic." Quint saw her smile in the moonlight. He unbuttoned the top button of her shirt.

Marissa kept her hands behind her head. She smiled a slow, warm smile, and moved her chest slightly. "You ever dive the cliffs at Painted Rocks?"

"The twenty-five-foot jump," Quint said. "And the thirty once."

"But not the fifty-foot?"

Quint shook his head. "My God, no." He turned on his side and looked at Marissa in amazement.

"That's right," she said. "And I want to tell you that if you ever go off a cliff that high, you should keep your legs together if you don't want water up your bodily orifices."

"My God! I never had the nerve."

"Also if I were you, I'd try to protect my private parts. Me, I managed to land on my chest. Splat! I was seventeen years old at the time, and after that my breasts just flat stopped growing."

Quint unfastened the second button. He ran his finger softly on the outside of her shirt. He avoided her nipple, which he could see clearly pushing against the fabric. Her breathing quickened. "What would you like me to do?" he asked. He watched her face.

"I like a man with imagination, but for starters you might try the next button."

"This?" Quint put his hand on the button.

"See what happens."

Quint unfastened the button. He put his finger on her shirt and moved the tip of her nipple slightly one way, then the other. "This looks promising."

"Oh, sure," Marissa said. She turned her head to one side.

"Lots of time." Quint kissed her softly on the lips. Humper was slow, masterful. Quint told himself to watch his pacing. Not too fast. Humper always listened to their breathing.

Quint undid the rest of the buttons and took her shirt-tail out. She sucked in her breath—Staab's women did that—when his hand brushed a nipple. She arched her back, stretching her skin tight against her ribs, flattening her small breasts. The pancake dive at Painted Rock hadn't done anything to her nipples. She had extraordinary nipples; they were dark brown and wide and the middle as thick and as long as the end of Quint's little finger.

Jim was overwhelmed by the warmth and softness of Marissa's long body. He forgot all about Humper Staab and had a real Montana whing-ding with the graduate student in his arms. Shee-it!

Later, Quint noted that Marissa's pussy did not pout the way Humper Staab's women's sometimes did. It looked

mysterious, desirable—tantalizing, even when it was flushed
and sweaty after a hard sprint. Quint thought he detected
a hint of a smile there under jet-black pubic hair. Marissa's
pussy looked like a wanton, perspiring Annie Oakley.

9.

Alistair Jones said yes to Quint's request for an interview
in Milan. This surprised Quint and annoyed the UN press
officer, a Nigerian. The Third Worlders in the UN despised
the Western media because their reporters asked real
questions. The Italians and the French could not be controlled, and the Americans were animals. The Third Worlders had a deal going. They called a conference about this
or that issue; their travel was paid for and the United
States picked up the tab. But these damned Western reporters kept asking what was being accomplished? The
Third Worlders just wanted another bottle of wine, please,
and more salmon. The UN did a study of the world press
and gave top marks to TASS because the Soviets made it
a point to agree with everything the Third Worlders said,
no matter how crocked.

The Italians provided Jones and Quint with a comfortable
room for their chat. Since the UN inspector was British, the
Italians served bad tea instead of their own good, strong
coffee. The Nigerian press officer looked on sullenly while
an Italian waiter poured. Jones loaded his tea with sugar
and cream to mask the taste. "You'd probably have preferred
coffee."

"Oh, no," Quint said. "The tea is just fine."

Jones looked at the Nigerian. "I think I'll be able to handle
the questions."

The Nigerian was irritated. He wanted to know what kind
of questions Quint was going to ask. He also wanted to hear
Jones's answers. The Nigerian didn't like the English. He
looked at Jones, looked at Quint, and walked to the door.
"I'll be outside if you need me," he said. The UN was angered

at the continued appearance of the Vrienden bus—and bomb—at inspections made by Leonoor Lund's team. The Nigerian knew Quint had been riding the bus.

When the Nigerian had gone, Jones said, "I can't guarantee that I'll tell you anything you can't find in the press officer's kit. These people are wary of the press. They're getting tired of the Vrienden out there showing up with their bomb."

"Maybe I can learn something, maybe I won't." Quint took out a small notebook with a spiral wire binding on top.

"I guess maybe the real reason I agreed to be interviewed was because you're riding the Vrienden's bus. I was curious."

Quint grinned. "The little blonde's a livewire, I'll give you that. Cute as hell."

Jones blushed. "My God, I can't believe I'm that obvious."

"No, no, I don't think you understand. Listen, I'm sort of traveling with Anita's girlfriend, Marissa—the one who's studying the group. Women talk, you know how it is."

"I see." Jones knew about Marissa Stanley. Thomas Cunningham had briefed him on every rider on the Vrienden bus.

"For what it's worth, I think she's genuinely attracted to you."

Jones was pleased. "What is it you want to know? Let's see if I can help you out."

"My assignment is to do a story on the Vrienden and their bomb. What I'd like to know from you is what you really think about this whole business."

"I can't tell you what I think for publication."

"That's fine," Quint said. "So what if you tell me what you really think, and I agree to disguise the source? I'll use what you say in the spirit in which you said it." He folded his notebook.

Alistair Jones was obviously still feeling good about Anita Hawkins. "Done," Jones said. "Do you know how much plutonium it would take to match the bomb that leveled Nagasaki?"

"I have no idea," Quint said.

"About ten pounds."

"Oops."

"There are about thirty countries that can produce plutonium for weapons if they choose." Jones took another sip
of tea. "Only about half of these countries have signed the
International Treaty on Non-Proliferation of Nuclear Weapons—which means the United Nations is entitled to monitor
their fuel supplies."

"Well, hell, that's a start," Quint said. He was beginning
to understand the drift of Jones's concern.

"There are 90 inspectors to monitor 315 nuclear facilities
around the world. We work in teams."

"What do you do in there?" Quint nodded his head in the
direction of the reactor.

"Because of the radiation, the spent fuel is stored in large
cooling ponds. These ponds are monitored by cameras, very
similar to those in a bank. We inspect slides produced by
the cameras. We look at seals to make sure they haven't
been tampered with. We look at alarms and guard systems.
And we audit records to make sure what goes into a reactor
is accounted for at the other end. Credits and debits. We're
sophisticated bookkeepers. The point the Vrienden are making with their bomb is that it's really impossible for us to
prevent some country from joining the nuclear club if it has
the determination."

"They're proving the technology is available to anyone."

"For making a bomb. Precisely," Jones said.

"What can you do when you find a screw-up?"

"We write a report to our director. He then forwards a
copy of the report to the accused facilities and asks would
they please fix things. We have no power of enforcement."

"None?"

Jones put his forefinger on his chin. "None. So who are
the nuclear powers, do you think, Mr. Quint?"

"The United States, the Soviet Union, China, Britain, and
France, I guess." Quint knew about the Indians and the Israelis, but he wanted to hear Jones tell it.

"We have to add the Israelis. They've been running a secret
research facility at Dimona on the Negev since 1964. It produces plutonium. It's free of international inspection or ac-
countability. The South Africans are one of the world's largest

producers of natural uranium. In 1970 the West Germans helped them build a small plant at Valindaba more than capable of producing enough uranium-235 for weapons. They popped one in 1978."

"They did?"

"They did, their protestations to the contrary. The Indians completed their Bhabha Atomic Research Center at Trombay in 1964. They used Trombay-produced plutonium for their first bomb in 1974. That was the so-called peaceful explosion, remember? The Indians are said to be pacifists."

"I remember."

"Well, then they built another one at Tarapur. More plutonium. It's impossible to tell how much of that stuff they've used for bombs." Jones leaned forward and poured them each another cup of tea. People didn't understand the dangers. It was incredible. Quint was a journalist and had some influence. Jones pulled a package of Marlboros from his jacket pocket. "Do you mind?"

"Go right ahead."

"Would you care for one?"

"Don't smoke," Quint said.

Jones lit a cigarette and inhaled deeply. "The bleeding Pakistanis just went nutty over that one. Their prime minister said Pakistanis would eat grass if necessary to get their own bomb. Well, now they have two sources of plutonium. We're entitled to inspect one, at Karachi, which is Canadian-supplied. They supply their own fuel for the other and don't have to let us in. Somehow Harold, Leonoor, and I always draw Karachi. We've inspected it four times in the last two years." Jones had already smoked his cigarette. He lit another quickly, and took another hit before he continued. "You and I could fly to Karachi and by tomorrow night we'd have enough plutonium to fit in the Vrienden's bomb out there. That place is like a cafeteria."

"I wanted to ask you about that bomb."

"It's real. All it lacks is plutonium."

"How do you know that? I know they have their list of scientists who say it's real, but how do you know for sure? Although one night when we were smoking on the bus, Wim took it apart and put it back together, and I must say it was impressive."

Jones leaned forward and rested his chin on the heel of his hand. "I haven't seen the bomb myself. It would cause a big fuss if I walked over to the bus, and I'd be in the newspapers and everything. Wim van der Elst took it apart like that at the Oktoberfest in Munich. I have an acquaintance, a professional photographer, who watched the whole thing. He shot pictures with a Nikon. The Vrienden urge people to take pictures. Van der Elst took the bomb apart where the light was good."

"And what did your acquaintance say?" Quint asked.

"You understand, Mr. Quint, that this man gave the pictures to people who are experts. These people know nukes."

"You British have nukes."

"Indeed we do. The nuke people were especially interested in the characteristics of a metal globe used to hold the plutonium inside the bomb."

"And?"

"If the Vrienden had four kilos of plutonium, Mr. Quint, they could take out London if they wanted—New York. Isn't that a what-if?" Jones looked at his wristwatch. It was time for him to be going. He'd gotten carried away, and forgot to ask Quint about life aboard the bus.

That didn't matter. Jim Quint had voluntarily answered the main question.

Quint went for his wallet and pulled out his card. "I'll send you a copy of the article when it's published. You can judge for yourself if I'm a good writer and someone you can trust. If you ever feel you want to say more about the bomb—or anything related to it—then I'd like to hear." Quint pointed at the card with his finger. "This is my agent, Leo Tull, and his number. He knows how to get in touch with me when I'm on the road. This is my home address in Maryland."

Jones took the card. "I just might have occasion to drop you a note one of these days. One never knows."

Much to the annoyance of the Nigerian press officer who had accompanied them to Milan, Leonoor Lund and her colleagues continued their habit of mingling with the Vrienden and local environmental groups. Bernt Walther had asked Mrs. Lund, obliquely, whether or not this was a wise practice. Mrs. Lund, who was a sociable woman, pretended not to understand his implication. Her English wasn't the best.

Bernt Walther knew it was boorish and pointless to press Leonoor Lund on the matter. The media attention was tiresome, but he was willing to ride it out.

Harold Woods enjoyed the mingling. He was a talker. He liked to tease. He liked to slap backs and laugh loudly. Har! Har! Har! That was Harold Woods. Despite their dislike of nuclear energy, the Vrienden took to him. It made them laugh to see him make fun of himself as he walked their way. Woods said, "It's the nuke man, the dirty nuke man, gonna getcha!"

Jones, according to habit, found his way to Anita Hawkins to pick up their aborted Antwerp conversation. "How was the ride across France?" he asked.

"The Alps were hard on the bus, not to mention the riders." Anita rubbed her behind.

"I had a hard trip too, had to eat that airline food, then the Italians gave us a briefing." Jones looked to the heavens as though pleading to God. "We were talking about unilateral disarmament."

"An idea you find amusing."

"I didn't laugh out loud," Jones said. "I'm always willing to listen. Tell me how it would work."

"Let's see, how would it work?" Anita took Jones by the elbow and turned him slightly. "I like your jacket. Where'd you buy it?"

"London," Jones said.

"I would begin by having the Americans deliver an atomic bomb to a neutral site administered by the United Nations."

Jones held his arm out to look at the buttons on the sleeve of his jacket. He looked at Anita. "What would happen then?"

"Then the Soviet Union would turn one in."

"Two less warheads in the world."

"Yes."

"Aren't you talking about multilateral disarmament here? Everybody agrees to get rid of their bombs at once."

Anita turned Jones the other way to get another angle on his jacket. "No. I mean unilateral. Somebody has to begin. Somebody has to start. If somebody decides, acts, then the others will follow. It's madness not to. We could get this terrible thing out of our lives forever, all of us."

"After the Russians, I take it, the British would turn one in, then the Chinese. Don't tell me the French as well."

Anita was undeterred. "The French too."

"You'd have to convince me." Jones looked at his wristwatch and frowned. "I don't think they like us talking to you like this, so they rush us."

"Alistair, let me ask you a question, flat out. Do you love your wife, or have any feeling of affection for her at all?"

Jones laughed. It was an absurd question.

"Do you like living with her?"

Jones shook his head sadly. "You just can't imagine what married life's like for me."

"Then do yourself a favor and come live with me."

"On the bus?"

"On the bus. On the *woonboot*. Wherever."

"Just like that. Go live with you."

"It's obvious you want to spend more time with me than five minutes every other week. I can see it in your eyes. We might look at the world a little differently, but we both have fun every time we talk. I want you to come. There's no better reason in heaven, Alistair. You do it because you want to and I want you to." With that, Anita Hawkins gave Alistair Jones a nice kiss on the mouth.

Behind his back, Jones heard the Nigerian press officer say it was time to go.

10.

There was nothing in the MI5 security file on Alistair Jones that said anything at all about Debra's lips. Except for that it was a perfect dossier, professional in every sense. But the only thing Jones thought about when he stepped off the train at Amsterdam was that at last, finally, after fifteen years, he was going to escape Debra's lips.

Over the years of their marriage, Jones had learned to hate his wife's lips. They were pathetic, anemic excuses for real lips. Little things, they were. But the hysterical bullying venom that issued through those portals was unmatched in anything imagined by Dante. The lash of her tongue was harsher than de Sade's whips. Jones endured. When she was not in the grip of emotion, she was intelligent and could be good company.

Alas, her moments of sanity were rare. Debra Jones preferred the charms of paranoia. She was constantly on the watch for slights of any kind. These slights, whether real or imagined, were immediately seen as the acts of enemies. Debra was forever being thwarted by these enemies. If they were female, they were bitches. If they were male, they were sexists. Why don't they like me? she demanded of Alistair. Why? Why? They don't respect me. Why? They disagree with me. She loved the warmth of rancor's spotlight. Where these abuses seemed on the wane, Debra got listless; but she always arose from these periods of lethargy determinedly, to invent more slings and arrows.

Alistair Jones knew intellectually that his wife's aberrations were probably psychotic and that she must certainly be a statistical anomaly within the larger population of women. Yet he began, in spite of his better instincts, to wonder whether or not it was the occasional appearance of a woman like Debra who set women back everywhere— caused the ERA to fail in America, caused women to have to wear veils in Moslem countries, caused baby girls to be killed in China, and so on.

Jones would never, ever, forget his wife's lips. They were the lips of a woman who knew everything and could do no wrong. They moved like two hyperactive, bloodless, soulless worms. If they did not complain of slights, they ordered and bullied. Nobody knew what to expect next. The worms bullied her parents, bullied her two sisters, bullied her brother. Debra's lips had Alistair hopping about like a Sandhurst cadet.

It was with the terrible vision of his wife's lips in mind that Jones stepped between the yellow trams gathered in front of Centraal Station. He was, as Harold Woods put it, going to ride shotgun on an unarmed atomic bomb. He wouldn't have to return to Austria as he did between inspections. He would have a holiday from Debra's lips.

Alistair Jones began his hike down the Harlemmerstraat to the Brouwersgracht. A fitful breeze slipped across the red brick streets. It was seed time, growth time. The awful doubts and fits of anxiety that he had had earlier were gone. Cunningham had briefed him thoroughly. Keep it simple, Cunningham said. Put yourself in the shoes of a man running away from life. Think the way he would think. Become him. But also be yourself. You are what you are. You can't become somebody else overnight. Relax, Cunningham said. Have a good time. Cunningham said most men would envy him his assignment. It would be like a little holiday for Jones, he said. A little time away from Debra, and after the bomb was nipped he could go home again, back to the routine. That wouldn't be so bad, would it? Cunningham was sorry Debra couldn't be told. She would understand, he said. Jones was doing this for Queen and Country.

Thomas Cunningham had no way of knowing that Alistair Jones was, in fact, running away from life. This was an anomaly that Cunningham could later lay squarely on the blokes at MI5. Why hadn't they told him about Debra's lips? It was crucial, critical that he know about Debra's lips, and it was nowhere to be found in Jones's dossier. Nowhere.

Alistair Jones was a British agent. He was part of a tradition. His mouth tasted as though it were stuffed with cotton, but he became more confident with each step toward the Brouwersgracht. On behalf of his country, Jones was running off to live with an American girl sixteen years his junior. He was wearing the jacket Anita had admired in Milan. She'd like that.

Jones heard the music before he saw the *woonboot*. He checked the address of a nearby café. Yes, this was it. The Vrienden were listening to American country and western music:

> "*I've felt the ruts*
> *Down six long roads*
> *Left six good women*
> *Like six squashed toads.*"

Hearing that, Jones retreated swiftly to a bar across the street, Cor's Place.

"Yes, sir?" Cor was a broad, blond, mustached Dutchman in his late twenties.

"A beer, please," Jones said. "You ever spend much time with Americans?"

Cor poured Jones's beer, dumping the draw straight to the bottom in the Dutch manner. He wiped the foam off with a plastic paddle. "There was an American writer named Quint who hung out here for a few weeks. If all Americans are like him, I think you can say Americans like to have a good time. He said his grandfather was a Montana moonshiner. He gave me a recipe for buffalo steak. He wrote it on a napkin, laughing all the while. He said I could get everything I need to make it here except panther piss."

"What?"

"Corn whiskey that goes in the marinade."

Jones sipped the cold Amstel and watched the *woonboot*. He stepped outside to listen to the music coming from the Vrienden tape deck:

> "*Faster horses, Younger Women*
> *Older whiskey, more money.*"

He sighed and walked slowly across the narrow street and hopped onto the stern of the *woonboot*. The music got louder. He caught a glimpse of faces through a porthole. He saw Marissa, Anita's graduate-student friend, but not Anita. What if she wasn't there?

The door opened. Tom T. Hall's robust voice burst forth:

> *"Faster horses, Younger Women*
> *Older whiskey, more money."*

Anita Hawkins, with big eyes, warm and welcoming, stood before him. "Well, Alistair Jones, you come on in. Marissa said she saw you standing there. My God, Marissa, would you look at this. Alistair's wearing a necktie!"

Jones was stunned. He cursed Thomas Cunningham. Of all the bloody...These kids learned English listening to Yank music. He loosened his tie, thinking maybe that made him look a little American. He thought of Robert Mitchum.

He had no trouble at all receiving Anita's embrace. No American could have done that better. Not Paul Newman. Not Robert Redford.

Anita gave him a kiss that was of the angels to a man married fifteen years to Debra's lips. Anita drew back, beaming. "Well, would you look at this, everybody. Alistair Jones, come to share a bunk with a Vriend. Me." She kissed him again. Jones blushed. He couldn't help it; he was pale complexioned. Anita took him by the shoulder and turned him in a slow circle. "Here he is, friends, a nuclear security inspector lately defected from the service of the United Nations."

Jones went with the flow. He allowed himself to be displayed by the happy Anita as though he were some kind of trophy—a springbok dropped at two hundred yards, a nuclear inspector stopped cold with a pair of blue jeans and a B-cup bra, no mascara.

Jones shook hands with the Vrienden thumbs-up, the way he'd seen American blacks do on television. Jones thought it was a vulgar way to shake hands. A joint was thrust in his direction. The apple thus thrust, Alistair considered briefly, then, in the service of his country, bit. He took a big draw, too long and hard; he stood trying to look calm while his lungs seared.

Anita introduced him to one Vriend after another. Jones had been taught that it was polite and civilized to remember names. There is nothing more important to a person than his name. Jones had seen the faces before but now, on their turf, it was different. "I'm not good at names," he said.

Anita pulled him down with her onto an enormous bean bag stuffed with irregular chunks of foam rubber. "It'll take awhile, but the names will come. Right now I want you down here with me."

"Oh!" Jones was pleased.

"Tomorrow we'll go shopping."

Jones looked uncertain.

"We've gotta get you out of those UN duds, Alistair."

"Well, sure," he said. She'd liked this jacket in Milan, hadn't she? Jones blamed Cunningham. MI6 should have told him how to dress.

"You'll be a new man." She nuzzled his ear. She smelled wonderful. "You don't mind our playing some country and western, do you? Jim Quint stayed behind in Milan to write. Gave Marissa the old I-gotta-be-left-alone-to-work routine. Isn't that right?"

"He'll be back," Marissa said. "Back in Lost Horse, they say boys from Bison are so horny they can juggle branding irons and unzip their pants at the same time." She turned up the volume on the tape deck.

Alistair Jones was both excited and alarmed by the provocative ways of these American women. What Jones needed, he knew, was an American man, someone he could talk to and confide in.

Just then, as though by the intervention of Providence, the door to the *woonboot* opened and there stood a curly-haired man, a case of beer under each arm. "Hello there. My name's Gerald Murrant." He put the beer down and extended his hand to Jones.

"Alistair Jones."

"You're Anita's friend, I'll bet. What do you say we have a beer and smoke a little?" Murrant was affable, genial.

"Sure," Jones said. He liked Murrant. Murrant was just what he needed.

11.

It was the time of the full moon, and so an auspicious time, Quint knew, a time when deer graze at night in meadows just outside of town, when lovers come together in Bozeman, and Bigfoot stalks the Bitterroots. Quint's father had sown alfalfa at the time of the full moon—there was a special calendar in the milkshed with the phases of the moon marked on it. Quint stayed loose under a full moon.

But Quint was not in Bozeman or the Bitterroots. He was in a fleabag hotel in Milan. The hotel, shunned by travelers who knew it, was owned by a cranky old man who drank red wine all day from a thick ceramic mug and cursed Communists. He was a widower, but his wife had once had an affair with a Communist and the old man never forgot. He said Communists had chronic flatulence, which impaired their ability to think straight. This flatulence came from eating cabbage, food for Slavs.

The wiry little fart, Quint called him.

Two things happened that night—actually, one of them the next morning—that were memorable. The first was the hallway scene Quint wrote for Humper. This was prompted by a mild rebuke from his editor concerning the quality of his last Staab title. The letter read:

> Dear Jim,
> Yes to your proposal to do another Humper. However, I must tell you we all think your last effort could have been better. The sales were okay, but we think you were holding back. People read these books because they get off on sex and violence. You have to give them what they're looking for if you expect

them to buy more titles. Let it flap, Jim. Let Staab
really hump a few women. Show us some blood. We
know you can do it.

Quint reread the letter and felt a flutter in his stomach.
Were his publishers about to give Humper Staab the old
New York garrote? Were they stalking Humper, setting him
up with this letter? Was this the sweet kiss? Humper could
yell if he pleased, threaten, but if the members of the New
York tribunal said no, then it was no—Humper was dead—
and off they'd go, laughing, the bastards, for a sushi lunch.
Quint just couldn't give Humper Staab up—the name was
too delicious. He'd never be able to come up with another
one as good. If Quint's own nerve was to blame, if he had
failed to give Humper proper nitty-gritty...
Jim Quint resolved not to let that happen. He wrote under
a pseudonym, after all—who was to know? If they wanted
sex, sex they'd get. He'd give them clits that throbbed like
trombones, tungsten tits. He decided to write a Humper
based on two outrageous scenes, one sexual and one violent.
He would have started with the sex, but writing sex scenes
made him horny. Quint didn't know how to get laid in Milan
at that hour, and he wasn't interested in hookers. He would
write the violent scene first and save the sex for later.
It was eleven o'clock at night when he sat down at his typewriter—wearing a fedora for the proper mood—and prepared to grapple with the muse. He got out a bottle of Chianti
and a hunk of Lebanese hashish that looked like a giant piece
of fudge. He said to himself, everything's cool, Humper my
man, everything's okay. Old Jimbo is gonna come through.
Quint pretended he had steely, cold, killer eyes.
Two hours later he set about, red-eyed, to put it on paper,
hammering away at his Olivetti, trying to avoid words with
b's because the Olivetti skipped on b's.
The big violence scene took place in a long concrete hallway that sloped to the ground level of a parking garage. This
was to accommodate federal wheelchair laws, there being
no elevator. Humper chased a wart-faced neo-Nazi down
the ramp, which was awash with human blood, littered with
corpses and parts of corpses—entrails, heads, arms, feet. A

human ear looked like a poignant dinghy floating in the blood. Humper couldn't stand up and neither could the Nazi, who had thrown away his empty machine gun and Luger. Staab's knife was far down the ramp, protruding from the forehead of a surprised corpse. Humper and the remaining creep struggled down the concrete ramp doing belly flops and pratfalls. The Nazi's face plunged into a pile of freshly extruded feces. He puked. Both Humper and the Nazi were reduced to rapid crawling, like huge, awkward dogs. But the Nazi was no match for Staab.

The Nazi tried to get on his feet, but whack, whack, Humper smashed both his kneecaps with karate chops. (Quint wondered if that was possible.) Humper grabbed the asshole by the throat and smashed his skull against the iron railing. The Nazi still blinked, so Humper, who had been a power forward on the Stanford basketball team, dribbled his head against the concrete.

The episode was appalling and preposterous, but Quint thought it was grand, and started laughing. Two in the morning and he couldn't stop. His eyes began to water.

At last the wiry little fart banged twice on the door and shouted, "Stop laughing, signor."

This made Quint laugh all the louder. He didn't want to add to the image of crackpot Americans, but he couldn't stop.

The landlord banged harder on the door. He cursed Quint in a rising, tremulous Italian that bordered on the hysterical. "Signor! Signor!" He alleged that Jim Quint's mother sold her favors, that his father was gay, that his sister had herpes.

Quint grabbed the Italian phrase book he had bought in London and stated loudly the first phrase he came to, spelled out in phonetics for frantic travelers. *"Ho perso il mio passaporto."* I have lost my passport. He continued laughing and whooped even louder when he saw the next phrase in the handbook.

"No! No!" the landlord shouted. He kept banging. *"Communista! Communista!"*

"Dov'è il consolato britannico?" Quint shouted. Where is the British consulate? He had to bite his knuckles or risk being thrown out on the street.

The next morning, the landlord seemed to have forgotten about the fracas. "Signor, *telegramma*," he said. He took a big slug of wine from his mug, a little drama for Quint's benefit. He handed Quint the envelope.

It was from Leo Tull, Quint's agent. A writer had an assignment from *Playboy* magazine to do a story on NATO. The writer's wife was seriously ill. The British had given the writer an appointment to interview the British defense minister. That appointment had been changed to Quint's name. It was now Quint's assignment. Quint should go to London in ten days and phone one Arthur Zalburg at *Playboy*. Solid money, solid, Tull said.

Quint thought, Hot damn. Good for you, Leo! First virtuoso blood and guts, now this. Solid money, and Amsterdam just across the channel. There Lost Horse Marissa waited, a woman who knew how to work a yellow-bellied goofus.

Even though it was two in the afternoon, Jim Quint ordered an English breakfast. He assumed it was impossible for anyone to muck up a breakfast. He was wrong. The broiled tomato was anemic. The eggs were melancholy. But he needed to eat. He had to eat something. He hogged the bacon in quick gulps so he wouldn't have to taste it. He gulped the coffee, which was even worse, and burned his tongue in the process.

Afterwards, he claimed the only vacant telephone booth in front of London's Euston Station. He dialed 157, ran his fingers along the glass of the red metal booth. The telephone booth was solid, built like a bunker.

"International operator. What country, sir?"

"The United States." Quint gave her the area code and number. "Person-to-person collect, please. Hugh Hefner's paying for this one. I wish to speak to Arthur Zalburg. My name is Quint, that's a Q as in queen." Quint waited for the call to go through.

"This is Arthur Zalburg. I'm glad you called, Mr. Quint."

"Leo Tull wired me in Italy. He said I should go to London and call you."

"We have an appointment for you to interview the British defense minister at his home in Torquay tomorrow. You should be able to catch a train down there this afternoon, shouldn't you? His London office will give you the details."

"No problem," Quint said. "Can you give me the gist of what kind of story you're after?"

"Story?" Zalburg asked.

"Leo's telegram said you had a writer with a sick wife on his hands and you wanted me to do a NATO story of some kind."

"Oh, I'm sorry, Mr. Quint. I think Leo got things a bit confused. Bob Kline's the writer; you may know Bob. His wife's having a hysterectomy. She'll be fine and he'll be coming over later to do the story. But it took him months to arrange this interview with Scoble, and we wanted a professional to do it."

Article for *Playboy*. Solid Money. Quint thought, Aw shit, Leo. "I see," he said.

"We'll pay you four hundred dollars plus expenses for the interview. I'm told it's beautiful there in South Devon—the English Riviera."

Quint sighed. "Sure, I'll do it. And I do know Bob Kline. What's he looking for?"

"He wants you to get Scoble's opinion on American proposals for a change in tactics in Europe. This is for conventional weapons. The Americans want to do away with an established front line and fight with high-tech weapons. The Germans are going to be pissed. Can you do that, Mr. Quint?"

"Sure, I can do it," Quint said. Four hundred bucks for a couple hours, work. Probably not as much as *Playboy*'s girls got for modeling their boobs, but what the hell.

"This will be for background only, Mr. Quint. Kline says the British are waiting for the Americans to screw it up themselves. That way the British won't lose IOUs to the Germans. They want the Germans to help them fight subsidized French turkeys."

"Listen," Quint said, "if you ever need a good writer, you might keep me in mind. I had a lead article in *Rolling Stone* a couple of weeks ago about a group here in Europe with their bomb."

"You're the guy who wrote that piece? I read that. You do good work!" Zalburg sounded surprised. He had assumed Quint was another graceless hack.

"While we're on the phone and all, I wonder if you people might be interested in the drug and sex capital of Europe?"

"Which is?"

"Amsterdam. I could do a piece on the hashish trade and throw in the window ladies and all. Anything goes in Amsterdam."

"Oh?" Zalburg sounded interested.

"It's right up there with Hamburg as far as the sex goes."

"I tell you what, Mr. Quint, I can't give you a yes or no answer here on the telephone. Your idea does sound interesting. I'll reread your *Rolling Stone* piece. Can you write me a proposal with some specifics so I can share it with the people here?"

"Done," Quint said. "You'll have your interview shortly." Quint hung up.

He took the fast train to the industrial city of Bristol, just south of Wales. The train turned south from Bristol through Weston-super-Mare, Taunton, and Exeter, before it arrived at the resort city of Torquay. There were palm trees in Torquay—not exactly your splendid date palms of Southern California or coconut palms of Hawaii, but a kind of palm nevertheless. A high wind was coming off the Atlantic and it was getting dark when Quint stepped off the train. Quint turned his back to the rain and wondered what kind of palm tree could survive weather like that. It was, he had to admit, a handsome place. The town of Paignton was in the middle of the bay, and at the south end, the fishing village of Brixham.

Quint bought himself a couple of bottles of Mackeson's ale and took a taxi to his room at Kathleen Court. He watched a snooker match on BBC1. Tony Knowles, young and ambitious, played Cliff Wilson. Wilson, white haired and half blind, peered across the table through thick-lensed glasses. The kid was good, though, and in one game made a run of one hundred and four points before he fouled. Tony Knowles and Cliff Wilson were so good at avoiding anomalies that they were on television. They were professionals. Heroes.

Quint found Sir John Scoble to be a polite, thoughtful old Tory who, at sixty-two, was enjoying the power he had so long pursued. He had a stout, John Bull stomach that suited him. He had thin, white hair, balding on the front. His pale complexion told Quint he rarely saw the sun. He wore pale-rimmed glasses. His necktie identified him as a graduate of Balliol College, Oxford, a training ground for generations of British politicians from the upper class. Sir Harold Macmillan, the former Prime Minister, was a Balliol man.

Sir John's manservant poured sherry, and the two men sat watching the storm grow in intensity across the bay far below. Great columns of spray shot off the concrete breakwater on the far side of a neat little yacht basin.

Sir John took a sip of sherry. "You know, Mr. Quint, one of my ancestors, also a John Scoble, built a fort called Berryhead at Brixham on the far side of the bay there, against a possible invasion by Napoleon. Yes, he did. Your own Fourth Infantry Division practiced amphibious landings at a beach near here in preparation for the invasion of Normandy." Sir John cleared his throat. "It's very hard for us British to communicate with you Americans, you know. But the stakes are very high. We have an obligation on both sides of the Atlantic to do our best."

Quint removed his notebook from his jacket pocket.

"Now, it was my understanding when I agreed to give this interview that it will be for background only. If you want to know what I'm thinking, it will have to be that way. I do hope you understand."

"I understand."

"Now then, you want to know the likely British position on your American proposals for new combat tactics in Europe. Should Soviet tanks roll, according to this plan, then high-altitude reconnaissance aircraft will guide rockets carrying conventional warheads to destroy Soviet bases and supplies. As the Soviets advance, NATO forces will attack here, retreat there."

"That's it," Quint said, although he had learned about the proposal just that minute.

"This requires fewer troops, perhaps, but more sophisticated weapons—which you Americans would be pleased to supply, of course." Sir John looked to the ceiling as if pleading to God for assistance. "Would it really hurt for you people perhaps to give us British a scrap here and there? Maybe a tiny little contract? But those kinds of trade-offs can be negotiated. The real problem, Mr. Quint, is that you're asking the Germans to give up a front line. Germans living in Hamburg or Frankfurt aren't going to like that. And what Germans living in Hamburg or Frankfurt don't like, German politicians aren't going to approve. The Germans have a veto in NATO."

"We Americans always plan ahead," Quint said.

"The Germans will insist on a front line with tactical nuclear weapons to back it up. They know from experience what it's like to be occupied by Russians. You American chaps were the ones to pop the bombs first. We've been trying to replace the cork ever since. All this conventional warfare stuff is a lot of talk, really. The bomb's the problem."

"Yes, the bomb."

"Neither the British, the Americans, nor the Russians will use the bomb. The point of having it is so you won't have to use it." Sir John shook his head. "You notice I excepted the French. Those bloody sods are apt to do anything." He took a sip of sherry and leaned forward. "But the French won't use it either, nor will the Israelis, and we all know the Israelis have nuclear warheads. These are complicated games we're playing—with taxpayers footing the bill. The real horror, Mr. Quint, is if some nutter should get his hands on some plutonium—someone responsible to no one and nothing except his own misguided imagination."

Sir John refilled their glasses. "Did you read last week where some bloody sod from the IRA walked into a classroom where a man was reading the Bible to a class of ten-year-olds and shot him full in the face with a shotgun?"

"I read that," Quint said.

"Can you imagine?" Sir John said. "Can you just imagine what that kind of mind might do if he got his hands on a little plutonium? But this is off the subject of NATO, I suppose."

Sir John's manservant came back into the room. "Excuse me, Sir John, but I have someone on the telephone. He says it's urgent, sir."

"I shan't be but a few minutes, Mr. Quint." Sir John rose and left Quint to sip sherry.

When Sir John got back, he looked shaken, stunned.

Quint assumed this was some disastrous turn of events for the British government. He rose to his feet quickly. Kline would have to make do with what Quint had already. "If you would like to end the interview, that's fine by me, Sir John. I believe I have everything I need."

"If you don't mind, Mr. Quint, thank you. I think that would be best. I've just received some shocking news." He took a sip of sherry. "It's been quite pleasant talking with you."

Quint shook hands with Sir John and left. As he stepped out, he looked back and saw the British minister of defense with a sorrowful look on his face.

Sir John stood at the window looking out at the storm.

SECTION F

12. *So there they were, two agents of Her*

Majesty's Secret Service, detailed to watch a demented American sitting hunkered over a portable typewriter wearing a fedora and smoking what the agents assumed was an illegal substance. They didn't care what he smoked. Hash was cop work. These two were spooks. It was cold and wet out, and they were forced to stand in the shadows and watch the American. They clutched their balls under their trench coats to keep their hands warm.

"You know, Perry," said the first. He pulled the collar of his coat higher up on his neck. "We're going to have to stand here all night, do you know that? Freeze our bums. They're not going to bring this chap in tonight. We could be having a pint somewhere."

"Why is it other chaps draw people who sleep? We get a bloody nutter. The bloke's not going anywhere. Look at him." Perry's breath came in frosty puffs.

Inside, Jim Quint was smoking up a storm, getting worked up for his big sex scene. He would have Humper poke many bad guys with his fabled knife. There would be love-moats and womanly tunnels beyond count. Quint would call this one *Humper Staab Sticks It In*. He would give Humper two women—throw him to the beavers, so to speak. Quint was tickled.

Perry said, "Look at that, will you, the bloke's got the giggles. Americans really are strange. Lucky we got rid of 'em." Perry wanted to smoke but couldn't, because the American might spot them. Perry was a British agent, a professional. He had his LIDMC to think about. British agents had a tradition.

Quint decided to lay out some possibilities. What this woman's nipples looked like. What that woman did when she was coming. A butt here. An arched spine there. Later, he would see if he could make any sense out of it. Quint took another hit of hashish. This book would gross them out. No editor would dare fold Humper after this one.

Quint wrote, "Humper looked squinty-eyed over the landscape, an experienced prospector. To his left, a rounded hill dropped steeply into a humid, dark ravine. Up ahead, her gash was split, glistening, a seam of gold in a brushy arroyo." Quint signaled a triumphant thumbs-up at the end of that sentence. Humper, old pal, Quint thought. There were all kinds of ways to hook and string together two women and one man. This was going to be fun—like playing with tinker toys or an erector set. "Beth's poop chute had a perfect, neat little shape, an impact crater on the Sea of Tranquillity." Quint was pleased.

The first secret agent said to Perry, "He's supposed to be a writer. What do you suppose he writes?"

Perry shifted from foot to foot. "Probably telling the folks back in California what curious people we are, closing the pubs for tea in the afternoon, shouting at one another in Parliament like bloody footballers."

"He's having a good time at it. I'll give him that."

"How in the world can he tolerate all that smoke?" Perry didn't care what Quint was smoking. He was envious. He wanted a cigarette. Standing in the cold wouldn't be so bad if he had a cigarette.

Quint wrote, "Up close, Beth's tongue was an erotic beast—one moment sensitive, delicate, the next hard and demanding. It wallowed, turned, reveled, rooted, in the warm slough between Janet's thighs. The tongue caressed, foraged greedily on the fun spot, breathed fire, slurped sweet lovejuice."

He wrote six pages of that kind of thing, typing in quick bursts, laughing, staring at the darkness of the courtyard. Then he read it, once, twice, three times. He had a lot of goodies on paper, but there was no spark, no flash. He shrugged. He'd go to bed. The odds were he'd wake up in the middle of the night, pumped, ready to run it through his Olivetti.

He poured himself another glass of bitter and thought about the two men who were standing under a tree at the far end of the courtyard. It was cold out there, raining. The men stood in the dark, talking. They didn't even smoke. If they had been Americans, Quint thought, one of them would have been smoking. Quint couldn't imagine why they were standing there. He assumed it was the curious British habit of closing pubs at 11 p.m. Tradition had pushed these two men onto the street. But they didn't want to go home. They wanted to chat. So there they stood, cupping their balls to keep their hands warm. Quint thought that it was such madness as the British pub laws that had lost Their Various Majesties the Empire.

Quint decided the next day he would go to Foyle's, said to be the largest bookstore in the world, and browse among the acres of delicious books. He closed the curtain and turned out the lights. He looked outside at the two men. They stepped out of the shadows and stood for a second under a street-light—Quint could see them clearly—then walked away.

Quint was standing there waiting his turn to cross the street to Foyle's when a black Ford Sierra pulled up at the curb. There were two men in the front seat. The driver adjusted the Sierra's rear-view mirror. His passenger lit a cigarette and rolled down the window. He looked up at Quint.

"Mr. Quint? Mr. Jim Quint, the journalist?"

Quint was surprised. He glanced down the street at Foyle's, then down at the man. How could a stranger in Soho know his name? "That's me," Quint said. He felt a hand on his shoulder. There was a man standing behind him.

Quint turned.

"Would you please get in the back seat, Mr. Quint." The man was about Quint's age and wore a herringbone tweed jacket and an English gentleman's hat.

What was going on here? "I'm going to Foyle's to look at books. You want to drive me to Foyle's?"

"I'm afraid we're prepared to use force if necessary, Mr. Quint."

"You guys are high rollers. I've got about fifty pounds on me."

The man in the tweed jacket smiled.

His colleague on the front seat leaned back and opened the rear door.

"Get in, please, Mr. Quint," Tweed Jacket said.

"The fuck you say." Quint turned in the direction of Foyle's.

Tweed Jacket casually kicked him behind his right knee. It was neatly done, quick as a mongoose. Quint's leg buckled. He fell against the open door.

"Shit! The last time anybody did that to me was in the fourth grade."

"Inside, Mr. Quint."

Quint knew he was dealing with a professional. He slid onto the rear seat of the car, followed by Tweed Jacket.

Tweed Jacket said, "You may call me Thomas, if you like."

"I don't suppose that's your real name, is it, Tom?"

Thomas laughed.

"I'm a journalist, a man of letters, an American citizen." Quint took his passport from his jacket pocket, then started to laugh. His man-of-letters line was too much. "My name is Secret Agent Humper Staab."

"We know who you are," Thomas said.

"Do I get to talk to my embassy, or is that asking too much?"

"No."

"I'm to be taken to the Tower, then, is that it?"

Thomas made an involuntary sucking noise with his mouth. The driver looked back at Quint through his rear-view mirror.

"It was treatment like this that pissed us off in 1776."

Quint suddenly recognized the two men in the front seat. They were the men who had stood all night under the tree across the courtyard from his room. He realized they must work for the British government. He thought of Alistair Jones running off to join the Vrienden. He suddenly felt secure. He hadn't done anything wrong. This was fun.

Background, maybe, for Humper or one of his other characters. "Hey," Quint said. "You two guys are the ones who stood under a tree outside my window last night."

"They did what?" Thomas asked. He suppressed a smile.

"I stayed up half the night working on a skin scene for a book. These two were standing under a tree across the court feeling themselves up."

"Doing what?"

The driver and his companion pretended to ignore the conversation. Their LIDMC's were exposed.

"Standing with cupped balls to keep their hands warm, I suppose. I wondered if they were gay boys having a tête-à-tête."

The driver kept his eyes on the road. His associate gave Quint a bland look. "Write porn, do you?" he asked.

"After a while they started jigging up and down," Quint said. "Grown men."

The man on the front seat twisted sharply.

"Perry," the driver warned.

Perry glanced at Thomas.

Thomas said, "You guys playing with your Lid-Mac's, were you?"

"You people are always sending American travel agents colorful brochures telling us what a civilized place this is. I was embarrassed." Quint shook his head. "They don't even do that in Cleveland."

He settled back on the seat. These guys deserved it. He hadn't done anything wrong. The Ford soon stopped in front of a block of brownstone row houses. He got out as he was instructed and preceded Thomas up the steepest stairs he'd ever seen. The driver and the other man stayed behind in the Ford.

Quint and Thomas went up, and up, and up, ducking their heads at low overhangs at each flight. A neat little sign at each point pictured a possible fractured skull and said "Mind your head." On the sixth floor, at the very top, Thomas opened a door and motioned with his hand for Quint to enter.

There was a card table in the center of the room with a rolling swell in its composition top. Tucked under the table were three folding metal chairs. There was an old refrigerator in one corner. The yellow wallpaper was marked by water stains and brittle with age. Heavy brown curtains were drawn over the windows.

On one side of the room there was an old couch, its shapeless cushions nearly threadbare. A small, balding man with a little paunch sat on the couch smoking a cigarette. He fingered a Zippo cigarette lighter with his left hand. The plump man took a drag on his cigarette.

He watched Quint. He said nothing.

"Would you please take a seat, Mr. Quint." Thomas began pulling the folding chairs from under the card table.

Quint sat. He saw there was a mirror on the wall. It was set into the wall, not hanging from a nail. Quint gestured at the mirror. "Two-way, I assume."

Thomas looked at the plump man, then back at Quint. "As you've obviously figured out, I'm an employee of Her Majesty's Government, an officer of MI6. Do you know what MI6 is?"

"Humper Staab saved their butts three or four times."

Thomas ignored that. "We're interested in learning more about a British citizen named Alistair Jones. I assume you've been reading the papers. Can you tell us why it is you lived with the Vrienden?"

Quint sighed. "I had an assignment from *Rolling Stone* magazine. My editor there is Jeff Grigsby, he'll tell you. He's the bastard who's really responsible. Is this being taped?"

"Where did you first meet Marissa Stanley and Anita Hawkins?"

"At Worms, Biblis C."

Thomas looked at the cigarette smoker as if seeking the latter's approval. The little man moved his head slightly. It was fine by him.

"What was your relationship with Miss Stanley?"

"We had ourselves a little Montana whing-ding," Quint said.

Thomas wet his lips.

Quint said, "She makes me feel like a jackrabbit with a hard-on." Quint winked at the cigarette smoker. Cowpoke to city boy.

"When did you first meet Alistair Jones?"

Quint thought about that. "I interviewed him in Milan."

"For *Rolling Stone* magazine?"

Grigsby'd love a piece on this roust, Quint thought. He said, "Yes."

"When did you see him next?"

Quint shrugged. "Mostly he hung around a little blond Vriend named Anita Hawkins."

Thomas looked at the floor then up at Quint. "Did they talk about that on the bus? What did they say?"

"Well, Marissa said Jones had been giving Anita the eye ever since an inspection at Norgent-sur-Seine. The Greens were there—the French version—and the Vrienden. Here was this very proper Englishman, they said, falling all over himself to talk to this little American sweetie. The Vrienden thought it would be good press to recruit him, so to speak."

Thomas looked at the plump man. "How did they propose to do that?"

"Propose? The guy was ready for it. Anita propositioned him the same day I interviewed him in Milan."

"Propositioned him?"

"She asked him if he wanted to shoot a little beaver. Something like that."

"Shoot a little beaver?"

"You'd probably express it differently," Quint said.

The plump little cigarette smoker snubbed out a butt in the saucer that served as an ashtray. He opened a new pack: Marlboros. He was a Marlboro man.

Thomas said, "Did Jones say anything in your interview about the problems of stealing plutonium? You know, a 'What If' kind of thing?"

"What?" Quint remembered the look on John Scoble's face.

Thomas repeated his question.

"He said there's a reactor at Karachi that's like a supermarket. He said the two of us could break in there and take what we wanted, like lifting a hunk of cheese or a pork roast. What's happened?"

Thomas looked at the plump man. "He told you that in Milan?" he asked Quint.

"Are the Pakistanis missing plutonium? What's happened?" Quint folded his arms and leaned back on the rear legs of his chair. That wasn't good for the chair, but he didn't care. "Well, I tell you something, pardner. You've got my name, rank, and service number. You can jaw away until your bladder fills up, but you're not getting jack from me until you tell me what's going on. That, as they say in Bison, is final."

Thomas looked at the plump man.

The plump man inhaled a lungful of Marlboro smoke and said, "It'll probably be in the papers tomorrow. One way or the other they're going to get onto it." He was an American.

The Brit named Thomas said, "Alistair Jones is dead. So are Wim van der Elst and Anita Hawkins. The Dutch police say Jones apparently shot and killed the other two in some kind of quarrel, then committed suicide. The murder weapon was in his hand."

"What?" Quint looked naturally to the plump man, a countryman, for help.

"Marissa Stanley is missing," the plump man said.

"The bomb?" Quint looked at Thomas.

"Missing," Thomas said.

"Oh boy."

"Would you be willing to take a polygraph examination over what you've just told us?"

"A lie detector? Bring it out if you like."

Thomas looked at the cigarette smoker. The plump man nodded. He approved.

"LaTrobe," Thomas said. He turned to Quint and said, "You're privileged."

"You are," the plump man said.

"I am?"

The plump man said, "Watch."

The door next to the mirror opened. A large man with a wrinkled, traveled face stepped out, pushing a mobile tray of electronic gear. He looked at Quint, at Quint's interrogator, and at the plump cigarette smoker. He shook his head sadly. His eyes were like those of a morose hound. He breathed heavily. His lips were chapped, like scraped bark. He moved his bulk with drama. He did not merely occupy space; he was someone to be reckoned with, dealt with. He stepped back inside and brought along another folding chair.

"Hello," Quint said.

The sad-faced man shook Quint's hand but didn't volunteer his name. He had thick, slow fingers. He said, "No man lies to me."

Quint said, "I'd sooner take the devil."

"I'll be attaching these clips to the ends of your fingers," he said to Quint. "They won't hurt. They measure galvanic skin response. You'll feel nothing. But if you lie to me, I'll know it."

"Whatever," Quint said.

"I'll begin with ten questions. I want you to tell the truth. Then I'll ask ten more. I want you to lie. Then I'll ask you the identical questions as this gentleman asked." He motioned to Thomas. "And perhaps a few more."

This last comment seemed a mild rebuke, but Thomas seemed not to mind.

"Go for it," Quint said.

"What is your full name, please?"

"James Allen Quint."

"Where were you born?"

"Bison, Montana."

Quint watched several needles zig-zagging on graph paper that inched slowly from the machine. He followed the instructions of the man with the wrinkled face. When he was asked to tell the truth, he told the truth. When he was asked to lie, he lied.

When it was over, the man with the wrinkled face studied the graph paper and said, "This man is telling the truth."

"See?" Quint said to Thomas. "No need to be so dramatic. All you had to do was ask."

"I'm sorry if I seemed harsh, Mr. Quint. You must believe me when I say I've got a lot on my mind."

The plump man rose and put his arm around Thomas. "Worry won't get you anywhere, Thomas. These things happen. We do our best; that's all anybody can ask. There are answers, and we will find them."

"Why us? Why us?" Thomas said. "One more. My God, why couldn't he have been one of yours or a West German or somebody? I just don't believe this is happening."

"You did what you thought you had to do," the plump man said. "We all approved, myself included. You didn't have any regrets at the time you did it. You thought it was the right thing to do, and that he was the right man for the job."

"Yes."

"Well, then. So something went wrong. You couldn't have known. You couldn't have foreseen. Could you, now?"

"I guess not," Thomas said.

The plump man turned to the polygraph operator. "Our man's ready. Any time, any place, he says. He's itching for action."

The polygraph operator scoffed. "I don't need to use this machine. I know liars. I know them by the look in their eye. When a man lies, I know it."

"Our man's good."

"He can lie to young polygraph operators, perhaps, students. I've seen him on videotape and read his dossier. I know what he is." He shook his head sadly and rose to his feet on painful joints.

"Oh yes? What's that?" The plump man smiled.

The polygraph operator, melancholy, kind, rested a hand on the little man's shoulder and whispered something in his ear.

The plump man paled. He cleared his throat. "Well, I suppose that's possible. Anything's possible."

The morose old man whispered in the plump man's ear a second time. The plump man's jaw tightened. He looked at LaTrobe in disbelief.

Thomas—Thomas Cunningham—stood and screwed on the top of his pen. "Thank you for your time, Mr. Quint. Mr. Farr here has volunteered to take you to Foyle's or wherever you want to go." He gestured to the plump man.

"They call me Georgie." Farr got his coat out of the closet.

Quint said, "Good luck, Thomas." Quint followed the plump little man down the steep stairs.

"I would have been irritated too," Georgie Farr said when they got to the sidewalk. He began patting his coat pocket for cigarettes. He opened a new pack. "I have a rented car."

Quint fell in beside him. "Why didn't you say anything?"

"It's his country. The Brits have such a record of screwing up. He wanted me to know he knew how to ask questions."

"How did he do?"

"He did all right." Farr stopped and took Quint by the arm. "I'm a desk officer of the Central Intelligence Agency. We refer to it always as the Company. Okay?"

"Sure," Quint said.

"Thank you." Farr was a pudgy little fellow but a brisk walker. He strode along: Heel. Toe. Heel. Toe. Tap. Tap. His polished Florsheims glistened. "I've always liked London," he said, "wonderful city. There's no reason we should be formal. Would you please call me Georgie?"

"Jim's my name." Quint had to hustle to stay with Georgie.

"Jim, the Chairman of the Board is concerned that we have a small problem on our hands."

"A deviation from the norm."

"I see you know the language. I hope you don't mind a little walk; my car's twelve or fifteen blocks away. I'm under doctor's orders to take a hike every day. Blows the fat out of your veins."

"No problem." The little guy sure was a walker, that was true. "We're talking about the big Chairman of the Board here."

"My Company has a director, Jim. There's just one Chairman. Keep in mind we're talking about a possibility. Just a possibility. People are understandably concerned." He flipped a cigarette and scrambled for another.

"Some possibility." Quint stretched his stride to keep up.

"We have to be very, very discreet when we look into something like this. You can understand that, can't you, Jim?"

"Of course."

"We have representatives who routinely interview travelers who have information that might help our enterprise. If a businessman or scientist is returning from someplace interesting, why then, we talk to them."

"Debriefing." Quint had learned that lingo for his Humper Staabs.

Farr smiled. "Yes, that's the term. This business today was sort of a debriefing. No real harm done, Jim? The man on the machine is named LaTrobe Blue. He's said to be the best in the world. There's only one liar said to be capable of beating him."

Quint was interested. "Who's that?"

"An American representative of the Company. A fabulous talent. This man was on temporary duty in England once as an instructor at a school where Blue's students were being trained. Blue wasn't there at the time, and the American bet the students they couldn't catch him in a lie. He relieved them of their paychecks."

"My God!"

"Yes. From that kind of nonsense myths grow."

"But the American liar has never faced the master."

"No, never," Farr said. "Blue felt humiliated and embarrassed by his students' failure. We've actually had foreign firms in our business ask if we couldn't pit our liar against LaTrobe, man to man."

"Who'd win?"

"I have no idea. LaTrobe wants to accept but the Brits won't let him."

"Well, why is that?"

"They don't want to squander his reputation on a foolish bet. LaTrobe's getting older, they say, and he isn't what he used to be." Farr's voice trailed off and he walked in silence, lost in thought.

Quint wondered what it was that LaTrobe Blue had whispered in Farr's ear. Quint adjusted his long stride to the little man's pace and waited for Farr to speak.

"Now then, Jim, in a possible anomaly such as we've been talking about, the rules are that I have to conduct a discreet preliminary investigation and get the Chairman's permission before I proceed."

"Rules?"

"Alas, Jim, there are rules for everything. I have to give something called a show-cause report. I have to show cause why the Company should risk an inquiry that might be leaked, to the press. The Chairman has to worry about stockholders."

"Huh?"

"A chairman can't afford to frighten stockholders. It's that simple."

"Oh, boy." The good old U.S.A., Quint thought. My country.

Farr lit another cigarette. "This is a preliminary phase. An informal thing, no big deal."

"I see," Quint said.

"You shared a berth for several weeks with Miss Stanley, didn't you?"

"Yes." They were halted by a red light.

"Then you spent some more time with her on the boat in Amsterdam."

"Yes."

The light was theirs. Farr stepped forth again with his quick tap, tap, tap strides. He looked up at Quint. "I've seen your young woman on video tape. She's a fine, fine-looking woman. An educated woman. Smart. It's been my observation that one's testicles direct and the feet follow when one is dealing with a splendid find. You'll be wanting to find out what happened to her."

"When a Bison man meets a Lost Horse woman in Worms, sparks fly."

"What reason have you dreamed up to go back to Amsterdam?"

Quint laughed. "I was going to write another Humper Staab, and there's a chance I could score with a magazine article about drugs and sex there."

"You might learn something I can use, you never know. Will you keep your eyes and ears open for me? If you hear something you think might interest me, why, give me a call. We have three people dead here in unusual circumstances. That bomb of theirs is missing. We ought to be very, very sure about something like this."

"I could do that," Quint said.

"If you learn something, you're going to have to get in touch with me. I'd like to give you some simple instructions now. This may sound like heavy Company stuff, but it's only routine."

"Routine."

"Absolutely," Farr said. He recited a telephone number.

"What area code's that?" Quint asked.

"Virginia. Please listen. Now what was the number? Please give it to me."

Quint repeated the number.

"If it's urgent, say 'bison stampeding.' If you say you're stampeding I'll be paged on my little bleeper and I'll get right back to you. Always, always make sure we know how to contact you. Use public telephones if you can."

"What if a poacher's standing there with a high-powered rifle trained at my head? You know, movie stuff."

"After you've given the operator the status of your call, a buzzer will sound. Say whatever it is you have to say. It'll be taped. Whatever you have to say will be confidential between you and me. If anything happens to me, your call will go to the Company director—also in confidence."

Jim Quint was amazed by this nutty turn of events. But he was game; this was fabulous background for Humper Staab.

Farr stopped suddenly and began looking at the sides of buildings. He began rummaging through his coat pockets even though his current cigarette was barely started. He pulled out a booklet guide to London. "Page thirteen for this section," he said. He began leafing through the booklet. "Yes, here it is." He studied the map. "I should have turned right when we came out of the safe house." He looked dismayed. "I'm not always this addle-headed."

They must be thirty blocks from Farr's car by now, Quint thought. Were they going to walk? Quint didn't mind. He liked a good hike now and then.

Farr looked up and down the street. He was irked. "This street's normally loaded with cabs. They're all over the place. What happens when you need one? Where are they now?"

Farr was willing to go to some lengths to help out his heart, but walking thirty more blocks wasn't one of them.

"Oh, one more thing, Jim. I have a French friend in Amsterdam, Jacques de Sauvetage. If he happens to look you up, I'd appreciate it if you'd help him all you can."

"Just a routine matter?"

"That's right, Jim. Routine. I find it hard to believe I did this."

"And de Sauvetage is with?"

"Ahh, there's a cab. The Sûreté, Jim."

"That bit of bad news back there, from LaTrobe Blue. That didn't have anything to do with me, did it?"

"You?" Farr looked surprised. "For heaven's sake, of course not. It has to do with a disconcerting possibility, an anomaly perhaps. A routine matter, Jim. Routine." Farr slipped onto the black seat of the cab and waited for Quint to settle. "Poor Thomas," he muttered softly.

13.

It was getting dark when Jim Quint, Lost Horse Marissa ever on his mind, turned right from the Prinsengracht onto the Brouwersgracht. Alistair Jones and Anita Hawkins were dead. Pangs of anxiety clutched at Quint's stomach. He hadn't realized how much he cared for Marissa until she was missing. If he found her, he swore he'd let her know, swore he'd make it up to her. The street lights were on, their yellow light low and heavy over the brick street. The light was a dappled gold, shimmering and sparkling on the water. The closer to the *woonboot* he got, the faster Jim Quint walked. If Marissa were still alive, she'd be counting on him.

He walked past the *woonboot* in the darkness. He turned. He walked back and squatted by the boat. What was different? The cabin light was out. He'd always recognized the *woonboot* at night by its cabin light. He looked over his shoulder for landmarks. Yes, there was Cor's Place.

Quint hopped onto the deck and tried the cabin door. Locked. He was down on his hands and knees peering through a porthole when a man spoke behind him. "He said you'd be here, Monsieur Quint."

"What?" Quint stood and rubbed his knees.

"The *woonboot*'s locked. The Vrienden are gone."

"Were you standing there all the time?"

"Oh, no. I was watching from Cor's."

Quint leaped ashore and shook the man's hand. "And you are?"

"Inspector Jacques de Sauvetage."

Quint had to look up at de Sauvetage, who must have been six foot four. "Of the Sûreté, I'm told."

"Oui, monsieur."

De Sauvetage had an elegant, calm, reassuring manner about him. He was thoughtful, civilized. He had wide, pale, intelligent eyes. His face looked drawn. He was too thin. He could have used another helping of potatoes, Quint thought. De Sauvetage wore a fedora. His trenchcoat was resplendent with buttons and buckles, straps and belts.

"Is that trenchcoat a Burberry?"

De Sauvetage grinned. He was pleased. "Do you like it?" He opened the front so Quint could see the plaid lining. "Let me buy you a drink, Monsieur Quint."

"Sure," Quint said. He followed de Sauvetage across the street. "Fabulous coat. I always wanted to buy one of those— a Burberry, not just another trenchcoat. Here I am a writer, a world traveler. I've lost my luggage, been screwed by exchange rates, and afflicted with loose bowels on polite occasions. That's Eric Ambler stuff: trenchcoats and fedoras. In the end I always chicken out, decide it's stupid to spend that much money on a raincoat."

"Some day you'll buy yourself one."

"Humper Staab wears one. That'll have to do for now." They settled into a table.

De Sauvetage ordered jenever and beer for himself and Quint. "Monsieur Farr said you'd be looking for the young woman who was traveling with the Vrienden, Marissa Stanley."

Cor brought them jenever in small frosted glasses and glasses foaming with Amstel. "A knock and a head, gentlemen," he said. A knock and a head was jenever with a beer chaser.

"I don't know what happened to her, monsieur, but let us toast truth and good endings."

"I'll drink to that," Quint said.

"We've accounted for most of the Vrienden and their friends. They all say Marissa knew what happened to the bomb. They say Wim and Anita knew what happened as well; Wim and Anita were shot in the head, as reported in the newspapers. Monsieur Jones apparently committed suicide."

"Oh, Lost Horse, where the hell are you?" Quint was sore at himself for having stayed behind in Milan.

"Jones didn't leave a suicide note."

"Should he have?"

De Sauvetage took a sip of jenever. "They almost always do. They want to get everything off their chest. They want to have the last word. They want to spite somebody. They want to make martyrs out of themselves. There's always a reason."

"No note," Quint said.

"None. Of course, you could argue that this was a sudden, impassioned act. Maybe he caught Wim and Anita in bed together. Under those circumstances people don't always write notes."

Quint looked out at the silhouette of the empty *woonboot*. "It's hard to believe he'd have found Wim and Anita in bed. Wim was in love with Catherine, a real beauty."

"She sits windows, I'm told. The other thing, monsieur Quint, is that Alistair Jones had no reason to own a pistol. Why did he have a pistol? If it was a lover's quarrel and he went to all the trouble to get a pistol, then we'd likely have a suicide note. He would have had time to brood, time to plan his exit."

"It doesn't follow, does it?"

"No, it doesn't. I think it's worth asking a few questions, don't you, monsieur?"

"I'm not going to leave Amsterdam until I find out what happened to Marissa."

"Did you ever meet an American black man named Leonard Poteet, called Teets by his friends?"

"I met him briefly the day I got on the bus. He used to supply the Vrienden with hash, although I suppose you know that."

De Sauvetage smiled. "This is the drug capital of Europe, monsieur."

"You'd like me to ask him a few questions."

De Sauvetage raised his glass of jenever for another toast. "If you wouldn't mind, Monsieur Quint. You're both Americans. He knows you."

There was something about the impeccably dressed Jacques de Sauvetage driving a Citroën 2CV that struck Quint as incongruous. It turned out de Sauvetage was something of a talker when he got started. "A Dutch friend loaned me the Citroën for my stay here. There's a certain satisfaction in pushing off from your doorstop like Thor Heyerdahl. Nice section, this. Look at those handsome doors." He gestured loosely to one side.

Quint looked, but saw only a confused jumble of doors and white window sills as the 2CV zoomed over the brick cobbles on loose shock absorbers. The tires rumbled on the streets as the Citroën leaned into the corners. De Sauvetage followed one canal, turned down a second, and onto yet a third. Quint held on tight. He was disoriented. Each bar, each café, each block looked like the one just past.

"Not far," de Sauvetage said. "Lovely city, isn't it? The clubs here stay open until six in the morning, Monsieur Quint. This one is quite popular. It is the future, I'm told. Or something." De Sauvetage passed his hand across his tired eyes. "The Melkyweg is the most famous. They have movies there, music, stalls where you can buy hashish."

De Sauvetage looked drawn in the yellow light that flickered across his face as they passed dim street lights. He was a man of substance, of breeding. He was aware of larger duties, a sane man in a time of madness.

The narrow row houses in the Centrum District—many of them five and six stories high—were built by Dutch masons in the fifteenth and sixteenth centuries. The tall buildings blocked out the night light on the narrow streets. The streets were too narrow for two-way traffic, too narrow for sidewalks. When there were sidewalks, parking was prohibited by phallic-looking upright metal posts humorously called Amsterdamers.

The streets flanking the canals were lighter, gayer in mood. De Sauvetage turned onto one of them, pushing the two-cylinder Citroën as though it were an Alfa Spyder. What Quint liked best about the city was that the canals were never far away. He remembered walking a canal once when he was in Amsterdam on a story about avant-garde artists. He found a stretch of the Prinsengracht so quiet in the early morning that when he closed his eyes and listened to the mallards jabbering on the water, it was like being in Montana in November.

De Sauvetage slowed the car, looking for a niche to park the Citroën. They were at the Zoom Club. De Sauvetage swung the car onto a sidewalk unprotected by Amsterdamers, and killed the engine. He unfolded from the tiny car and checked the creases of his trousers. He adjusted his Burberry, giving the elbows and sleeves a slight tug. He checked his fedora. He was ready. He reached into his jacket pocket and pulled out a card, which he handed to Quint.

It was a membership card to the Zoom Club with Quint's name neatly typed in. The card, Quint saw, was dated.

"Why, you Gallic rascal, you. This card was filled out two days ago."

De Sauvetage laughed. "The Sûreté makes do with what it can. I think you should go inside first, monsieur. You lived with them. You know some of their friends. I only know them from their pictures. I'll go for a walk and come in myself in a half hour or so."

"Better there should be some time between us."

"When you see me come in, ignore me." That said, the worried-looking Jacques de Sauvetage strolled down the

street with the unhurried, calm manner with which he had
apparently been born.

Behind him, Jim Quint looked at his membership card to
the Zoom Club. He put the card away and smoothed his
mustache with the back of his forefinger. He began humming the *Third Man* theme, doing his best to imitate the
sound of that famous zither.

De Sauvetage turned around and called back: *"Bonne
chance,* Monsieur Lime."

Quint stepped through the main door of the Zoom Club,
membership card in hand. He found himself in a small foyer
where coats could be checked at a counter on the left. The
foyer opened into a room filled with young people dancing
to taped music. This was free dancing, dancing without part-
ners.

In front of the door and the dancers stood the largest Asian
man Jim Quint had ever seen. He was as tall as de Sauvetage,
but had massive muscles that pulled at the fabric of his dark
blue shirt. He wore a yellow tie. He had a small head on a
huge body. His face was delicate, round, and soft. He had
dimples.

The Asian glanced at Quint's card. "Have a good time,
meneer," he said.

The first room was a rectangle about twenty feet wide and
forty feet long. The walls, ceiling, and floor were painted
white. There was no furniture. Loud rock and roll played
from huge speakers built into the walls. Slides of animals,
buildings, posters, aphorisms, abstract art, naked women—
that, and more—flashed across the walls and ceiling.

It was there Quint lingered first, watching the faces and
forms of young people dressed in World War II flight jackets,
plastic trousers, and boots of every description. He recognized nobody.

The second room was larger, with tables and chairs and
an oval bar in the center. Six bartenders were trying to cope
with the be-leathered young people standing three deep
around the bar. Those gathered in this larger room had their
choice of three movies being shown on the walls—Steve
McQueen, Humphrey Bogart, or Alain Delon. The movies,

shown with Dutch subtitles, flickered soundlessly, part of the ambience of drugs and music, sound and sights.

Quint spent more than his alloted half hour looking for a familiar face. He was about to give up when he saw Leonard Poteet standing alone, basking in a hashish high. His eyes were closed. He was snapping his fingers to the beat of the nearest source of music. He didn't see Quint coming.

"Remember me, Leonard?"

Poteet opened his eyes. "It's Teets, man. Oh, you."

"Jim Quint."

"The magazine guy. You start calling me Leonard, Jimbo, and you'll have these folks thinking I'm gay. This ain't Philadelphia."

"Sorry."

"That's cool, man. See that dude over there?" He nodded his head in the direction of de Sauvetage, who had entered the room.

"I see him."

"That man is a cop of some kind. I've got an instinct for cops."

"He's a tall one," Quint said.

"I like his coat, man. Wouldn't you like a coat like that? And would you dig that hat? You take that hat and put it on old Teets's dome and chicks'd turn hair-up six blocks away. Class. You have to give him that, a classy cop."

"I'm trying to find Marissa, Teets."

Teets shook his head. "You been reading the papers? If I were you, man, I'd leave it alone."

"I have to try, Teets. It's one of those things."

"Rumor in this town has it those Vrienden dudes done got themselves into some heavy-duty traffic. I'm talking negative berries. Deep, hard, negative berries."

"Can you help me, Teets?"

"She's a fine chick, man, there's no arguing that. Beats hell out of me why she'd want to hang out with a washed-out fart like you." Teets took Quint's hand and inspected it close up. "Look at that skin. No color." Teets threw Quint's hand back, a reject.

"Tell me, Teets."

"Like I hang out with dudes who move stuff. I hear stories.
These folks'll smuggle anything, don't make a shit to them.
They ain't the C fucking I A, man; they're not very good at
keeping secrets. One of them smuggles something different,
they talk."

"What are they saying?"

"Well, these Dutch dudes are saying the Vrienden did a
little number on a nuclear power plant in Pakistan. They
sneaked their empty bomb down there and loaded it up—
sort of like at a gas station." Teets looked amused.

"What?" Quint leaned closer to Teets.

"That's it. The Englishman there in the papers, you know,
the one who killed Wim and Anita. He's the one who did it.
He was the main man."

Quint shook his head in disbelief. "Why would they do
that? The Vrienden are pacifists."

Teets kept an eye on de Sauvetage. "You know, I bet Mr.
Cool there has heard this stuff too. I'll bet that's why he's
in the Zoom tonight. They say that English dude knew his
stuff."

"I interviewed him once."

"Then you know what his job was. The papers said he and
an American were supposed to be the best in the world."

"Why would Alistair Jones help them steal plutonium? He
was a security expert. That was his life."

Teets grinned. "He did it, man. He pissed in the bong. He
was English. Maybe that explains it."

Quint looked disgusted. "A rumor like that has to be easy
to come by, with all the stories in the papers."

"The rumors started before the dude killed himself—if
that's what happened."

"Well, who helped them move it?"

Teets shook his head. "Man, I don't speculate on stuff like
that with three people dead. If that chick of yours knew
about it, she's tit deep."

"Have you any idea where I might find her?"

"Not Marissa, I don't, but I saw the window chick Wim
hung out with. Now there's a fine-looking woman."

"Where did you see her, Teets? Where?"

"I don't know, man. She was sitting in one of them windows waiting for someone willing to fuck her for fifty guilders. Probably more for her."

"Where?"

"I wish I could remember the street for you. I was just boogying along and there she was sitting in one of those windows. I don't think she recognized me."

"Thanks, Teets. I mean it."

"All the best to you, man." Teets grabbed Quint by the shoulder. "I've got some good Lebanese red, if you're interested."

"I don't think so tonight." The band of Quint's panama was already bulging with joints.

"Whatever," Teets said. He closed his eyes and went back to snapping fingers.

Jacques de Sauvetage was a sensitive man. He waited for Quint to tell the story his way. The inspector turned the Citroën onto a gaily lit canal. There were many Amsterdamers on the streets, bundled up, walking briskly, or riding bicycles. Dutchmen in the bars drank Amstel or Heineken. Later, they would sway together, arm in arm, shoulder to shoulder, singing drinking songs—accordions, tubas, oompah-pahs, *bier* and good friends.

"Teets have anything to say?" de Sauvetage said at last.

"Yes, he did," Quint said.

"Had some hashish for sale, I suppose."

"Lebanese, but I said no."

"The Dutch police tell me he sells first-rate smoke at fair prices."

Quint told de Sauvetage everything Teets had told him, doing his best to recall the conversation in detail, word for word. That was a skill Quint had developed as a journalist. There were times when it wasn't the smartest idea to be seen scribbling notes.

When he finished, de Sauvetage said, "What do you think of that story, monsieur?"

"I'd say it stretches credibility to think Jones would pull a stunt like that. Still, you never know, I guess. Teets admired your trenchcoat and hat."

"American black men appreciate style, although theirs is not exactly mine. Those hats of theirs, those shoes." De Sauvetage braked for an unlit bicycle that appeared suddenly from shadows. "You don't have to dodge bicycles as much in America, do you? Everybody has a car." He zipped around a woman in tight leather pants. He watched her butt through the rearview mirror.

"We used to dodge deer back in Montana. Nice butt on that one."

"Oui, monsieur, well shaped. Informants working for the Dutch police have heard that same rumor, with some variations."

"That little man in London. What's his name?"

"Georgie Farr."

"Has Georgie Farr heard this rumor?"

"Oui, monsieur."

"What do the Pakistanis have to say about this?"

"They have assured both my country and yours that everything is fine. Nothing is out of line."

"Why would the Pakistanis lie about something like that?"

"You must remember we are dealing with Muslims. Who knows what to believe? By the way, would you like to go to the Hotel Krasnapolsky? I have a room there and we can talk in private."

"Sure," Quint said.

"Monsieur, you strike me as a man who believes this is a logical world."

"Anything's possible, I suppose." Quint retrieved a joint from the band of his panama and lit up. He offered it to de Sauvetage, but the Frenchman grinned and shook his head no. That was too bad. It was good hashish and deserved to be smoked by a Frenchman in a trenchcoat. Quint grinned lazily at the craziness of the world. "I'm not giving up until I find Marissa."

"We should not ignore this rumor, monsieur, no matter what the Pakistanis say. There are people out there who will

do anything. Out of revenge. Out of loyalty. Out of madness.
Out of stupidity. Monsieur, this is serious business."

"I'll help you any way I can."

De Sauvetage gripped Quint by the knee, a gesture of
thanks. "Teets said Catherine is working a window in one
of the red-light districts here. That ought to be an interesting
job for you, monsieur."

"Whatever."

"Finding a particular window woman in Amsterdam won't
be easy. There are scores of them. All a woman needs is a
room with a street-level window, a red light bulb, a negligee,
and a clean bedspread. They don't keep set hours. And if
you walk by a window and the curtains are drawn but the
lights are on, then she's entertaining a customer."

"That means a lot of walking."

"Oui. The famous district in Hamburg is more concentrated. In Amsterdam there is one main area and two or
three smaller ones. You might have to make a couple of
passes down a particular street or alley to make sure. Three
or four times would be better. You'll have to be systematic."

"I'll truck till my rods give out." Quint felt he was being
treated as de Sauvetage's equal, a colleague. He liked that.

"Monsieur?"

"I don't mind a little hike, Inspector. I've got my Nike go-
fasts on and my pins work just fine." Quint took another hit
on his joint. He felt he was being sucked into some mad
netherworld.

"Fine, then. While you're doing that, I'll be drawing on
information from Interpol and working with a colleague in
the Dutch police. To help us out, my Dutch police friend
gave us this."

When they got to de Sauvetage's hotel room, the tall
Frenchman spread a map of Amsterdam's Centrum District
out on the coffee table. De Sauvetage's map showed the old
town, laced with canals. The map covered about fifteen
square blocks in the heart of the Centrum. Each street was
marked by tiny lines indicating shared walls. Someone had
made a check, in a neat hand, by each row house, indicating
how many windows were being worked in that building.

"How much do they charge?"

"Fifty guilders," de Sauvetage said. "Fair rate, do you think?"

"I was just curious, is all," Quint said.

14.

Quint started his quest in the streets and alleys off the Oude Zijds Voorburgwal and the Oude Zijds Achterburgwal—two canals in the heart of Amsterdam. This was the old area of Amsterdam, the Centrum. The area around the Voorburgwal and the Achterburgwal had once been heavily fortified and later became the sailors' quarter. Over the years it had turned into one of the most famous red-light districts in Europe.

Just across a large square from the Queen's Palace was one of Amsterdam's finest department stores, de Bijenkorf. To one side of de Bijenkorf, by the entrance to the parking garage, there was an alley.

Jim Quint stepped down this alley and began his hike.

Catherine was a window lady. This meant she had a room rented at close to street level. Quint found that the windows, as in the first alley behind de Bijenkorf, tended to be grouped in clusters—to encourage browsing, he assumed. It was a festive market; Quint felt in a good mood. He wasn't interested in a be-condomed fifty-guilder screw, but that didn't make any difference.

He found that the proprietress of a window, looking her best, usually sat in a velvet chair. Maroon Persian carpets seemed to be the fashion among the hookers. The drapes, often dramatic white lace over scarlet velvet, were neatly drawn at each side of the window.

In Quint's first hour of hiking, he got to see several women, having accepted a commission, pull the neat little bows that held the window drapes. It was madame's pleasure to pop the bows. This was done with a neat flick of the wrist, very often accompanied by a sly grin at passersby. Quint thought this was wonderful. It was suggestive, worldly, free.

There was one hazard to hiking the alleys and streets of Amsterdam that Quint hadn't counted on. At first he thought Amsterdamers were looking for lost change, perhaps, or a gem somehow popped from the grasp of a diamond cutter. What they were looking for was dog manure. Quint had been in a lot of dumped-upon streets in the world, but Amsterdam took the cheese. These weren't little oopsies or squittles of shit. Oh, no. Quint half expected to round a corner and see a squatting mastodon grunting its relief or wildebeests doing their duty.

Every once in a while Quint saw a swift streak of odious brown or bilious yellow, evidence of an uncautious walker. He imagined a fastidious Englishman, used to clean streets and walking head up with his little hat on, suddenly skiing wildly on one heel, cursing dogs as his head struck the pavement.

The trick, Quint realized, was to keep his eye on the pavement and watch the women in the windows at the same time. The settings and costumes in the windows varied, as did milady's beauty, her fee, and the promise of dreams delivered.

The Dutch had a liberal imagination and thought this was all civilized and charming, in its way. Those involved were adults. A deal was struck, a service rendered. It was fun to cruise the windows and speculate. One woman wore a garter belt and silk stockings, the next a baby-doll nightie, the third a leather bikini.

Dissenters inevitably likened the windows to a market. Quint found this tiresome after a while. It had become a cliché. Still, he understood their point. For example, one window might have potatoes in it, for the man who demands big boobs and doesn't mind a little starch. There might be asparagus in the next window, a slender lady for the man who doesn't mind waiting in line or spending a few extra guilders. Quint thought of all kinds of vegetable lines. Humper could meet women with breasts like hybrid squash, buttocks like pumpkins, nipples like fresh radishes, fingers like green beans. Would green beans work? Quint decided not.

What man in his right mind would want his balls caressed by green beans?

Men from all over Europe cruised the windows, taking their time. (It was not in bad form to have a look as long as one didn't gawk.) They shopped around. There was much for a man to consider when he invested his guilders. Each made his decision with the ghost of Dr. Freud peering over his shoulder.

Only in the most competitive alleys, Quint found, did anybody bother to sit before mid-morning. At about eleven or eleven-thirty, more women appeared in their windows. This, Quint assumed, was for Amsterdam businessmen grown eary of Wiener schnitzel for lunch. The women opened their curtains in numbers in the afternoon. Afternooners, Quint reasoned. In the late afternoon, the women waited to be reviewed by Amsterdamers commuting by automobile. The men waited for their turn at major streets, inching their Opels and Talbots forward.

Quint hiked up and down canals, in and out of alleys and side streets. When the traffic was thin, a woman didn't have much to do except maybe knit or read magazines and romantic novels. A woman absorbed in a crossword puzzle or needlepoint doesn't look that hot to trot; those windows on the street level usually had large rearview mirrors rigged on their windows so the women could watch for oncoming traffic. This gave them time to knock off such private pleasures as the picking of noses and behinds, time to start looking Rubenesque if they were overweight, or urgent if they were older.

Quint found Catherine at the far side of dusk on his second day out. She was sitting in a window in an alley behind the Hotel Brouwer, where the Blauburgwal meets the Singel. Catherine saw Quint through the window and had a housecoat on by the time she opened the door.

"God, Jim, I hope you're here looking for the people who killed Wim and Anita."

"I sure am. And for Marissa." Quint was prepared to swim oceans if necessary, climb mountains.

"Marissa's hiding out in the Brouwer just around the corner. She's afraid to come out for fear Gerald Murrant will find her. She said you'd come. Mr. Brouwer's watching for a man in a panama. Room number five."

Marissa Stanley was so relieved to see Jim Quint when he stepped into her diminutive hotel room that she let him have it with a burst of relieved laughter and took him full in the face with a plastic squirtgun. "Oh, you Montana bastard! Where have you been? I thought you'd never show up. How d'you like my gat?"

Quint wiped the water off his face with the back of his arm and gave her a kiss. "The best endings, love, are in the nick of time and the hero gets the girl."

Quint stepped aside as Jacques de Sauvetage, who had answered Quint's call from Catherine's and met him in the hotel lobby a few moments earlier, followed him into the room. "Marissa, this is Inspector Jacques de Sauvetage of the Sûreté."

"Charmed, mademoiselle." The elegant de Sauvetage bowed deeply in his handsome trenchcoat.

"Marissa, you must tell the inspector what happened to the bomb."

"Won't you have a seat, Inspector?"

De Sauvetage sat on the chair in front of the sink. His long shins bumped the edge of the ancient single bed upon which Jim and Marissa sat, each cross-legged. "Mademoiselle, I would like to tape what you say. I need it for your country-men and for others who are concerned. You understand what I mean?"

"Tape it, certainly," she said.

De Sauvetage opened his slender briefcase and adjusted the built-in recorder. "Whenever you're ready. Tell it how-ever you like."

"It's easy enough to tell. To put it bluntly, Alistair had left an awful wife and just plain went nuts for Anita. There was nothing he wouldn't do for her. Nothing. You should have seen him. He was lovestruck; there's no other way of putting it.

"One night the four of us, Wim, Alistair, Anita, and myself were smoking Moroccan out of a pipe. The others had gone to a rock concert. Alistair hadn't had as much experience smoking as the rest of us, and he was pretty high. We got onto the subject of unilateral nuclear disarmament. Wim and Anita both thought it would work. Alistair just laughed. He said sure, if the Americans hand in their bombs, the Soviets will just fall all over themselves turning theirs in as well. Anita said people are smarter than Alistair gave them credit for, and that it was possible to prove unilateral disarmament would work. Alistair literally began giggling at that." Marissa stopped here and looked at Quint, then at de Sauvetage. "You must believe me, this is exactly how it started. I will never forget it."

"Continue, *s'il vous plaît*, mademoiselle."

"Anita said if they could get some plutonium for the Vrienden bomb they could arm it and turn it in on behalf of the PLO, the IRA, and the Red Brigade, all the radical nasties and terrorists in the world. She said they could do it before an enormous press conference held at the United Nations in New York. There, in front of the television cameras, she said, they could turn in their atomic bomb and challenge the nuclear powers to do likewise. She said if all the peace groups and churches put as much pressure as possible on their governments, why then, something might happen. She said she knew they wouldn't turn over their entire arsenals at once, but suppose they turned in one each, just to shut everybody up? There is a bottle of red wine and some paper cups in the closet there, Inspector."

Marissa waited while de Sauvetage poured them each a paper cup of wine. "Anita likened this to Eve biting the apple, only in reverse. In this case it was the pear of hope, the desire to preserve the human species, and plain old common sense. She said only something imaginative and shocking would make people pay attention. Otherwise, she said, we're doomed to repeat the same old crap. The only other thing that might shake people up would be if somebody actually blew up a city." Marissa paused here and took a sip of wine.

"I remember watching Alistair when Anita was outlining her fantasy. Wim was working on a half-liter bottle of Grolsch and listening. When she finished, Alistair took a big hit on the pipe. He said he could steal the plutonium and load it for them."

"For unilateral disarmament, mademoiselle?" De Sauvetage clearly didn't believe that was possible.

"No, no." Marissa laughed. "He thought that was preposterous, a pipe dream. Nothing would come of it. On the other hand, he said, if they turned in a loaded atomic bomb at such a press conference, it *would* prove what he'd been saying all along, namely, that there are real dangers in the proliferation of nuclear facilities. He said there was an outside chance that the gambit would encourage negotiators at the disarmament table."

"But he didn't give that much hope, did he, mademoiselle?"

Marissa shook her head. "I think he mostly said it to please Anita. But he did think his point—a critical one, he thought—would be proven. Perhaps some good could be done. He said he would do it only if he were in charge. Only the four of us would know, plus a fifth person, someone experienced in smuggling contraband. Wim said no problem, he was sure Gerald Murrant would help us all he could." Marissa stopped, unable, momentarily, to continue.

"Oui, mademoiselle, it was very likely Gerald Murrant who killed Anita and Wim."

"I wasn't even a Vriend. I was just here taking notes for a paper nobody'll ever read anyway. He'd have gotten me too, Jim, but I was on the other side of town. Missed my tram."

"Good for you," Quint said.

"This tram system is confusing to a girl from Montana. Never have figured out how many numbers on the strip to put in the little puncher thing."

15.

Georgie Farr had never before attended a meeting of the National Security Council. That had always been the job of Angus Garvey, who was DCI—Director of Central Intelligence—or one of the other Grand High Muckamucks at Langley. It was the Company's mandate to provide intelligence on the activities of foreign governments for the President and his Secretary of State.

This was a Code Two morning, meaning that the Council was faced with an urgent decision. Farr was on the line. Owing to his position, he would present the Company's case. He would make the recommendations.

Farr drove to Langley, where he got his notes out of security so he could review them. Farr went over his notes, neatly typed on special cards stamped "Top Secret." He typed them himself so as not to expand need-to-know even to his secretary.

Garvey arrived at nine o'clock. He stepped into Farr's office and sat down without saying anything.

Farr looked up from his notes. "Angus."

"We'll have to be going in a few minutes. We'll go in a limousine; you'll have a few more minutes on the way over."

"The President will be there, I suppose."

"Of course. This is a Code Two. I want you to take your time, Georgie. Go step by step: explain the evidence and your logic every step of the way. Leave nothing out. They're going to ask some pretty dumb questions, but be patient. You're going to wonder how some of them got where they are. Ride it out. There can be no Op investigation without their approval. It's in your charter, a show-cause report, then NSC approval."

Georgie Farr knew all that. Garvey just wanted to be sure Farr remembered. Georgie Farr was Georgie Farr.

"I'll be careful," Farr said.

"The President will be sitting at the end of the table, but remember, Wyland is National Security Adviser; it's his

Council." Terry Wyland wanted to replace Angus Garvey with Garvey's second in command, John Tarnauer. Garvey suddenly winced and sucked in a deep breath through clenched teeth.

"Ulcers?"

Garvey fumbled with the snap of his briefcase and retrieved a bottle of green tablets. He gulped two and waited, holding his breath against the burning. He relaxed. "Tarnauer will be in charge when I have these things operated on next week."

Farr said, "Yes, I know. I'll do my best."

"You have to understand, Georgie, neither Wyland or the President officially like the idea of The Op. It was originally a French idea, and the last administration went along with it. Everybody knows the French are assholes. If it's French, it's suspect. The Op's an easy target."

"We wouldn't want people to think wine drinkers could have decent instincts."

"You've been in government long enough, Georgie, to know it's necessary to understand the dynamics of something like this. You're suggesting a disturbing anomaly, believe me."

"An atomic bomb," Farr said, lest Garvey forget the unadorned word.

"If I were you, I'd avoid hard words like that in the Council, Georgie. These people prefer language that's a little more subtle, maybe."

Farr looked at Garvey and burst out laughing. What else could he do?

Garvey gripped his small friend around the shoulder, for they were friends, had been for years. "If you get into trouble, you can count on some help from me—but maybe not too much." Garvey wasn't about to give up his defense industry IOUs and the women.

Ordinarily meetings of the National Security Council were brief and routine. Reports were delivered by the various agencies involved; a summary of these was prepared by the President's national security adviser. At other times, such as in discussions of American positions in disarmament talks, the meetings were long and complicated. Terry Wyland sent a classified memorandum to the principals involved. This memo gave the day's agenda and specified whose attendance was required and who might send a surrogate. Sometimes the Council members received a simple code so that an issue might be debated before it was published in the *Washington Post*.

The stewards at the Executive Office Building, having been informed that this was a Code Two morning, had added more coffee pots to the Council's conference room. The sweepers had been called in to tech the room yet another time to ensure that Soviet agents weren't listening in from across town.

As Angus Garvey had said, they were all there: President Robert Lyle; Vice-President John Reeve; Secretary of State Littleton Davis; Secretary of Defense Willard Thompson; the admirals and generals of the Joint Chiefs of Staff; everybody.

They met in a large room that had an enormous polished cherry table as a centerpiece. The floor was carpeted blue, and blue curtains were drawn to foil parabolic snoopers. Cool colors, Farr supposed, so as to encourage cool thinking in times of national crisis. There were four huge silver coffee pots on a narrow table on the wall opposite the entrance to the room. On Code Two, the admirals and generals had to serve themselves; stewards were not allowed inside.

Farr declined to serve himself coffee, although he wanted some in the worst way. He didn't want to have to pee in the middle of his presentation.

As members of the Council began settling into their seats, Garvey took Farr by the elbow and led him to a man dressed in a brown suit with a pale yellow shirt. "Terry, I would like you to meet Op Two, Georgie Farr. He'll be giving our report this morning."

Wyland had thin, colorless lips and neat little bags under his eyes. He shook Farr's hand. "Pleased to meet you, Mr. Farr." Wyland was wary of Farr, a career man whose politics were unknown. Wyland had sold bonds before he was appointed National Security Adviser. He worried about discipline, worried that he wasn't respected, worried about reelecting Lyle.

Farr was shown to his seat in the center of the table just before Lyle entered.

The Council members rose when the President stepped through the door. Lyle was said to look like the actor Frank B. Ryan, famed for his portrayal of General William Tecumseh Sherman, the man who charmed the world with the sacking of Atlanta and who coined the phrase, "The only good Indian is a dead Indian." (President Lyle's press secretary, David Meyer, a humorous man, said Sherman had had it easy with Rebel sharpshooters. He ought to try dealing with southern congressmen sometime.) Lyle had Frank B. Ryan's commanding, handsome beak, his shrewd, quick eyes, and his expressive mouth.

Editorial cartoonists, of course, seized on this resemblance. As other presidents had, Lyle soon came to look like the cartoons—an imperious beak, domineering eyebrows, a strong jaw. Lyndon Johnson had a beak, tiny vindictive eyes, and ear lobes bigger than the Buddha's. Richard Nixon had a ski-jump nose and a sweating upper lip. Gerald Ford had an earnest forehead, Jimmy Carter, a saint's lips.

Lyle scowled and sat. He wet his lips. The amiable chatter ceased. Georgie Farr found himself barely able to breathe. He was an intelligence officer, not an entertainer, and had never before experienced stage fright. But reporting to the President was an awesome duty. To his relief, Farr saw that each participant had a glass of cold water in front of him and that there were crystal pitchers of water in the center— expensive cut glass. Water wouldn't race through his bladder like coffee. Farr yearned for coffee, loved the caffeine rush. But coffee, he knew, would race through his bladder. He couldn't risk it.

Terry Wyland rose at his end of the table, looking pious and serious. "Mr. President, gentlemen, we have a Code Two this morning at the request of Mr. Garvey of the Central Intelligence Agency. This is a report by The Op pursuant to regulations, seeking our permission to conduct an investigation in Europe."

President Lyle relaxed his thoughtful grimace so he could concentrate on what was being said. The eyes around the table turned to Angus Garvey and the pallid, scholarly-looking little man beside him.

"Mr. President, colleagues," Wyland said, "our report this morning will be given by Mr. George Farr, who is the American representative in The Op."

Everybody around the table, including the President, laughed at the introduction of George Farr. They had in the past received many reports from Georgie Farr, delivered by Garvey or Tarnauer. Farr was well known, although they had never seen him before. He was said to be one of the most brilliant officers in the covert section. George Farr? Georgie fit him.

"Georgie Farr," Wyland amended, to laughter from everyone at the table, including Farr himself.

Farr stood and removed his notecards from his jacket pocket. He got his bifocals out and put them on. That was better; he could see the notecards much better. He tilted his head forward and surveyed the faces watching him. "Mr. President." He nodded toward Lyle. "Mr. Wyland." He nodded toward the chairman at the opposite end of the table. "I'd like to begin with a brief review of Le Op, then get on with my report. You'll please note that your summary is classified top secret." Farr realized, too late, that he should have used the English definite article. "For some years there had been a fear that weapons-grade plutonium might somehow get lost or stolen. If this material got into the hands of revolutionaries, terrorists, zealots of one kind or another, or a psychotic, then we could have a problem on our hands. These people are responsible only to themselves; there is no moderating influence of the state. We all felt threatened: ourselves, the British, the French, the Chinese, the Soviets. We established The Op so we could share tips, bits and pieces of information that could avoid trouble.

"The leadership rotates every two years. The Soviets were first, then the British had a turn. Op One is now a Frenchman. As Op Two, I'm up next. Each country has different rules for its participants. For example, I have to get your permission to actively investigate a rumor."

"A wise precaution," Wyland said.

Farr looked at President Lyle, then back at Wyland. "I do have the authority, with the permission of the director, to do a covert preliminary investigation. That's been done in this case."

Georgie Farr told the President and the Council the circumstances and reasoning leading up to Thomas Cunningham's decision to send Alistair Jones across to watch the Vrienden bomb. He gave the President and his men a careful, detailed report. "It was an Op decision. We all participated. I agreed," he said.

President Lyle put the palms of his hands on the table, fingers spread. "My God, is that the man who was found dead when that bomb was stolen?"

"Yes, it is, Mr. President." Georgie Farr then told the President the details of the Amsterdam rumor.

President Lyle licked his lips and leaned forward on his elbows. "Alistair Jones was a British agent?"

"I'm afraid he was, Mr. President."

Lyle put his hand over his face. "The British Prime Minister has to call an election within a year. Was that part of your discussion?"

"No, sir. There are always rumors of plutonium on the black market. We wanted to keep an eye on the bomb."

Wyland said, "That's why the Company's required to get our permission, Mr. President, to make sure that kind of thing doesn't happen to us."

"Jesus!" Lyle said. "How long do you think it will take the British press to find out Alistair Jones was a British agent?"

Farr said nothing.

"Did you say we have an agent on Mrs. Lund's team?"

"Yes, Mr. President. His name is Harold Woods. He's been in the intelligence business for years. He began by spying on Mario Savio and the Berkeley Free Speech Movement for the FBI. Woods reports to myself and to the director." Farr turned over a notecard and surveyed the table. He continued:

"A person in Jones's position is rather like a bank inspector—he's privy to makes and models of locks. He knows how buildings are wired, where the records are kept. He knows how to handle the equipment that handles radioactive material."

"What did Harold Woods say about this man?"

"Woods said it was his opinion and that of the Hungarian team leader, Leonoor Lund, that Jones had been losing touch for months."

"Losing touch?"

"Woods said Jones was paranoid over security. He said Jones bored him and Mrs. Lund to death with stories about how easy it would be for some screwball to get his hands on some plutonium." Farr paused and looked around the table. "I have to admit, I was nervous when I came in here this morning. I decided not to drink coffee so as not to have a full bladder in the middle of all this. I think I need coffee." Farr was right in assuming the Council could use some relief. He retreated to the silver coffee urns and poured himself a cup.

Georgie Farr took a sip and wondered why he couldn't make coffee like that. "From the moment of Jones's reappearance in Holland, the Amsterdam police began hearing street rumors that Jones and van der Elst had taken the bomb to Pakistan and armed it with plutonium at a reactor near Pakistan. The rumor was specific. I would like you to listen to this interview with a young woman, a doctoral candidate at Columbia University—a non-Vrienden—who was present when a decision was made to load the bomb. This was taped yesterday in Amsterdam." Farr punched the on button and watched faces as Marissa told her story to Jacques de Sauvetage and Jim Quint.

When the tape finished, the silence hung like burning sulphur. "Did you ask the Pakistanis about this?" Lyle asked.

Farr nodded to Terry Wyland.

Wyland said, "I took care of that myself, Mr. President. Colonel Al-Zakbar was enraged that we should ask a question like that. Didn't we think the Pakistanis had good sense? Didn't we think they were honorable men? Did we think they would try to cover up something like that?"

"Mr. Farr?" the President asked.

"I don't have any answers for you. All the evidence leading up to the Pakistani denial suggests real danger. The evidence is circumstantial, yes. But we could have a dead psychotic who had the education and imagination necessary to arm the Vrienden bomb."

Wyland said, "The Pakistanis are adamant that nothing has been tampered with. Nothing is missing. Colonel Al-Zakbar gave me his personal assurances."

Pain stabbed through Farr's bladder. He shouldn't have taken a chance with the coffee. "I'm only asking that we make certain. Surely we can make some effort to pin things down a little, the dangers being what they are."

"Mr. Wyland was assured," the President said.

The pain again. This is how the world will end, Farr thought. "Who in this room can guarantee for certain the Pakistanis are not lying? Why would they lie? I don't know." The pain struck once more.

"What do you propose we should do, Mr. Farr?" Wyland asked.

"We should ask for a reinspection by the UN. In the meantime, we should get some people into Amsterdam. There's a reason we should be wary of blindly accepting the Pakistanis on this."

The President said, "Take your time, Mr. Farr."

"The Indians have a bomb. Pakistan then bought what it needed to build a uranium-enrichment plant which could be used to fabricate fuel for weapons. The Pakistanis dug a huge tunnel in the Baluchistan Mountains near the Afghan border—perfect for underground tests. They built themselves a deuterium uranium reactor for which they provided their own fuel. The UN asked for permission to inspect it. The Pakistanis said no. Their plant at Karachi was open to inspection, however, since it was Canadian supplied."

"The significance of this?" Wyland asked.

"The Pakistanis have no reason to divert fuel from the inspected facility at Karachi. If we reinspect and find the plutonium records have been tampered with, we'll know it was likely someone from the outside, and not the Pakistanis, who did the stealing."

"I see," Wyland said.

"I might add here that Alistair Jones inspected the Karachi facility four times before he ran off to the antinuclear group."

Wyland said, "Mr. Farr, do you have any idea of what the reaction of the world community would be if word got out that we're even worried about such a possibility, much less have people out there asking questions? In view of the Pakistani denials, I don't see how we can justify having Company agents wading around in the murk. Is the French Op One still investigating?"

"Yes, he is."

"Is he reporting to you the progress of his investigation?"

"Yes, sir."

"Mr. President?"

President Robert Lyle pursed his lips. The responsibilities of his office weighed heavily upon him. There was an election coming up. The day had not yet arrived when he could not learn from British screw-ups. The Pakistani assurances to Wyland were the key. No plutonium, no bomb. No plutonium, no risk. He was still safe. "I agree, Terry," he said. The President rose, looking wise. The meeting was at an end.

"We're dealing with people's lives here," Farr muttered. Garvey took him by the arm and gently guided him into the hallway. Pain twisted Farr's bladder. God, his bladder! Farr looked about, his eyes blind with pain. "Where the hell's a john around here?" He felt like whipping it out and urinating on the carpet.

16.

Angus Garvey was only going to be gone three or four weeks; nevertheless, John Tarnauer moved into the DCI's office. He was acting director. The office was there with all its trappings, for him to use if he pleased. It was like a new toy he couldn't resist.

Farr smiled when he read Tarnauer's inter-office memo. Beneath the from, to, subject, and date, was a one-sentence request for Georgie Farr's presence in Angus Garvey's office "at 1100 hours this date." It was signed John Tarnauer, Acting DCI. Farr handed the memo to his secretary, Barbara Mannes, who had been with The Op since its inception. "What do you think, Barbara?"

Barbara read the memo and winced. "The principal wants to see you."

"Brother Wyland's work, do you suppose?"

"I wouldn't be surprised."

Farr looked at the clock on the wall. "I think I'll go for a little walk."

Tarnauer looked at home behind Garvey's power desk. He was nattily dressed, impeccable. He wore large gold cufflinks. His suit, his posture, the calm, assured look on his face said: My name is Tarnauer, bureaucrat of bureaucrats, look upon my office, ye mighty, and despair.

"Well, Georgie, won't you have a seat?" Tarnauer didn't bother to get up.

Farr sat. "Nice office."

"Yes, well. Angus could be away as long as a month, we're told, and all the DCI's messages are rigged to come in here." Tarnauer looked at the courtyard outside the window. There was a white pebble walkway in the courtyard, which was landscaped with mosses, ferns, and elegant bonsai: tiny cyprus trees, miniature pines. "Georgie, I'm afraid we're going to have to put American participation in The Op on hold until Angus gets back from the hospital."

"Oh?" Farr said.

"Terry Wyland talked this over with the President, and neither one of them thinks it's right for us to be involved in this potentially risky business while Angus is in the hospital. Everybody's got a right to be sick."

Farr laughed. "Are you telling me this is because of Angus? You're doing this out of concern for Angus Garvey?"

"Georgie, Angus is on medical leave. I have the authority to do this, it's on paper."

"No, no. I'm not questioning your authority." Farr waved his hand. "Why don't you just call Angus and hear what he has to say?"

Tarnauer looked serious. "On this phone? To an open line in a hospital?"

"We can drive over there, if you want."

Tarnauer said, "We both know we won't be doing that, Georgie."

"So what am I supposed to do until Angus comes back?"

"I don't care, Georgie. Do crossword puzzles. Take long lunches."

"How about Barbara?"

"Your secretary? The same for her, crossword puzzles, and she can go shopping if she wants." Tarnauer reached under the desk and hit the stop button on the tape recorder. He leaned forward over the huge desk. "You know what your problem is, Georgie? You've been in the Company thirty years, I looked at your record. You have a reputation as having a brilliant mind. But you're all duty, duty, duty. They call you a mongoose sometimes, do you know that? You're little and quick and smart. But where has it gotten you? Have you ever stopped to think of that? A little PR goes a long way, Georgie. Those people over there are playing a high-stakes poker. All they want to be sure of is we don't hand the *Washington Post* some fuck-up to rub our noses in."

"We're talking about an atomic bomb here."

"Is that asking too much, Georgie? Those people don't know what you're going to do next. You're brighter than Angus Garvey. Did you ever stop to think of that? Here you are getting your plug pulled while he's in the hospital."

"What happens if I go on working?"

"We can fire you or transfer you, if we want."

"Angus wouldn't let you do that."

Tarnauer shrugged. "We'll see."

"What if The Op people in Britain or France have a question?"

"Answer their questions. We just don't want any American action initiated on this bomb business. If a newspaper story breaks that an investigation is under way in Europe, then we say we're being advised of its progress. If the British or someone get lucky and retrieve the damned thing, we'll take credit for being part of The Op."

"Just like that."

"That's what we're going to do. Georgie, use your head; we just can't get people all worked up over having a little plutonium around. We need the power."

"For all we know, that thing's like a cocked pistol aimed right at our heads."

"A cocked pistol without a bullet. If there were a real and present danger, if the Pakistanis had said yes, there is some plutonium missing, why then, we'd empty Langley, put everybody in the field. We'd be out there with flags flying and bugles blowing. As it is, we've got a missing hunk of metal. The Europeans are looking for it. They've got a few smarts too, you know."

Farr stood. "Well, I guess that's it, then."

"I'm sorry, Georgie." He watched Georgie Farr leave the office. He was worried by the look on Farr's face. Tarnauer asked himself, What if Farr is right? What if he is right and we're wrong? Tarnauer bit his lip. He was ambitious. His nose had an instinct for the buttocks of powerful men. Mmmmm. Kiss. Kiss. John Tarnauer liked his perks. Nevertheless, this business of a possible bomb bothered him.

Tarnauer picked up the phone and made a call. Just to be on the safe side. He'd send Len Meara to Jamaica, and maybe de Leeuw. They were old friends. Professionals. He could trust them to do a job.

Georgie Farr went to the cafeteria and had a big piece of apple pie with a hunk of vanilla ice cream on top and a cup of coffee. The pie tasted so good he had a second piece. Georgie's heart had been giving him trouble again, and he'd been warned about his diet. He was getting a little plump. Right now, he didn't care. The pie and ice cream tasted good. He walked back to his office.

"Well?" Barbara asked.

"He suspended our participation in The Op until Garvey gets back, but we'll go on working as before."

"You want to explain that?"

"Tarnauer's got it on tape that he suspended my active participation in The Op. If anything goes wrong, the Com-

pany and the President are protected. He and Wyland can
fire me if I don't watch it. Insubordination and all that."
Barbara said, "I thought Angus has friends on the Hill."
Farr shrugged. "Those people aren't any good. I don't have
anything to give them except a lot of grief." Farr paused at
the entrance to his office. "Did you read the FBI workup on
our friend Bison Jim Quint? He writes paperback adven-
tures. A Walter Mitty. A dreamer. My God!" Farr's heart
fluttered momentarily. He closed his eyes.
"Are you feeling all right, Georgie?"
Farr took two breaths and fumbled for his pills. "I'm fine,
thank you." He got the plastic top off the bottle and took
two, quickly. He sat down. "Did you know that in the middle
of this Alistair Jones fiasco, Harold Woods convinced the
Vrienden that he was a famous old radical from the 1960s,
that he once gave Lady Bird Johnson a moon?" Georgie
pretended to remove his pants and bent over to demonstrate
for Barbara. "He told them he had been an agent of the peace
movement for years, working inside the establishment. Yes,
Harold Woods."
"That man! Really?"
"Woods is famous for his ability to lie convincingly. He
was on temporary duty in England a few years ago at a
British intelligence course. He got to drinking bitter with
some young British polygraph operators."
"I've heard the story," Barbara said. "He won every bet."
"Well, maybe most of them—depends on whether Har-
old's telling the story or somebody else." Farr laughed.
"But he's never faced LaTrobe Blue."
"That he hasn't," Farr said.
Harold Woods had asked Farr for the New York loon list—
for Alistair Jones, he said. Woods was in communication
with Jones. Harold said Jones was concerned about a young
New York black named Leonard Poteet. Poteet was a hashish
peddler who had spent a lot of time with the Vrienden. Did
Poteet have radical or criminal associations in New York?
Jones wanted to know, Woods said. Farr wondered why the
request for the loon list had not come through Thomas Cunningham. Jones was a British agent, after all.

The request was outside of channels. Farr wondered why. Georgie thought he felt another quick flutter. He wasn't supposed to overdo it, he knew, but just to be on the safe side, he started digging for his bottle of pills.

Barbara said, "Oh, I forgot, the Interpol report on Gerald Murrant came in while you were talking to Tarnauer." She slid the report across the desk. "Maybe this'll make them change their minds."

Farr read the report. "I'll ask Tarnauer, but I don't think it'll do any good. Everybody around a President agrees with him. Pretty soon he thinks he can't make a mistake. It's considered un-Presidential to admit error. I'm afraid it's been a costly tradition. Right now, I think the smart thing for me to do is talk to Jacques de Sauvetage and Jim Quint. Can you please see if you can get them on the phone for me?"

Barbara had read Jim Quint's file. "Bison Jim, the stoned writer?"

Farr sighed. "That's the guy." Quint seemed like a nice enough person, maybe a little eccentric. One of his eccentricities—curiously enough, the smoking—was just exactly what Georgie Farr needed. Farr hated to do this to Quint, poor bastard, but he didn't have any choice.

17.

Jim Quint could tell by the expression on Jacques de Sauvetage's face at the telephone that something had gone terribly wrong. Georgie Farr apparently spoke good French, because de Sauvetage lapsed into long, passionate soliloquies in his mother tongue. His drawn face looked more and more worried. When de Sauvetage spoke French, he looked repeatedly at Quint as though sizing him up.

Quint knew he was at the heart of the problem, but it was impossible from the context of the conversation to tell how.

Finally, de Sauvetage said, "Oui, oui, Monsieur Farr. We have no other choice. I understand. I'm sorry this has happened." He looked at Quint. "No, no, monsieur, think nothing of it. We do what we must do. We are human beings first, Frenchmen and Americans second. Oui, monsieur. Let us hope we look back on this as an awful dream. Oui, oui. I don't even try to understand anymore, monsieur. I try not to judge. It is not your fault; you did your best. Oui."

De Sauvetage handed the receiver to Quint. "Monsieur Farr would like a few words with you."

"Jim Quint?" Farr asked.

"Me," Quint said.

"I'm afraid we have a small problem, Jim. The Company has to sit this one out, I'm afraid. I ask you please to put yourself in the hands of Inspector de Sauvetage. He is a civilized, thoughtful man, a professional. He will tell you what you need to know. You must do this, Jim. You must."

Quint blinked. "Where are the hatable Company representatives? They're supposed to be all over the world. The stockholders are paying you billions of dollars and you're drafting *me*? What is this?"

"I asked you a favor in London, Bison. The situation is now desperate. The stockholders need you."

"I think you know you're going to have to give me a better answer than that." There was a long silence during which Quint listened to long-distance hiss. "Hello, Mr. Farr?"

"You recall that device we were talking about?"

"Yes."

"The Chairman of the Board and his close associates have been assured no fuel has been made available. Until they have direct evidence that fuel is on the market, they're staying out of the action. They're seeking permission to double-check the inventories of the people who made the assurances. If fuel is on the market, all representatives will be made available, no problem."

"That's insane."

"Company policy," Georgie Farr said.

"What is wrong with the Chairman's mind?"

"There's a corporate meeting coming up next year. He doesn't want to panic stockholders."

"If he doesn't do something now, he may lose one of his franchises—Washington, say, or New York. I wonder how he'd like those apples."

"Bison, listen. These people get where they are by knowing the ways of stockholders. They learn to protect themselves. Their first instinct is to play it safe. We're long past the days of Andrew Carnegie and John D. Rockefeller. You want to tell me about yourself, Jim?"

"What do you mean?"

"Tell me about your family."

"Lived on a little farm in Montana."

"What else? Anything out of the ordinary?"

"Well, I don't know."

"I've got a file on you here in front of me, Bison."

"What does the file say?"

"According to this, you're the first member of your family to go to college. You're not ashamed to have been a Montana farm boy or anything like that, are you?"

"Hell, no!" Quint said.

"It says here your father spent time in jail for making whiskey. You embarrassed about that?"

"Only if he made bad whiskey."

Farr laughed. "I guess what I'm trying to say here, Jim, without sounding like an idiot, is that there is no free lunch. In most countries of the world there is just no way a farm boy can receive the education and the opportunity to become a writer. You receive, and there's a chance you could be called upon. Right now I'm desperate for a man who knows what happened in Amsterdam and is free to travel. He cannot be a Company representative."

"Me?"

"You," Georgie Farr said. "I don't want you to go down there as some kind of volunteer. I want you to be paid for your work. There is a way this can be done; Jacques and I have worked it out. I want there to be a record after this is finished—no matter what happens—that we weren't all standing around playing with ourselves."

"You want a record."

"Absolutely. The only sure way to do that is to put you on somebody's payroll."

"You sly little man."

Georgie Farr laughed merrily. "Let's hope that in the end this is all a bad joke and I'll look like a foolish little man."

"If I go to work for the Company, and it turns out I have a hand in saving a Company franchise, I want the Chairman, in a televised press conference, to accidentally let it be known that he's a fan of Humper Staab adventure novels."

"You want what?"

"I'll want him to have read all the Humpers first so when he's asked about the books, he'll be able to recall amusing scenes and say how much he enjoys Humper after a hard day's work. It's a small enough price for him to pay for screwing up like this. Good help's expensive these days."

"I give you my word, Bison, that I'll do everything possible. Can you please put Jacques back on the phone."

De Sauvetage took the receiver and listened to Farr. "That is no problem at all. I'll take care of it. Oui. Au revoir, monsieur." De Sauvetage hung up. "I think Georgie Farr may be right. You Americans are in some trouble."

"We never do anything the easy way in the U.S."

"Monsieur, what do you know about Jamaica?"

"I like reggae," Quint said.

"At the western tip of Jamaica is the village of Negril that has in recent years become popular with young people from Europe. There is a seven-mile-long beach—Negril Beach— and an area called the West End where spectacular cliffs are said to drop straight down to a beautiful sea. The water has cut tunnels and caves under the cliffs, and this is a favorite spot for scuba divers. You mentioned reggae, do you know about the Rastafari religion?"

"Some," Quint said. Murrant had said his sister lived in Negril.

"The Rastas, Monsieur Quint, are black men who believe we are living in the state of Babylon. Their God is Jah, a variant, no doubt, of Jehovah in the Old Testament. Ethiopia is the promised land. Emperor Haile Selassie, the Lion of Judah, is a prophet, said to be a direct descendant of Moses. It is their wish, monsieur, to return to the promised land one day. Their religion, curiously enough, revolves around the smoking of ganja, or marijuana, and they are very good at growing it."

"Ahh," Quint smiled.

"The hashish smuggler, Gerald Murrant, flew marijuana into the United States for almost eight years. He flew it in from Colombia, from Mexico, and from Negril, where it is grown in commercial quantities in small patches in a swamp called the Great Morass."

Quint listened carefully. He could sense it coming.

"When Gerald Murrant's habits became too widely known in the Americas, he moved to Europe and turned his old contacts over to his sister, Robin. Your American authorities have, of course, been watching Mademoiselle Murrant. They believe she landed her small plane in the Great Morass a month ago and is still there."

"Gerald Murrant didn't get involved in a shootout or anything like that?" Quint asked.

"No, monsieur, nothing like that."

Quint smiled. "But Georgie Farr thinks it's possible that Robin Murrant's plane may be used to take the Vrienden bomb into the U.S."

"Oui, monsieur. Into Florida, Georgia, or Alabama; perhaps I should tell you now that I'm the French member of an international organization called Le Op, named after your atomic scientist J. Robert Oppenheimer, who was in charge of the Manhattan Project that developed your atomic bomb. We in Le Op exist for the reason that it is possible for something like this to happen. When a rumor arises, we share information. We are all of us at the mercy of fanatics. Each country has the option of either joining or not joining the investigation of a rumor or possibility. This is very sensitive, monsieur. We are pledged only to openly share information.

"Georgie Farr is Op Deux. The man in London who questioned you is Thomas Cunningham, Op Quartre. There is a Russian, Op Trois, and a Chinese, Op Cinq."

"And Op Un?"

"Op Premier, monsieur."

"You?"

"Oui."

"The man in charge."

"Oui. President Lyle and his advisers are reluctant to actively investigate the missing Vrienden bomb. The Paki-

stanis deny that any plutonium is missing from their Karachi
facility. They are adamant. Op Deux is forbidden to partic-
ipate under threat of losing his job. He may only share information."

"Farr wants me to go to Negril."

"Oui."

"There's more than one way to skin a beef, eh, Inspector?"

"You are a high-spirited man, monsieur. You see irony
everywhere. Good intentions? You smile—just wait. Truth?
You laugh—watch. Do you have a religion?"

"No," Quint said.

"Politics?"

"No, no, Inspector, you don't understand. Barroom truths
and great causes are not for me. I don't graze in a herd or
fly in a flock."

Inspector Jacques de Sauvetage had done his best. He
hadn't had time for a proper background investigation as
MI5 had run to assure the quality of Alistair Jones's LIDMC.
He only had Georgie Farr's word that an FBI check of Jim
Quint was negative. "'Sauvetage' means salvage, rescue,
monsieur. It is time for me to honor my name. Georgie Farr
can't hire you, but I can. I'll pay your salary out of the
American contribution to Le Op. Jim Quint, raise your right
hand. French law requires that you take an oath of alle-
giance."

Quint raised his right hand.

De Sauvetage recited a pledge in French. "Monsieur?"

"Hell, yes," Quint said. He smiled. He hadn't understood
a word.

"Good luck, Jim Quint. You are now an agent of the Sûreté."
De Sauvetage poured them each a glass of red wine. "A
toast." His face was grave, worried.

"*Vive les français,*" Quint said, "a people almost as mule-
headed as us Americans."

"*Vive les américains,* my friend, for whatever we Europeans say about you Americans, you've always been there when
we needed you most."

Quint said, "It's settled, then—I'm off to Jamaica?"

"Oui. You will be assigned to my section, monsieur, Section E."

Quint grinned. "I worked in sports for a while when I was with newspapers. I was even with the women's section once. What's Section E?"

De Sauvetage laughed. "Section D, Section E, they're all the same. They could be this; they could be that. A, B, or C, monsieur, there's no reason for you to know for this one mission."

"You should put me in Section F for symbolic reasons."

"Pour le fumeur? For the smoker?"

"I was thinking of a straightforward Montana expression," Quint said.

De Sauvetage shook his head. "Alas, monsieur, there is no Section F."

Quint tried on his Humper Staab steely-eyed look. Jim Quint, a Section E man. Esprit de corps surged through his body like a hit of Lebanese red.

"You might be pleased to know there is one aspect of this that is a first for the Sûreté."

"How's that?"

"We have never to my knowledge had an American agent on the payroll. I can remember Nigerians, Mongols, and Venezuelans, but never, never an American."

"An anomaly."

"Oui. We gave you Lafayette. You gave us the American Expeditionary Force and the Fourth Infantry Division at Normandy. We owe you one more."

"Then it's quits with us preposterous Americans, eh, Inspector?"

"No, no, monsieur, despite our differences, never quits."

"I'll do my very best," Quint said.

"I would go with you to Jamaica myself, but I am French. Paris is my city. I love her dearly. Until I know the truth, I must remain in France. You are lucky to be from Montana. Where is that place? I'll need it for your personnel file." De Sauvetage was amused by his American friend.

"Tell payroll I'm from Bison, Montana," Quint said. "Folks there worry about rustlers in four-wheelers."

"I must tell you that I was suspicious of Gerald Murrant and so requested a profile from Interpol. The Interpol computers watch for connections. Murrant has had contacts with two known agents of the KGB."

"The KGB?"

"Oui, monsieur. This puts him in *la Catégorie Trois.*"

"Category Three?"

"A possible KGB agent, monsieur. The Soviets regard us French as irritants. We are independent. We have our own missiles. We have our own bombs. But they hate you Americans."

Of all the flotsam and jetsam of Jim Quint's past, of all the faces and memories, there was one voice he would never forget: a Montana herald announcing the acceptance of challenge by brave men. Quint associated this voice with summer heat, dust, horse dumplings, pronto pups, the smell of beer and urine, cars and pickups parked at odd angles in nearby fields. The challengers wore sturdy Levi's, cowboy boots, and splendid Stetsons. They strode about the rodeo grounds with numbers pinned flapping proudly on the backs of their shirts; their wives and girlfriends changed diapers in the shade of the bleachers and talked about the latest episode of "As the World Turns."

The echoing voice-oice-oice of the rodeo announcer-ouncer-ouncer was a sweet and poignant memory. Jim Quint, the dreamer, high on hashish and settled back in a soft chair, remembered that voice now. It told of cowpokes from Kalispell and Sandpoint, Umatilla and Coeur d'Alene. There were 'pokes up from Bend and down from Medicine Hat. The herald's voice echoed across the arena, urging the folks to give a cowboy a little hand.

Quint lived in fantasy. He had been that way since childhood. He closed his eyes and heard the announcer now calling his name. Quint's countrymen had a side bet riding on his number. It was time to drop the jokes, time to put Humper Staab aside.

Out of the center chute, a cowpoke out of Bison, Montana, riding a brahma named Vile.

L'homme sérieux de la Sûreté clenched his teeth. His name was called:

Bison-son-son Jim-im-im Quint-int-int.

BOOGAHS
IN BABYLON

18. *Jim Quint took a taxi from Montego Bay to*

Negril because he wanted to be alone. He needed time to think. If he had been paying for it himself, he would have had to endure two hours of lurching and swaying on a Jamaican bus. The idea of being packed into a bus with sweating Jamaicans babbling their crazy lingo was too much. The atlas said Jamaicans speak English; Quint soon learned the truth—a fast-talking Jamaican might as well be speaking Urdu or Finnish.

The taxi moved out of Montego Bay and followed the coast to the western tip of the island. The road twisted and turned, came back on itself, and snaked along the water. The taxi passed huts, coconut palms, goats, and heavy-bodied, big-horned cattle that stood alone, unmoving in the heat. Yellow-brown mongrels slept on earthen yards in front of small huts, and on trails that led back from the highway. The dogs remained inert as the taxi rushed by. It was too hot to look up.

Negril was farther than Quint had anticipated; it didn't look so far on the map. After about forty-five minutes, the driver pulled to a stop at one of the three-walled huts beside the highway that sold bananas, salt fish, orange juice, Red Stripe beer, and pineapple soda. It was then that Quint saw black clouds boiling and roiling behind them.

"Will it rain?" he asked.

The driver grinned. "Dis August, mon. Rain ever day."

They each bought a piece of salted fish that had been soaked in pepper oil and drank a cold Red Stripe. The rain caught them before they got a mile from their break. The sky turned black; great, thick slabs of lightning raced above the ocean, turning everything momentarily white. This was followed by a sharp, cracking boom directly overhead that startled Quint. The driver laughed and turned the radio louder. They passed two boys prodding a donkey loaded with stalks of sugarcane. The rain eased somewhat; the boys nodded at the car. One chewed a hunk of cane. The other carried an enormous machete.

The road straightened out when they reached a long lagoon that was Negril Bay.

"Negril Beach dere, mon," the driver said.

"All along here?"

"Seven miles. Where you want to go, brotha?" The driver turned on the front seat.

Quint wet his lips; the taxi plunged into a shallow lake in the middle of the road. "I need a room where I can stay for a night or so while I find a place I like."

"Ya, mon. How much you want to pay?"

"As little as possible," Quint said.

"The Red Ground District. Me got a friend dere."

"The Red Ground, sure." Robin Murrant was supposed to have lived in the Red Ground.

Before the lagoon reached its western hook, they came to a narrow bridge. On the beach side, at the base of the road embankment, there was a market of small stalls. The Negril was a dark, noxious brown. The brown stopped where the water reached the lagoon. In the lagoon, the splendid green water had turned silver gray under the tropical storm.

"Why is that river brown like that? Is it sewage?"

The driver glanced at the river. "No, mon, de rivah dere downhill from de watah."

"The swamp in there?"

"Ya, mon, de Great Morass. Rastas fly herb from dere."

"Marijuana?"

"Irie."

"You call it ganja, don't you?" Quint asked.

"Ya, mon. Ganj."

They moved left at a traffic circle at the end of the bridge. There was a cream-colored stucco building at the far side of the circle. "Movie theater, grocery store, disco," the driver said.

"Disco?" Quint was curious. He looked back. "What's it called?"

"The Soon Come." The driver winked at Quint. "Means 'be right back' or 'be dere soon.'"

Quint grinned. A rusted Oldsmobile with a door missing and a Morris with a trunk missing were parked in a shallow lake that had formed in front of Miss Brown's, an eatery of unpainted boards and a corrugated tin roof. They passed two more hut-like Jamaican cafés and a vacant lot full of waist-high weeds before the driver turned left at the Wharf Club. The Wharf Club had once been whitewashed and it had a composition roof, rather than the ubiquitous corrugated tin. Black faces peered out at the rain from the dark interior. The street, unnamed and barely large enough for the Toyota, wound uphill toward the Red Ground. The road was flanked by tropical undergrowth on both sides: small, unpainted one- and two-room shacks nestled among ferns, vines, coconut and ackee trees, avocado trees, and bushes—squat bushes, tall bushes, thin-leafed bushes, fat-leafed bushes. The shacks and thatched bamboo huts were joined by a network of trails, which were bisected by narrow, unnamed dirt streets or streets paved with broken rubble.

They passed the Dragon Inn—a combination bar and grocery—and more tiny homes in the forest before the driver turned left down a narrow lane packed hard by bare feet. A hundred yards later, he turned down another narrow lane. At the end of this lane, he stopped before a house shrouded and obscured by palm fronds and foliage still wet with the rain. The rain slackened momentarily, then stopped as Quint got out of the car.

"How much should I pay him?"

"Offer him eight. You can stay at the beach for fifteen. Settle for ten."

Quint got his valise out of the trunk and paid the driver. He wanted the taxi to wait a few minutes, but before he could say anything, he was alone. The Red Ground got its name from the soil, which was now sodden with water and slick. Two Rastas with dreadlocks hanging to their shoulders sat on the porch of a small house playing dominoes.

The one on the left took a leisurely hit on an enormous joint.
"I'm looking for Lester," Quint said. "I was told I could rent a room for tonight."

The man on the left handed him the joint. "Sinse, mon. Spliff like this make you feel good."

"When will Lester be back?" Quint took a hit.

"He be in Sav, mon. Take dis room back ere. Cool, mon."

Quint gave the spliff back and flopped his valise in a small bedroom that had been partitioned off from the rest of the house. He glanced through the open door: the house was a hive of tiny bedrooms. A door at the rear opened onto a packed earthen yard. A large black woman and five small children were gathered around a large pot that simmered over an open fire. They were protected from the rain by a thatched lean-to.

"Shower in de yard dere, mon," one of the Rastas said behind him. Quint could hear the sound of dominoes being shuffled on the floor.

The shower, Quint could see, was a piece of corrugated tin surrounding a copper tube lashed to a tall stake driven into the ground. The top of the tube was bent earthward to rinse sweat from waiting bodies.

"No watah dere now, mon. Latah." The Rasta stood to shake hands. "Me called Rodney."

"Jim Quint." They shook. The second man's name was Lewis.

Quint sat on a wooden bench. He didn't know what to do next. The two Rastas played dominoes and smoked ganja. He heard a buzzing.

Mosquitoes. "You got mosquitoes?"

"Ya, mon, rainy season. How long goin' be?"

"I'm not sure. I'm down here looking for a young woman named Robin."

Brother Rodney grinned. "White girl?"

"Yes."

Rodney laughed. "Dem girls like de big bamboo, mon."

"Makes 'em scream," Lewis said. He grabbed himself by the crotch and grinned. One of his front teeth was capped with gold that shone when he talked.

Rodney took a toke on the spliff and looked thoughtful.
He handed the spliff to Quint. "Lots of white women, mon—
Canada, Germany, Italy."

"Irie," Lewis said.

The word was pronounced "eye-ree." Quint looked puz-
zled.

"Irie mean nothin betta, mon," said Rodney. He played a
domino.

"All I know is, she came here a few months ago and was
living in the Red Ground District."

Rodney dug into a plastic bag and pulled out a handful
of ganja. He began rolling another spliff that was large on
one end, small on the other. "You find her if she ere, mon.
Small place."

Lewis lit the spliff. "Irie."

"You got pitchah, mon?"

Quint took the snapshot from his shirt pocket. "This is
about ten years old."

Rodney grinned. "Ya, mon, good lookin. Bet she would
like de big bamboo."

"How would you go about looking for her?"

"You talk to Babylons, mon?"

"The police?"

"Ya, mon."

"Tomorrow, maybe."

"If me be you, mon, me go see Timothy."

"Timothy?"

"Ya, mon. Him be Big Notch. Go to de Dragon Inn. Dey
got de coldest Red Stripe in Negril. Ask for Ragabones, him
get you Timothy."

"Irie," Lewis said.

Rodney handed Quint the spliff and laughed. "Dis time
irie mean dat ri, mon. Go two ri, Ragabones."

Quint had it figured. Two right turns and he would find
Ragabones. "I can always see Lester in the morning. Is that
cool?"

"No problem, mon."

"Later then."

"Cool runnings, mon," Rodney said.

"Irie." Lewis took a big toke.

Quint grinned and looked at Rodney, who was pleased to translate yet another version of irie. "Him say everting cool."

"Ya, mon," Quint said.

The Rastas grinned and went back to their domino game.

So there it was. Bison Jim Quint, a French agent, was in Negril. He was alone. The responsibility was his. He looked down the dark lane shrouded by coconut and banana fronds: Lord Jim country.

19.

Quint retraced the lanes that led to Lester's house, and turned right on the narrow street that led down to the village. There was the thumping of a reggae bass on a radio deep in the forest, but except for the shrill trilling of crickets, it was silent. There were no street lights, no traffic noise except for the puttering of a moped in the distance. He heard men talking, and soon saw the silhouettes of their bodies. There were three of them, Jamaican men wearing long pants and tee shirts. They were barefoot.

"Evenin," one said.

Quint said, "Pleasant night." He had a slight buzz from the ganj and walked slowly into the sweet, black night, accompanied by soaring cricket riffs.

Quint heard the reggae first. Then he saw two men urinating on the side of a small, unpainted wooden structure. Crude, uneven letters on a tiny sign said Ragabone's Dragon Inn. Quint saw that it was half market, featuring huge cloth bags of rice and beans, and half bar. The L-shaped bar was deserted; there were seven stools scattered about the tiny floor. A reggae tape thumped on a ghetto-blaster the size of a suitcase.

There was a woman in the market side, but nobody behind the bar. The woman wasn't concerned when Quint took a stool. She took her time with her chores, then stepped up behind the bar. The bar had a floor; the market didn't, and so was lower. "Ya, mon?" she asked.

"I'd like some rum, please."

"You want quatah and juice."

"Sure." Quint didn't have any idea what she meant.

She took a bottle of dark Jamaican rum from a shelf and used it to fill a half-pint bottle. She took a can of pineapple juice from the shelf and jabbed holes in the top with the ice pick she used to chip ice into a plastic cup.

"I'm looking for a man named Ragabones."

"Him be ere latah, mon."

Quint was on his second quarter of rum when four men came in to drink Red Stripe beer.

"How you doin, mon?" one of them asked Quint.

They each drank a Red Stripe, then moved to a room in the back. They sent for more beer and played dominoes, talking loud and fast in their Jamaican lingo. Quint heard them slap tiles loudly on the table. They played on a card table; the tiles scattered with each triumphant slap. After each slap there was a pause while the dominoes were straightened.

Then another slap.

Quint decided Ragabones could wait. He finished his rum and stepped into the moist air. A dog barked. Another reggae tape played in the distance. As one tape receded, another took its place. Most of the homes sitting back in the darkness were lit by candles and kerosene lanterns. The farther he walked, the more people were gathered in the street. They stood in threes, fours, and fives, men here, women there. Their skins were the blackest of black. Until he was upon them, Quint saw only clothes that moved like ghosts—a yellow blouse, a white tee shirt, a pair of green shorts, but no arms, no legs, no faces. They moved slowly and talked softly, their voices an old and sad murmur.

A bomb smuggler in Jamaica? No hurry, mon.

Quint passed a small thatched hut with three walls when a man's voice called, "Hey, mon!"

"Me?" Quint asked.

"Ya, mon. Come ere, mon."

Quint stepped into the hut, which was lit by a single flickering candle. He saw a bar with a wire screen stretching from bar to ceiling. Three Rastamen stood in the dark area in front of the bar.

"Me name Timothy, mon." Quint's new acquaintance held out his hand, thumb up.

"Jim Quint." A large spliff glowed in the dark. Quint saw a butt extended his way. He took a hit. How many Timothys were there? This must be his man.

Brother Timothy was stoned. "Dis is wat it all about, mon. Ain't dat ri? Dis is wat it all about. Smoke. Friends. A little talk."

"Ya, mon," Quint said.

"Irie," one of the Rastas murmured.

"Me name Timothy, mon. Me take care of you. Know what me mean, mon? You want herb, me get it for you. Want pussy, dat too. How long you been ere, mon?"

"Just a while ago," Quint said. "I'm looking for a girl named Robin."

"Jamaican lady?" Timothy studied Quint in the yellow light.

"White girl. She was living here with a Rasta last year."

"Lookin for de big bamboo? Don't know her, mon." Timothy took a long draw on the spliff. The hut fell silent; the crickets took over.

"You remembah me, brothah. Me called Timothy. Me can get you anything. Good herb if you want, no stems, no seeds. You can buy us a Red Stripe if you want, only six Jamaican for all of us."

Quint nodded yes, aware of the black faces watching him in the candlelight.

"Ya, mon," Timothy said. "Earl?"

Earl had neither ice nor electricity, so the beer was warm.

"Dere's a pahty tonight at de Red Rose, you wan come wit Timothy?"

Quint took a sip of warm beer. "I'm not sure."

"Maybe you find lady dere."

"This a local party?"

"Ya, mon. Red Ground people. You want to get laid, mon?"

"I have to find this young woman."

Timothy grinned. "Why den, you should go, mon. You want go for a walk?"

"Sure, mon."

They finished the spliff and stepped out onto the road, where Jamaicans from the Red Ground strolled, their voices soft and gentle, a lovely murmur. The top of Timothy's head was well below Quint's shoulder. He wore a pair of purple swim trunks and a tattered baseball cap that said "Billy's Cocktails, Ft. Myers, Fla." on the front. Timothy had the physique of a Jets cornerback. He was also a leisurely walker.

"Slow down, mon. Walk too fast."

Quint slowed. "Habit, I guess."

"No hurry, mon. Where you go so fast?" Timothy looked up at Quint and grinned, his teeth a startling white. "Pahty never stops, if you know wat me mean, mon. Lots of time. Listen to de crickets."

"The party never stops," Quint said.

"Irie."

"You think somebody at the party might know her?"

"Who dat, mon?"

"Robin."

"Never know, mon."

Quint felt as though he were walking in a dream: the blackness, the crickets, the strolling people, the ghetto-blasters booming Bob Marley and Yellowman in the distance, his well-muscled, slow-walking companion. He wondered how it was possible for him to be here among these people, bearing this kind of responsibility. It was unreal.

"Feel good, mon?"

Quint slapped an insect on his forearm and said, "Irie."

They passed the Dragon Inn; Quint could hear the slapping of dominoes on the card table in back. Jamaicans played dominoes with panache, the way Julius Erving hit a slam dunk. A new source of reggae thumped heavily in a building nearby. Quint must have passed it before he met Timothy.

"Pahty over dere, mon. Red Rose," Timothy said.

"Are we going there now?"

"No, mon. Too early. We walk first."

They walked. Quint was introduced to small groups of Jamaican men whose faces were all but invisible. Quint enjoyed the drifty laziness of the stroll. He was still alert, though; de Sauvetage and Georgie Farr would be urging

him on. He slopped along, his sandals slapping against the
bottoms of his feet. Silhouettes of ackee, breadfruit, and pear
avocados dominated the shorter coconut palms, banana trees,
and tropical underbrush. Quint was introduced to some Jamaican girls, their faces jet-black and pretty.

When they were alone again, Timothy said, "Got to get
you pussy, mon."

The party at the Red Rose was held on a concrete slab
maybe twenty feet long and ten feet wide. A small hut on
the street side of the slab served as a bar. The music came
from a larger structure on the far side. The building with
the music had a large, open window, and an open door facing
the slab. Quint saw Jamaicans inside sitting on straight-
backed wooden chairs.

There was a concrete retaining wall on one end of the slab
and a waist-high metal rail at the other. Six or eight two-
by-fours were piled at the end of the retaining wall; the
young Jamaican women were gathered there. They wore
tight skirts or even tighter jeans stretched over extraordinary butts and narrow hips. There were ten or fifteen of
them, each one moving easily and gracefully to the taped
music. They chatted and danced in groups of three and four.
Quint thought they were grand. Their physiques were sleek
and hard, athletic and erotic at the same time.

A slightly larger group of young men was gathered at the
other end. Some mingled with friends, moving all the while,
others danced alone. Still others leaned against the rail.
Everybody danced. Nobody stood still. They danced with
their hips, their elbows, their feet, their heads; the bartender
was a shoulder man.

Another spliff was thrust in Quint's direction; he took a
drag. He was the only white face there.

No, there was one other. Quint saw a young woman looking out of the window on the far side of the dancers. The
face looked familiar. He grabbed Timothy by the shoulder.
"Look there!"

"Wat dat, mon?"

"The white woman across the way."

"No white lady dere."

She was gone. "Sure there was," Quint said.

"Me no see her, mon. You want rum punch? Buy Timothy a rum punch."

Quint's clock said it was seven when he was awakened by a goat bleating outside the open louvers of his window. He looked outside; a black goat, looking studious and a bit imperious, peered back. A rooster crowed in the distance and was answered by a bird on Lester's porch; a dog protested. Quint flopped back on the bed. He'd been in more tranquil barnyards.

Women began gossiping behind the house; a reggae tape joined a crying baby and the scolding of children. The Red Ground stirred to life. Quint decided he wanted a shower. There was no water pressure; a crude sign said to wait half an hour if there was no pressure. A plastic tub of baby manure in the shower persuaded Quint to forget it. He'd be sweaty in ten minutes anyway.

A few minutes later, he retraced his way through the narrow lanes to the street that led to Negril village. The Dragon Inn was open for business, although Quint couldn't see anyone inside. At the foot of the hill, a Wharf Club bartender told him the police station was a couple of hundred yards to the left. This was the southern hook of Negril Bay; the street led to the cliffs, rocky coves, and underwater caves at the extreme western tip of Jamaica.

Quint walked on the seaward side of the street. The beach gave way to sharp folds of lava at the village. The police station turned out to be a U-shaped structure. The open end of the U faced the street and the bay beyond that; the long sides were white and made of aluminum. The curved end of the U was made of plywood and wasn't much more than a passageway between the two sides. In the very center of the end was an open door; a Babylon sat on a stool behind a high counter. His cap hung from a nail on the wall. There was a bench for visitors.

The Babylon was reading a report, and finished his paragraph before he acknowledged Quint. "Ya, mon?"

Quint smiled. "My name is Jim Quint, and I'd like to talk to whoever is in charge, please." A small sign on the desk said "Cpl. Edwards."

Edwards looked briefly at the report on the counter. "And dis is about?"

"I'm looking for a young woman who may be living in Negril."

"Living wit a Rasta?"

"Maybe," Quint said.

"Ya, mon." Edwards straightened the papers and stood to file them in a narrow cabinet behind the counter. The splendid, dark blue trousers of his uniform had a red stripe down each side. The trousers had a thick red stripe around the waist as well; the black patent-leather belt was fastened by a silver buckle. The trousers were pressed to a sharp crease. The shirt, which Quint had thought to be gray at first, turned out to have thin blue and white stripes and silver buttons.

Quint mopped the sweat from his forehead with the back of his hand.

"Hot day," Edwards said.

"Yes, it is."

Quint was led down a short passageway to a large office whose door was open. A light-complexioned Jamaican with European features sat behind a large desk. He was about fifty years old with receding gray hair. The window was open; a large, slow fan on the ceiling ploughed through the humid air.

"Mr. Jim Quint, sir," Edwards said.

A larger, fancier sign than the corporal's said the man behind the desk was Insp. Richard Guy. He rose to shake Quint's hand. "Inspector Guy," he said. He motioned for Quint to sit in one of the two chairs in front of his desk. "Now what can I do for you, Mr. Quint? Do you have a crime to report?"

Quint told him that some months previous, a young woman named Robin Murrant had come to Negril from New Orleans and failed to return.

Guy sat back in his chair. "Miss Murrant. Yes, as I recall, we received an inquiry from the American Consul's office in Kingston." He called Corporal Edwards in a Jamaican patois that was too rapid for Quint to understand. "An interesting place, Negril. Don't you think so, Mr. Quint? Jamaica has a long and interesting history." Guy looked out of the window. "They caught the pirate Calico Jack Rackham right here on Negril Beach. Did you know that?"

Stories of pirates made Quint think of Long John Silver and Treasure Island. "What happened?"

Inspector Guy looked pleased. "It was in November 1720. He'd been looting some ships and had stolen some fish from the locals. He stopped here to party on the beach, you see. This is where the British got him. They hanged all but two of them in Mo Bay. Interesting."

"And what happened to the other two?"

"They were sentenced to hang with the rest until it was discovered they were women." Guy laughed. "They were both dressed as men and both were pregnant. Ann Bonney's father was a famous lawyer in Charleston; he came down and took her back. Mary Reid died of yellow fever in St. Catherine's."

"They smuggled rum in those days, I suppose," Quint said.

Guy nodded. "Ganja now." Inspector Guy wondered why the Americans didn't give up on the Murrants. They'd driven Gerald out of the Western Hemisphere. Robin didn't fly that much ganj. Why couldn't the Americans give Jamaica a break? The only thing the Jamaicans had to export was ganja. Well, there had been bauxite too before the recession. Why did the Americans insist on going through this charade?

Guy rose to accept a brown file from Corporal Edwards. He read the file while Quint waited. When he finished, he looked up, his finger on his chin. "The American Embassy in Kingston forwarded a request through Mo Bay that we try to find the woman. It says she is twenty-nine. Sergeant Crowley and myself investigated." Guy closed the folder.

"And?"

"Nothing. We were told she was staying in the Red Ground." Guy shrugged. "Lots of white girls live in the Red Ground. They go in there and you just don't see them. They live here, live there. We went to all the places where the local folks have rooms to let and ran a passport check."

"Then what did you do?"

"We checked the rooms in the village and along Negril Beach. Nothing, Mr. Quint. It's possible that she changed her name. If she's living in the mountains or the swamp, it's just impossible. All you have to do is chop yourself a clearing and build a little house. You can do everything with a machete. Grow yourself some ganja to peddle on the beach, and you're in business."

Quint sighed. "So what would you do if you were me?"

"First, give me your word that you'll let me know what you're doing. Ganj smugglers can be mean people."

"So you've got it," Quint said.

"Second, I'd find myself a room with local people. You'll be living with students, Europeans mostly. The beach is a good place to look; that's where the Rastas hustle their ganj. If Miss Murrant is still in the area, you'll eventually meet her on the beach or in the West End. The West End is the road to perdition, Mr. Quint." Guy coughed. "The people in the resort hotels are tourists; they're in and out in a week or ten days. Students stay for months or years."

"Where would you recommend?"

"Miss Wilma's on the beach would be good. Her rooms are a bit primitive, but cheap. You'll be right in the middle of things. You like bare breasts?"

Quint laughed.

"There'll be a lot of European girls at the Bar-B-Barn on your right and the Negril Beach Club on your left. You have to walk farther up the beach to see the rest."

"Naked ladies?"

"To your heart's desire. Go to Boobie Cay. You can see all you want out there. Mr. Quint, if your investigation gets close to ganja smuggling, you must tell me at once." Inspector Guy wondered why the Americans didn't give up worrying about a little pot.

20.

Except for Gerald Murrant, Brother Timothy was feeling real good, mon. He slept late, then fried himself a big plate of ackee and salt fish. The salt fish was a treat. Timothy had sold an overpriced wad of ganj to some Germans the day before. The Germans, who rarely got anything except hashish in Europe, had stupidly paid what he asked. Even then Timothy had mashed it tight so as to conceal the stems and seeds.

Thus armed with a pocket full of bucks, Timothy had gone for a slab of salt fish and a bottle of white Overproof rum in the market by the Soon Come.

Timothy didn't like Murrant. Why hadn't Murrant stayed in Europe? Why was he back in Negril pushing his weight around? Murrant had dealt with the Bigger Notch for years. Here he was telling Timothy to ease up on the tariff on his sister's ganj loads. If Timothy didn't back off, Murrant said, why then, he'd have a word with the Bigger Notch.

What could Gerald Murrant possibly say to the Bigger Notch that would hurt Timothy? Nothing. Timothy wasn't worried.

Timothy finished his breakfast and mashed a wad of ganj as small as he could. He stuffed it in a paper bag. He put some hand-carved coral on top, rolled himself a big spliff, and set out. He iried some friends on the corner by the Wharf Club, exchanged some cool runnings and ya mons with some brothers hanging out by Miss Brown's. He crossed the bridge over the river. Timothy was headed for the Sunset, well up the beach, but he cut to the beach as soon as he could. Brother Timothy didn't want to miss the Negril Beach Club, where German girls sunbathed without tops. The only American girls to go topless were the ones with good tits; the others were too shy.

Germans were a trifle cold for Timothy's taste, but German girls could have fabulous breasts. Timothy couldn't understand why they wanted tan tits. The American girls shaved their armpits; Timothy liked that. But German or American, it seemed like every girl who went to Negril wanted to try out the big bamboo. True, if you were just another burr-head nigger, it wasn't as easy. Grow dreadlocks like Peter Tosh or Jimmy Cliff—now that was another story. As far as Timothy was concerned, all women were pink in the middle. But the white girls were a special treat, like sucking on a ginap, a succulent fruit that was mostly one large pit. Timothy loved to suck ginaps.

They were playing volleyball at the Beach Club. Timothy was pleased to find six or eight well-oiled European girls stretched out on plastic lounge chairs, tits up. A Jamaican in a powerboat pulled a woman in a parachute. Tourists mingled with Jamaicans in the water, which was a splendid turquoise, startling in its clarity.

Brother Timothy spotted a couple without a suntan. The man wore a University of Manitoba tee shirt. The young woman had her hair braided in cornrows like Bo Derek in the movie *10*.

"You want to exchange, mon?" Timothy asked.

"I already changed my money," the man said.

"Oh. How about some smoke? You want herb? Ganja, mon."

"No, I think we've got everything we need."

"Me name is Timothy, brothah. Me take care of you, mon. Whatevah you need, see Brothah Timothy. Me be around."

"We'll watch for you," the young woman said.

"Cool runnings, mon." Timothy passed the T-Water, Miss Wilma's, and the Bar-B-Barn.

It wasn't too far past the Bar-B-Barn when Timothy heard somebody call his name. He looked up and down the beach, then stepped into the underbrush.

The Caribbean sun was blazing directly overhead when Jim Quint left the Negril police station. He walked the sea wall again and by the time he got back to the Wharf Club, his shirt was soaked with sweat. Quint was ready for a beer.

The Wharf Club was a venerable establishment, catering to Jamaicans living in the Red Ground and European students who lived with local families. It was dark inside and smelled musty. There was one customer, a sun-tanned white man in khaki walking shorts. He had a sweating Red Stripe in front of him. He motioned for Quint to join him.

Quint was relieved to find there was no reggae playing. The Wharf Club was not built for people with Visa and MasterCards. It was a good place to sit with a Red Stripe.

"Hot one," the man said.

Quint sat and turned toward the bar. The bartender, a young woman in a Bob Marley tee shirt, sat on a stool and stared out at the empty street. On the wall hung pictures of John Kennedy and the baby Jesus. "Red Stripe, please," Quint said.

The bartender looked at Quint, glanced back at the street again, and ran her hand across her forehead.

Quint faced his new companion. "Jim Quint," he said, and they shook.

"Name's Paul de Leeuw." De Leeuw opened a pack of Craven "A" Jamaican cigarettes.

"Beer cold?"

De Leeuw shrugged. "Colder in the Dragon Inn, but it's not worth the walk."

The bartender arrived with Quint's beer. "How long have you been down?" Quint asked.

"Three weeks," de Leeuw said. "What did the good inspector have to say?"

"Who?"

"Richard Guy."

"How did you know I talked to him?"

"I was walking down from the West End when I saw you go into the police station."

Quint took a sip of beer. "How did you know I talked to Guy?"

De Leeuw smiled. "Corporal Edwards was at his post when I walked past."

"I'm looking for a young woman who came to Negril and disappeared."

De Leeuw looked interested. "I see. What did Guy have to say?"

"He said he tried to find her last February."

"Maybe I can help you out."

Quint looked interested. "How could you do that?" He wondered how de Leeuw came to know Corporal Edwards and Inspector Guy.

"I'm a cop."

"That's how you came to know Guy?"

"And Corporal Edwards and all the rest. I know all of them. Introduced myself."

"What kind of cop?"

"Detective sergeant, Baltimore city."

"Really? A cop?"

De Leeuw laughed. "That's it. I did homicide for six years."

"And now?"

"Theft," de Leeuw said.

Quint turned his chair so he could watch the bartender while he talked to de Leeuw. "What do you know about smuggling?"

De Leeuw caught the bartender's attention with a wave of his hand. "Another Red Stripe, darling. What is it you want to smuggle?"

"I don't want to smuggle anything. I want to know about smuggling. What do you know about smuggling pot?"

"You're talking Jamaican ganj, I assume."

"Yes," Quint said.

"I'm no expert, but we cops have our magazines and I've known some guys who've worked in Miami."

"Tell me what you know?"

De Leeuw accepted a Red Stripe from the bartender and looked out the open door. "Most of the commercial marijuana is now coming out of Colombia. They unload it in Miami harbor. They used to fly it in and dump it at Key West until the cops started searching trucks on the causeway. In the late 1960s and early 1970s a lot of pot came from Jamaica—even more than from Mexico. But most of it comes from Colombia now—that and cocaine, which goes through Colombia from Bolivia. Is this the kind of stuff you want to know?"

"Exactly."

"A lot of pot is being grown in the United States now, which cuts down on the trade from Colombia. The thing about Jamaica is that smoking ganja is part of the Rastafari religion. They've had years of experience growing marijuana plants. They've developed a strain of sinsimillion here— you're talking no seeds, now—that's the finest pot you can get outside of India. Better than Thai sticks, even."

"If it's that good, there must be a market for it."

De Leeuw grinned. "Oh, yes, there's a market for it. It's very expensive stuff in the United States: ganj buds. What I'm telling you is that the bulk trade's from Colombia."

"All stems and seeds."

"Just about. The problem now is the federal government authorized the navy to help out the Justice Department. They've got these planes that patrol the Gulf at night. They've got satellites. They've got radar you wouldn't believe. A pilot's gotta pull his wheels up and fly belly to water to get under the radar."

"What do they do once they get there?"

"The pot comes in bales. The bales are covered with burlap and laced tight with metal straps. The pilot just dumps them in a field and flies right on back."

"I see," Quint said.

"What's your interest in this, anyway?" De Leeuw sounded casual.

"I said I was looking for a young girl. I am. I'm a pilot, really. I dump chemicals on potato fields or whatever. This company hired me to fly a plane back from Montego Bay, see. It seemed like a simple enough job. So I go to this apartment house where she's supposed to be, and she's not there. The manager said she'd moved to Negril months earlier, but sent her letters from Negril to be mailed in Montego Bay."

"That's a bit strange, wouldn't you think?"

Quint laughed. "Hell, yes. I called the company back and this woman who hired me apologized and said they had had no way of knowing that this girl wasn't still in Montego Bay. She said that the lease on the plane had expired and it was now stolen. She said they still wanted the plane. If I have to steal it, they'll pay me ten percent of the value of the plane."

"What kind of plane is it?"

"A Cessna."

"Is it worth a bunch of bucks?"

"It's a hell of a plane. A whole bunch."

"You tell Guy that part?"

Quint smiled and shook his head no.

"Good thinking. So how do you propose going about this, Jim?"

"I suppose if the plane's in Negril, it's probably being used to fly ganja to the United States. A decent pilot could keep it on the deck—fly low to the ground; it could be done. I think I should get to know the big ganja growers here. Find them, find the plane."

"That's what I'd do," de Leeuw said. "Do you have any kind of proof of ownership?"

"The title to the plane is free and clear. A Delaware outfit named the Sondheim Corporation owns it and used it as collateral on a loan."

"The Sondheim Corporation leased it to this woman?"

Quint nodded yes. "When she didn't come back with it, the people who made the loan got nervous."

"And hired you to bring it back."

"Ahh." Quint grinned. "That's exactly it. Go get the airplane. I've got the engine serial number, copies of the registration papers, copies of the title, everything. They needed a pilot to bring it back."

"You."

"No reason why not."

De Leeuw looked at the back of his hand. "No reason, I guess. There are a lot of pilots around. Why you?"

"They got my name off the crop-duster registry. It's a dangerous job; not a lot of us do it for a living. Can you imagine dropping down over a row of Lombardy poplars with a load of cut-worm spray? You have a hairy job to do or need a pilot, you check the registry." Quint wondered how he was doing.

"Pilots used to risk."

"I guess," Quint said. "You're down here on vacation, I take it."

"On vacation. Had a divorce; my wife took my daughter. Thought I'd go for the gusto." He took a drink of beer. "Well, what does your missing lady look like?"

"I'm not sure."

"You're not sure?"

"The Sondheim people sent me this ten-year-old picture. You can hardly see her face. The landlady in Montego Bay said she was about this high." Quint held out his hand. "Said she was a skinny little thing. The woman from Montego Bay was huge, so that could mean anything."

"Oh, boy," de Leeuw said.

"I know. I know. The landlady said she was living in the Red Ground. I figured that was all I needed."

"So did you ask Guy what he had on her?"

"He said he had looked for her, but couldn't find her. He didn't volunteer much."

"He probably did his best," de Leeuw said.

Rasta Timothy's head was upside down, its crown resting neatly in the sand, dreadlocks outspread, so that from a distance it resembled nothing so much as an enormous spider. The corpse, from which the head had been so neatly severed, lay nearby, arms and legs outspread in the manner of a tourist seeking a suntan. Rasta Timothy certainly hadn't needed a suntan. There were swirling loops of red in the sand near the corpse, where Timothy's arteries had pumped their last. Two flies danced a little dance on Timothy's open eyes. His big bamboo was stuffed in his mouth. Flies danced on the coagulated stump of that poor member as well.

There was Timothy's head, his disfigured body, and the footprints of running shoes, nothing more.

Constable Roy Davis took all this in, then retreated a few steps to vomit. He wiped his mouth with the back of his hand and started yelling at the gathering crowd to back up. Constable Davis saw another man cleaning his mouth. Served him right, Davis thought.

Davis kept the gawkers well away from the corpse. Inspector Guy would be pleased.

Inspector Guy chose to ride the trike to the beach where Davis waited. That was okay with Corporal Edwards and Private Ruggles. They drove it up and down the beach almost every day; they'd drive the Volkswagen bus. The trike—a bright-red, three-wheeled Honda—was still a toy to Guy, who rarely had an excuse to use it. Its three wide, nubbed tires left a waffle pattern in the sand. The trike could really scoot.

The report of Rasta Timothy's lurid demise worried Guy. Aside from the occasional poor devil who simply popped his cork and bashed someone's head in, there were no murders in Negril. In Kingston, sure. Take a walk in Trenchtown late at night and you risk your life. But Negril? Negril was a village. The locals and the tourists bargained together, got high together, slept together.

Guy knew it was possible to buy anything on Negril Beach, so inevitably there was a Big Notch, as Rasta Timothy had been, to take his cut. You could buy ganja—expensive in the summer, cheap in the fall. You could eat hallucinogenic mushrooms or drink mushroom tea—best in the summer. If you were a white male and wanted chocolate sex, the rate wasn't bad if you didn't mind risking herpes. The daily vista of German and French breasts on the beach was nice. The areas that had European girls got the most attention from his constables.

Had the Big Notch in Negril somehow crossed the Bigger Notch in Kingston? Rasta Timothy's mutilation sounded very much like the Bigger Notch's handiwork. There was little Guy could do when the Bigger Notch got sore. But if somebody else was claiming Negril, then Inspector Guy and his constables were in for it.

The Bigger Notch would not put up with this kind of outrage.

Inspector Guy resolved to be careful. He recalled his meeting with the American, Jim Quint. Quint had been asking questions about Robin Murrant. Would Quint have any business with the Big Notch in Negril?

Constable Davis and Constable Ruggles were keeping on-lookers out of the area when Guy reached the corpse. Constable Edwards waited, pad in hand.

"Nobody saw anything?" Guy asked Edwards.

"No, sir."

"You call Sav?" Savannah de la Mar was region head-quarters.

"Yes, suh. Morris is on his way."

"Once Morris leaves with the body, I want all three of you going up and down the beach. We're looking for people who might have seen or heard something." Guy found it hard not to look at the upside-down head, a ghastly sight.

Paul de Leeuw got on his rented motor scooter and went back to his room at the Negril Beach Hotel. He punched on the air conditioner, took off his clothes, and lay back on the bed. The cold air felt good on his sweaty body. It felt good to have a pair of cool balls. De Leeuw had once read that a man had to keep his balls cool to have a good sex life.

The question was, what should he do about the man who called himself Jim Quint? De Leeuw wondered where the Company came up with all these cockeyed rumors. Tarnauer ought to have better sense. De Leeuw sighed and dialed the hotel operator.

"I want to place a call to Kingston," he said. He gave the operator the number. "And could you send me up a quart of rum, a bottle of Coke, and some ice? Thank you." De Leeuw selected a paperback novel from a valise of paper-backs he had brought down with him. When you were on a job like this there was a lot of waiting. He spread his legs to give his balls more air and started another book. When the woman came with the rum, De Leeuw didn't bother to move. Another naked man was no big deal in Negril.

De Leeuw knew he had a wait ahead of him. It could take two or three hours to get through to Kingston. It was easier to call the United States.

It was only a forty-minute wait this time.

"Yes?"

"Chickadee here," de Leeuw said.

"I thought it was a canary."

"It's been Chickadee as long as I can remember."

"This better be important, Chickadee; this is a Jamaican telephone system, remember."

"I met this guy you should know about."

"Tell me."

"He says his name is Jim Quint. He's a bush pilot, he says, who was hired to fly a plane back to the U.S. from Montego Bay."

"So?"

"So he said the woman who was supposed to be in Montego Bay with the plane is gone and has been having her mail forwarded from Negril. His employer is supposed to have the plane as collateral on a loan. It's a stolen plane now, he says, and he stands to earn ten percent of its worth for bringing it back."

"I see."

"He's a pilot."

"I hear you. How did you meet him?"

De Leeuw took a sip of rum and Coke. "I saw him go into the station here and talk to Inspector Guy. He's the Guy in charge." De Leeuw laughed at his pun.

The man in Kingston didn't laugh. "How did you find all this out?"

"In a bar. I told him I was a cop on vacation."

"What did Guy tell him?"

De Leeuw thought about that. "He told him the girl was reported missing in Jamaica last February. When I told Quint I was a cop, he wanted to know about the smuggling business."

"He did? Ganja? What did you tell him?"

"I told him about ganja smuggling."

"What do you think?"

"He's probably a crop duster trying to score a buck on a stolen plane, like he says."

"Probably."

"You never know," de Leeuw said.

"He spilled his guts, just like that? Told you his whole story?"

"Seemed like it. This guy could be a real turd in the punchbowl."

Richard Guy didn't get home until eight o'clock that evening, but his wife Marian was unconcerned. She had been married to a policeman for more than twenty years; she was a patient woman. Besides that, she had heard people gossiping about Rasta Timothy's murder at the market where she had gone for soap and mosquito coils to burn at night. Timothy was the Big Notch at Negril.

Marian heard her husband take off his shoes at the front door, heard him pour himself a long shot of white Overproof. This was Richard's first murder since he had been posted in Negril. Kingston could be violent. Negril was different.

"Can you fry me an extra fish tonight, honey? I feel hungry."

Marian started cleaning the fish. "I bought extra when I heard about Timothy. Did Walter Morris come over from Sav-La-Mar? You should have had him over for dinner." Walter Morris told great dirty jokes; Marian wanted to set him up with her younger sister.

"He's still out there making casts of footprints. The killer wore boogahs, he says." Guy suddenly remembered that Jim Quint wore Nike running shoes, popular American boogahs.

"The people at the market say he was killed with a knife."

"Ear to ear," Guy said.

"They say it was the Bigger Notch from Kingston."

Guy was disgusted. "Bigger Notch. Bigger Notch. Everybody on this island has the Bigger Notch on the mind."

"Timothy was the Bigger Notch's man, wasn't he?" Marian began scaling an orange fish.

"Yes, he was." Guy watched a storm move across Negril Bay, changing the water from turquoise to dark blue to a pewter with silver highlights. Lightning danced and flashed in the distance.

"More killings, you think, hon?" Marian slipped her knife into the belly of a goggle fish, so named because of its eyes.

"Why is it these kinds of cases always make me hungry? Should we smoke a spliff, do you think?"

"Be good for you," Marian said. "When I heard Timothy had been murdered, I went to see Patrick."

Inspector Guy groaned. Patrick was an obeah, a seer, a shaman. In Haiti it was voodoo. In Jamaica, the obeahs were called men of science. Patrick kept cages of doves, as was the practice of obeahs. His mother had given birth to a frog, the story went. After the frog was born there were two bones in her womb she couldn't get rid of. Patrick's mother went to see an obeah, who removed the bones and made her pregnant, which was how Patrick had gotten his powers.

"What did he say?" Inspector Guy cursed himself for asking. He couldn't help himself. If he had a war of Bigger Notches on his hands, he was in trouble.

Marian didn't answer. She continued cleaning fish.

"Well?" Guy asked.

Marian rinsed her hands and sat across from her husband. "Patrick says there is an unspeakable evil in Negril."

Guy laughed. "Unspeakable evil. Do you really believe that nonsense?"

"You asked, didn't you?"

"I read the astrological chart in the *Gleaner*. What does that prove?"

"Patrick said this evil is so vile he couldn't talk about it."

Guy rolled a big spliff in the manner of all properly rolled Jamaican spliffs, fat on one end, skinny on the other. "He was just trying to scare the water out of you, woman, earn his fee."

"I don't think so, Richard. I want you to be careful." Marian took her turn on the spliff.

"It could be outsiders, you know." Guy told his wife about the pilot, Jim Quint.

"I think he's telling the truth, Richard."

"The truth? Do you think so?" Guy didn't want to be bang dulued, a term he preferred to "hustled," by some American.

"He went to you asking for your help. That's what it sounds like to me. I don't think he's a bang dulu."

"You never know," Guy said.

"I met my niece Peggy at the market today. Remember, she's the one who works as an operator over at the Negril

Beach Club. She said she placed a call through to Kingston today and one man called the other a Chickadee."

"Chickadee?" Guy asked.

"Gay boys, I suppose. I hope they don't start showing up at Negril. That would destroy the beach. Peggy says her girlfriend took this man up some ice and rum and he was lying on the bed stark naked except for a panama hat. She says the air conditioner was running full blast."

"He's paying for it."

"I suppose," Marian said. "How could he stand it that cold?" Marian always wondered about men's balls, silly things. How could men walk with those things flopping about down there?

21.

Rasta Philip's dreadlocks lay heavily on his sweaty shoulders. He took his time strolling up the narrow lane that reeked of fluids past—Red Stripe, rum, pineapple soda, urine, vomit, bile, blood. The dirt accepted anything. Bare Jamaican feet, except for an occasional painful encounter with a shard of bone or bottle cap, didn't seem to mind. The lane was slimy in the rain, rock-hard in the sun, a fermented compost packed solid by human feet.

Philip couldn't imagine why people would leave the Jamaican countryside to live in an awful place like this.

A teenage girl in cut-offs that were threadbare at the ass chewed on a hunk of sugar cane and watched Philip approach. "You want fock, mon? Me do anyting," she said.

"Where you get dat sugah, dahlin?"

"Pussy." The girl rubbed herself and laughed.

There were hives of tin-roofed shanties on both sides of the lane. Weary clotheslines made of baling twine were strung from tin roof to tin roof across the lane. Philip passed a group of pot-bellied children playing a game with bottle caps. There was a man with no feet, a man sitting in urine-soaked pants, a woman yelling at nobody in particular. Philip dodged faded cotton dresses and ragged trousers hanging from the lines. He had never been up this lane before; people watched him as he passed. Women gossiped with their neighbors across the way.

"You got de big bamboo, mon?" one of them asked.

Philip fucked the air with his hips and the women giggled.

"Me old mon try dat, him fock up him back," another woman said.

They all giggled.

"Jah will provide." Philip leered.

"Wit me old mon?" The woman looked incredulous. "Me have to ask him when him in, mon."

Her friend giggled. "Listen to dis woman complain. She got pussy like de cave at Sav-La-Mar."

They giggled again.

Philip passed more children, clotheslines, pissing dogs, sleeping men, and gossiping women until he came at last to a British racing green Austin-Healy bugeye sitting square in the middle of the lane. The polished Sprite was famous in Kingston. The police knew who drove it. The folks in Trenchtown parted like the Red Sea when it approached. Its owner could drive up this lane at sixty miles an hour if he pleased, zipping under hem of skirt, cuff of trouser. Kids, dogs, chickens, and fat women with laundry baskets on their heads all unconsciously listened for the distant roar of the dazzling green sportscar.

The bugeye belonged to the Bigger Notch, Sonny Holmes.

An old man and his grandson examined the polished chrome and admired the black leather seats and neat little toggle switches on the dashboard. There was an expensive leather case on the passenger's side that held the Bigger Notch's reggae tapes. The top was down but the tapes were safe.

Nobody screwed over the Bigger Notch.

Philip turned at the bugeye and saw a crude door that was painted red, green, and yellow with a framed photograph of Bob Marley in the middle. There was a man in a chair on each side of the door. They looked up at Philip, their jaws working on strips of jerk pork. They exchanged a spliff, saying nothing. Each had a bottle of Red Stripe.

"Ya, mon?" one of them said, smoke drifting out of his mouth.

"Me ere to see Biggah Notch."

"Who de fock?"

"Me name Philip."

"Wat de fock?"

"Me come from Negril, mon. Dis be about Brothah Timothy."

The man shook his head. "Brothah Timothy one damn fool, mon. Him be Big Notch den fock de dog propah."

"Ya, mon."

"Got more ere dan Timothy?" The man tapped his head with his finger.

"Ya, mon. Me no fockin fool."

"Cool, mon. Wait ere."

"Ya, mon," Philip said.

The other man gave Philip the spliff and they smoked, saying nothing, until the first man returned. The first man extended his hand, thumb up. "Me name Daniel." He didn't bother to introduce the second man, who suddenly began putting the top up on the sportscar. A raincloud was sweeping its way across the city.

He followed Daniel down a narrow hall. There were huge cracks between the crude planks on the floor. Philip could see bottle caps, broken glass, and scraps of paper on the dirt beneath. He could hear the drone of an air conditioner as he neared the end of the long corridor.

Daniel rapped softly on another door painted red, yellow, green, and black. "Daniel," he said.

"Ya, mon. Come in, mon," a voice replied from behind the door.

"Drop you pants, mon," Daniel said.

Philip dropped his trousers. Daniel checked the pockets quickly. "Okay, mon?"

"Sure, mon. Go in."

Philip stepped inside and was immediately bathed in cool air. An air conditioner hummed in one corner. There was one man in the room, a man with thirty or forty gold chains around his neck. He had gold earrings, gold rings on his fingers, gold bracelets around his wrists and ankles. He was very black and the gold looked fabulous against his skin. He smoked a big spliff and enjoyed Philip's obvious awe at the room. "Go ahead, mon. Look it ovah. Not'ing but de best for Biggah Notch."

The floor was covered wall to wall with a Persian carpet that had once been bound for the den of Jamaica's Prime Minister, Edward Seaga, and had disappeared from a Kingston dock. The walls were covered with velvet paintings of nude women. There was a leather sofa and three easy chairs, all made in Costa Rica, all stolen from a Kingston dock.

The Bigger Notch had a Japanese stereo system at one end of the room. There was an enlarged photograph of Bob Marley behind the sound system.

"You be Philip?"

"Ya, mon."

"Sit, Philip."

Philip sat in one of the easy chairs.

"Nice, huh, mon?" The Bigger Notch was pleased.

"Be nice." Philip patted the soft arm of his chair.

"Know wat happen Brothah Timothy?"

Philip nodded. "Me know."

"Daniel do dat for de Biggah Notch, mon. Folks, dem say Timothy look foolish as hell wid him bamboo stuck in him mouth like dat."

"Me been told," Philip said.

"Biggah Notch be hard mon, Philip. You must know dat. You wan be Big Notch of Negril, fine, mon. You want see how hard me be, mon, den just fock ovah me. Me have ears everywhere. Remembah dat. Me only want ganj out of dere. Wat if some nut drop a bomb on Cuba or something like dat? Tink of it, mon."

"Den Fidel's man, him come calling," Philip said. He wondered who had betrayed Timothy.

"Ya, mon!" The Bigger Notch smiled. "See, Philip, you smaht, den everting fine. You make few dollahs; I make few dollahs; Fidel, him make few dollahs; ganj folks, dem make few dollahs; folks in America, dey smoke ganj and get hard-ons. Little bamboos." He laughed.

"Ya, mon."

"Me had to do dat to Timothy, mon, dat way folks know what to expect. Fidel, him trust us. Fock up like Timothy, we lose everting. You make sure you have good Rastaman check dose planes out on de day of de flight. You understan dat?"

"Me be careful, mon. Is it still okay wit de girl Robin or Rachel or whatevah she's calling herself dis week?"

The Bigger Notch was amused. His gold tooth sparkled. "Sure, mon. Her brothah, Gerald, is going fly de plane out of dere. Me can't believe she did dat. Gerald's the smaht one. Nevah had fock-ups wit Gerald." Besides that, Gerald Murrant was the Bigger Notch's source of Soviet-made AK-47's. The Bigger Notch didn't really believe Murrant's story about Timothy's having fucked up, but AK-47's were harder to come by than Big Notches.

"Okay Brothah Hubert check that flight?" Philip wondered how the Bigger Notch knew Gerald Murrant was going to fly Robin's plane from the swamp.

"Hubert be fine, mon. You go now. You be careful, you be okay. Biggah Notch take care of you. No problems. Me throw de biggest Christmas pahty on de island, de best pussy in Kingston."

Philip grinned. "No problems, mon."

"Say, Philip, you know wat de tariff is for de Big Notch?"

"Ya, mon. Me know."

"You keep it dat way, mon, especially for Robin Murrant. Hear wat me say?"

"Ya, mon. Me hear."

The Bigger Notch got up to shake. "Cool runnings."

"Ya, mon. Cool runnings." Philip felt good. His interview was over. He was the Big Notch of Negril. He'd get all the pussy he wanted, just like dumb shit Timothy.

Brother Philip would swing the biggest, baddest bamboo on the beach. He just had to make sure folks flew ganj over Cuba, not a lot of other crap. If the Americans got too tight about the traffic, too upset, then Fidel had to deal with gringos.

Philip's first duty as Big Notch was to talk to the white-head pilot Rasta Timothy said had been asking questions in Negril. If the whitehead was planning on flying ganj, he'd have to know about the tariff.

22.

Brother Hubert used a soiled piece of string to tie his dread-locks into a huge ponytail at the back of his neck, then checked himself in a triangular shard of mirror fastened to the wall with bent nails. Hubert had a flint-black face, high, wide cheekbones, and narrow, Asian-looking eyes. His dreadlocks were worked into reddish-brown ropes. Hubert tied his dreads when he rode his 175-cc Honda. The rest of the time he let them flow dramatically over his shoulders so that he looked like some mad mix of Mephistopheles and a black pharaoh.

This fearsome, dramatic appearance never failed to im-press the European girls. When Brother Hubert got high, he was given to long, rambling philosophical soliloquies about the brotherhood of man and all men being equal. The young women, having learned about Rastafaris from Bob Marley and Yellowman records, expected many references to Jah, Haile Selassie, Ethiopia, Babylon, and spliffs of ganj. These Hubert provided, together with fierce brown eyes and a real mean bamboo.

Brother Hubert did more than poke white pussy, however.

Hubert knew about ganja. While other Rastas hustled smoke and turtle-shell bracelets on the beach, Hubert rode his bike ten miles into the interior and hid it in some un-dergrowth. While his brothers scored American dollars in front of the Negril Beach Club or Miss Brown's Café in Negril village, Hubert threaded his way into the Great Morass, his ten-horse Johnson making a sputtering pop, pop, pop while Hubert smoked a spliff of mountain ganja. The sputtering and popping of an outboard could be heard for miles in the leaden stillness of the swamp.

There were two kinds of ganja grown in Negril. The crop in the mountains took about five and a half months to mature, and the buds were far less impressive than those grown in the Morass. You had to carry water to the mountains. You had all you wanted in the swamp, plus a rich, black soil that produced fabulous-looking long, green buds filled with red filament. The buds were moist and pungent. Tourists went for them in a big way. So did the folks who lived in spacious apartments on East Fifty-ninth Street in New York, and rode helicopters to Kennedy Field.

The Morass buds brought good money. Ya, mon. Brother Hubert had these little patches on Morass islands—two acres here, five there. He tended the young plants from seed. When they got some growth on them, he separated male from female plants. No seeds. Good sinse.

Brother Hubert smoked mountain ganja and grew it in the swamp for the trade.

He passed the wrecks of four private planes that had crashed in the swamp, an eerie sight. Threading his way through narrow passages, he saw the trail of one aircraft less than a mile from the road. Jah had not provided for the pilot; his body had never been retrieved from the ugly brown water.

The second plane had split on impact and had been stripped; weeds now grew through the cockpit and fuselage. The third and fourth failed to clear trees at the end of preposterous fifty-yard runways hacked out of underbrush on islands of dry ground. When you run ganja, you take chances. You sit there in the cockpit staring at the trees at the far end of the runway, brakes on, engines screaming, tac wavering above the red line in a giddy tremor.

Then you pop the brakes and shoot forward, your eyes on palm fronds in the distance.

The planes lay rotting, here a wing tip, there a curl of aluminum sticking up from the murk—ghosts of gambles lost.

It was more than an hour before Hubert beached his small boat on an island. He followed a winding trail that tunneled through tropical undergrowth until he reached a field of ganja well over his head. At the far end of the field was a small bamboo hut with a thatched roof. The hut's windows were covered with mosquito netting. A small fire burned under a cooking grill in front of the hut. Women's underpants hung on twine stretched between two trees.

A jazzman with a Dixieland band held forth on a tape, drifting out into the Morass.

The Dixieland softened. "Hey, Hubert," a woman's voice called.

Hubert parted the mosquito net and stepped inside. A young blond woman in a bikini and a pair of tattered boogahs sat on a pillow. A curly-haired man who sat opposite her rose and extended his hand. "Gerald," he said.

"Hubert." Brother Hubert had heard about Gerald Murrant.

A yellow cat beside the young woman opened its eyes and looked at Hubert without moving.

The young woman took a sip of tea and scratched a mosquito bite on her thigh.

Hubert sat squat-legged.

Gerald also sat, prepared, it seemed, to let his sister do the talking.

"Did you bring the mushrooms?" she asked.

"Ya, mon." Hubert glanced at Gerald.

"I don't know why I'm so damned lazy. I could go out and gather them myself if I had any energy."

"No problem," Hubert said.

"Would you like some tea? It's good."

"Ya, mon." The white lady made strong tea, which Hubert liked.

"I got a dozen fish in the trap last night. I don't see how anything could live in water like this. It's beyond me."

Hubert sipped his tea, wondering if he should tell her the news. "Good tea," he said. "Say, mon, I tink we might have a little worry." He watched as Gerald Murrant leaned forward.

"Oh?" Robin asked.

"Brother Timothy got into a little accident wit a machete on de beach yesterday."

The white lady petted her cat and poured herself some more tea. "Is he badly hurt?"

"Him lost him head, mon." Hubert demonstrated with his finger. "Machete man stuff Timothy's bamboo in him mouth. Ya, mon!"

"My God!" The white lady ran her hand across her face. "The Bigger Notch?"

Hubert shrugged. "Dis one be no fun, mon, dat be for sure."

Gerald said, "The Bigger Notch doesn't fool around."

"Does that change anything for us?" she asked.

"Don't tink so, mon. Long as we fly ganj and nothing else. Still need a pilot."

"Gerald will fly the herb on Wednesday. If anything's changed, Bigger Notch would let us know, wouldn't he?"

"You can count on dat, mon."

Gerald Murrant stroked the cat.

"More tea?" She poured Hubert another cup. "Anybody contact you?"

"Nobody," Hubert said. "A whitehead in town say him pilot."

"A pilot?"

"Be same whitehead Timothy bring to Red Rose for you to see."

Murrant looked thoughtful but said nothing.

"You suppose you could load the bales this afternoon, Hubert?" Robin asked.

"This afternoon?" Hubert looked surprised. The flight wasn't scheduled for two more days. The Big Notch always wanted the cargo loaded just before takeoff to ensure that only smoke was being flown over Cuba.

"That way you won't have to make another trip out here. Just load it up and give the Big Notch his cut." She put her hand over her mouth. She'd forgotten Rasta Timothy's murder.

"Ya, mon. Rasta Philip, him be Big Notch now."

"Well, then load it up and do your thing with Rasta Philip. You know you can trust us. We might as well get it over with."

"No problem, mon. Me take care of it." Hubert would tell Rasta Philip and let him decide. Philip was the Big Notch.

"And could you gas my boat and make sure the engine has oil?" The white woman tossed him a set of keys.

"Ya, mon. No problem." Hubert knew the Americans had made things difficult for Gerald in the Caribbean. The lady could have found a pilot who would take on the trees. Maybe the whitehead in town. Why the risk? Hubert wondered if something curious might be going on. First Timothy was killed, now this.

Jim Quint rode yet another lurching, rusted hulk from Lester's to Miss Wilma's. He should have known he was in for it when the driver slowed the Ford, which had a hood like an aircraft carrier, and turned left toward the beach. Quint wondered how he knew when to turn. Then Quint saw it, a tiny sign, blanched and peeled by the tropical sun. The sign had once said "Miss Wilma's Sunset Beach Cottages." Had someone given a paint brush to a six-year-old? Cottages? Quint took a deep breath. Why was he here? Why wasn't he home with a cold beer watching a ball game on the tube?

The driver eased down two parallel ruts into a dirt compound. The outdoor shower, surrounded by the ever-present corrugated tin—this one leaning to one side like the Tin Man on a bender—was on the left. Miss Wilma's house was on the right. Miss Wilma, a round, quiet woman in a print dress, sat in the open doorway of her kitchen, which was on the seaward side of her small house. There was a weathered picnic table in the middle of the courtyard where the family ate its meals.

Dead ahead was a small building divided into diminutive bedrooms. When Quint got out, he saw there was a barbed wire fence on either side of Miss Wilma's property. The fence ran from the highway to the beach. A four-foot-high mound of Red Stripe and soda bottles was piled against the fence on the left.

Miss Wilma looked up at Quint, but did not move. Her face was passive. "Yes?" she asked softly.

"I'd like to rent a room by the week, if you have one."

"Seventy Jamaican a week," she said. Miss Wilma retrieved a key from a nail in her kitchen and, on slow haunches, led Quint across the courtyard to see his room. He stepped over a sleeping dog and leaned inside. The room contained a bed, nothing more. The walls were made of one-by-sixteens that had been cut by a machete, a dull saw, or a precise beaver. The edges of the boards were cut on a forty-five- rather than a ninety-degree angle. When they were nailed together on wormy studs, the crack was at an angle. This blocked out the light between one room and the next.

Quint pushed on the bed. Mashed straw, he guessed. "This'll be fine," he said. He was pleased to see the outdoor bathroom had a porcelain sink and flush toilet. When Miss Wilma had gone, Quint hung his shirts on nails driven into the studs, and lay back on the straw mattress. Something smelled odd. He smelled the pillow case. Was that it? Yes. The sheets too. Was it mildew? Possibly, but something more too.

Quint shoved his valise under the bed and lay back again. He was supposed to find the girl with the airplane. Inspector Guy had said he should mingle with students and Rastas. Go to Miss Wilma's. Well, he was at Miss Wilma's—in a room so small he could touch both sides with his knuckles.

Quint wondered what made the sheets stink. He thought about eating a Whopper Burger with cheese—loaded with onions.

Instead, he got up and took a walk to the Bar-B-Barn on one side of Miss Wilma's and had pumpkin soup filled with hard little doughballs that looked like blanched elk droppings. That, and chicken necks. Quint sucked the skin off the chicken necks and decided he should let people know he was a crop duster. Pilot talk led inevitably to airplane talk. Aside from the dumplings—which Quint had to pin on the bottom of the bowl and cut with the edge of his spoon— the pumpkin soup was pretty good.

He didn't have time to get far because the afternoon rain clouds were gathering. Quint was startled by a boom of thunder in the distance. He drifted across to the octagonal, thatched outdoor bar. He had a rum and tonic and watched the bartender roll a long rope of tissue paper with the palms of her hands. She stuck the rolled paper into the top of an empty Red Stripe bottle and lit it with a match.

"Mosquitoes," she said.

"Oh?" Quint's heart sank.

"If it rain, den no come soon."

"Will it rain?" Quint jerked from another pop of thunder.

"Soon come." The bartender laughed.

She had no sooner said that than it started to rain, but there was a patch of blue behind the black, rolling cloud.

Jim Quint had a trait of character, a personality tic, that expressed itself as a sudden rush of confidence, a feeling that things were about to go right. Quint called it "the feeling." If he got the feeling when he sat down at his typewriter, he'd have a good rip. If he got the feeling on a cold morning in the Sawtooths, he was certain he'd come upon a bull with an enormous rack. Sometimes Quint's prose really zipped, sometimes it didn't. Sometimes Quint got a shot, sometimes he didn't.

But past failures meant nothing when Quint was in the grip of the feeling. He got the feeling now; it came upon him suddenly, eerily, and was in control.

Jim Quint knew something would happen on Negril Beach. He would learn something.

It was eight-thirty when the rain eased and Quint could walk down the beach toward the village. He walked past Miss Wilma's, past a crazy lean-to made of corrugated tin, past the log where Joseph Byrd carved bamboo bongs during the day, past the T-Water, a resort hotel with air conditioners humming in the units.

The sea and sky were a fabulous silver. The light rippled and swirled, bounced and danced on the water. A lovely two-masted schooner was silhouetted against the silver. Lightning leaped and made spectacular horizontal runs against the dark clouds low on the horizon.

On the beach courtyard of the Negril Beach Club, a crowd of German tourists and passersby had gathered for a show of Jamaican fashions.

"These girls are all employees of the Beach Club," the announcer said. "And here is Miss Leah in a lovely summer wrap-around."

Miss Leah, a slender Jamaican girl with enormous buttocks, strode across the cement in the exaggerated strides of a ramp model and removed the wrap-around with a flourish.

"Revealing a lovely bikini," the announcer said.

The bikini was cut as thin as a G-string in back. The Germans applauded enthusiastically.

A young woman spoke just behind Quint on the beach. "If you stand around out here at night you'll be eaten alive by sand fleas."

"What?" Quint turned and looked at the sand.

"Worse than mosquitoes. You'll dig until you get scabs." The young woman sat on a plastic beach chair. She wore blue jeans and had her feet tucked under her thighs. "Want to join me?"

"Sure." Quint grabbed a beach chair of his own.

"Let me see your feet. Hold 'em up here."

Quint did and the young woman took a spray can from her handbag and sprayed his ankles.

"Now your arms."

Quint held his arms out, one at a time.

"Rub some on your neck and forehead."

Quint did that too, then squatted on a chair just like the woman. The odor of the insect repellent was familiar. Where had he smelled it before? Quint remembered: the sheets at Miss Wilma's. The sheets were washed by hand in a tub. Quint wondered how many sprayed bodies it took to saturate the sheets beyond hope.

"My name's Rachel," the woman said.

"Jim Quint." She was an older version of the faded picture in Quint's wallet. She was Robin Murrant.

"How long you been down?"

"Just got here," Quint said. "You?"

"Been here a while," she said. "What is it you do, Jim?"

"I'm a pilot. I spray insecticides and herbicides on crops in the United States."

"Oh?" She sounded impressed. "You must be a pretty good pilot."

"It can get pretty hairy if a farmer has a row of trees at the end of a field and there're a lot of power lines around. You smoke?" He fumbled for the band of his panama.

She accepted a spliff from Quint. "Are you down here because you're interested in flying a little ganja, Jim?"

"I'd listen to any proposition."

Robin Murrant looked at her wristwatch. "I have to meet my boyfriend inside in a few minutes. Where are you staying?"

"Miss Wilma's just up the beach." Quint wondered what he should do now. He couldn't let her get away.

But he did. She was suddenly on her feet, walking inside. "I'll get in touch, Jim."

Quint wondered if the boyfriend might not be her brother, Gerald. Quint stepped back into the shadows. He saw the curly-haired Gerald Murrant waiting for his sister at the edge of the Negril Beach Club dining room. Murrant was not smiling this time. He looked anxiously in Quint's direction.

Jim Quint, Montanan, creator of Humper Staab, knew he had to do something. His countrymen were counting on him. He started sprinting toward the dining room.

Murrant took his sister by the elbow and began guiding her toward the lobby at the front entrance of the beach club.

Quint did the first thing that came to mind. He drilled Gerald Murrant low and hard with a cross-body block, now illegal in football. He took Murrant behind the knees. It was a clip, a cheap shot. Quint had been a wide receiver for the Bison High School Buffaloes. He would have been sent off the field for a hit like that.

Gerald Murrant went sprawling. Quint hit a table with the side of his head and took a scalding tureen of conch stew on his shoulder. He got up to face Murrant.

"Why, Jim Quint, old pal!" Murrant kicked Quint in the stomach.

Quint dropped to his knees. He began making a breathless "hoop, hoop, hoop" sound. He couldn't breathe but he had a job to do. He gritted his teeth and stood.

Murrant kicked him a second time.

Quint dropped again, still making the "hoop, hoop, hoop" noise. The hoops rose in pitch, as though he were practicing some odd scale.

He stood, aware of the babble of German tourists around him. He balled his right fist, still hooping, and took a shot at Murrant's jaw.

Murrant took him by the arm and sent him sprawling face first across another table, crashing through plates of steamed fish and curried goat. Quint felt himself being pulled off the table by a black man who did not at all regard the scene as cool runnings. When his eyes were able to focus and he was breathing again, he saw that Gerald Murrant was gone.

There was an atomic bomb in Negril. Jim Quint didn't have any proof of it, but he knew it was there. He wasn't about to give up. No fucking way.

"You bet your sweet ass," he said as he was half dragged, half pushed out of the Negril Beach Club.

23.

When Jim Quint traveled, he ate what local people ate and drank what they drank. When he was in Ireland, he drank Guinness. When he was in England, he drank bitter. In Scandinavia, he ate his fish boiled or pickled, in France steamed or sauteed with a lovely sauce. In Japan, he once consumed what appeared to be a bowl of embryonic eels. In Bangkok, he ate creamed cloves of garlic. He ordered recklessly from menus he didn't understand—Turkish menus, Tagalog menus, it made no difference.

A few of the uncomprehending waiters tried to get him to change his mind, but mostly they regarded him curiously as he stabbed here and there at whatever strange script the menu was written in. The results were mixed. It was not uncommon for Quint to order three soups, or three salads. On those occasions he giggled and ate his meal manfully, the intrepid traveler. He had veteran bowels and carried with him a magic potion he said could turn helium into lead.

Whenever local folks drank tea, Quint drank tea as well. He had consumed various black teas from Sri Lanka and India, oolong teas in Asia, teas made from rose hips, teas made even from dried alfalfa. As for mushrooms, Quint had gathered morels in Montana in March and April; in October there were orange chanterelles in the foothills of the Bitterroots.

So it was that late the next morning, sitting in Miss Brown's Café contemplating just what he should do next to find Robin and Gerald Murrant—if it wasn't too late already—Quint saw a sign on the wall that said "Mushroom Tea, $3." That was about forty cents American. Quint decided he'd try some.

"Lotta mushrooms dis morning. Tea be strong today," the waitress said.

The tea was thick, black, and sweet. Quint knew there was no accounting for taste. But if the Jamaicans liked it, why then the tea must have its pleasures. Quint stayed with it. Perhaps Miss Brown overdid it with the sugar. A little less sugar might have been nicer.

A glow washed across Quint's face and he began to feel nutty, a little loose. Dreams and ideas floated by. He considered them briefly, then they were gone. Quint recalled the smell of sagebrush, the odor of juniper. Quint giggled. He saw there was a handsome Rasta, naked save for cutoffs, sitting in front of him with fierce black eyes.

"Ya, mon, tea good?" the Rasta asked. His eyes only seemed fierce. He was friendly enough.

Quint looked at his empty cup. "It's different, but I gotta say it's real tea."

"You should have one more cup, mon. Miss Brown's special tea. Dis be me third cup. Drink it straight down, mon."

"Why, sure," Quint said. He ordered another cup. He wanted to be neighborly. He drank it in one pull.

"Dem be magic mushrooms in dat tea, mon. Be good for you." Rasta Philip laughed deeply. "Folks, dem say you be pilot."

"That's right. My name's Quint. Jim Quint." They shook.

"Me name Philip. Me bet you be interested in flying a little ganj, huh, mon?"

"Well, I don't know." Quint knew he was sitting across the table from his big break. Rasta Philip obviously knew about the herb business. This Rasta was the connection. Quint's head swam. Images crowded in. He had to find Robin and Gerald Murrant. Here he was, drugged. Philip had a voice like the un-Cola man in those old ads, deep and resonant.

"Me be the Big Notch in Negril. Dat means me be boss here, mon. Know what me mean?"

"That tea made me high. All I ordered was mushroom tea."

"Dat be psilocybin, Mistah Quint. Magic mushrooms. Me be high too."

Quint giggled. "I'll just bet that you being the Big Notch means I have to pay you a little tax if I want to fly ganj out of here."

"Not so much, mon. A dollar and a half American for each ounce. I get some, Bigger Notch in Kingston, him get some, Fidel, him get some. Plenty left over."

"Do folks fly anything out of here except ganja?"

Rasta Philip's face turned serious. "No, mon. Only ganj. Fidel, him don't want othah crap going ovah him island. Mon try dat, me must cut him balls off."

The psilocybin had sent Jim Quint adrift. Everything seemed absurd. The very idea of him sitting across the table from a black man in dreadlocks was preposterous. Quint started to laugh. A woman with a child standing outside the window was ridiculous. Philip giggled; he was high too. Quint thought briefly that only a mind thus drugged could possibly believe the bomb story. The idea of lying was absurd. It was impossible for Quint not to tell the truth in his condition.

"There's something I must tell you, Philip, and I swear by Jah that it's true. You must believe me. There's a young woman named Robin somewhere near Negril. She has a plane and she's fixing to fly an atomic bomb over Cuba to the United States. Do you know of a woman named Robin fixing to fly a little ganj?" Quint giggled. It was difficult for him to concentrate. His mind drifted.

"A what?"

"An atomic bomb, mon."

"You be sure, mon?"

"Positive," Quint said.

Rasta Philip said nothing.

Quint said, "I'll bet she calls herself Rachel."

Philip looked surprised. "Ya, mon. How you know?"

"A guess," Quint said. "I met her on the beach last night. How do you know her name is Robin?"

"Brothah Timothy check her passport before him get him throat cut. Dis be business, mon."

"You want to see my passport?"

"Ya, mon."

Quint showed him his passport. People talked softly. Their voices drifted gently by. The air was warm and sweet. There was an absence of the sound of things mechanical—no cars, no airplanes, no refrigerators, not even, momentarily, any reggae.

"You telling de truth about dat bomb?"

"Yes, mon. On my honor as a civilized human being. There's been a dreadful, dreadful fuck-up." A goat bleated and Quint giggled. The goat peered at him through the door. There had been a peering goat at Lester's. Quint giggled. "An anomaly."

If Quint hadn't been drinking Miss Brown's mushroom tea, Philip would have ya moned him for a few minutes, then gone on his way. The image of Rasta Timothy's amputated bamboo came directly to mind. What if this whitehead was telling the truth?

"Now then." Quint leaned forward. "Before you conclude that I'm crazy because of this tea, let me tell you what I know and what I can guess, and you tell me whether I'm right or not. How about that?"

"Sure, mon," Rasta Philip said.

"That woman who calls herself Rachel is Robin Murrant and she inherited her ganja contacts from her brother, Gerald."

"Ya, mon, dat be so."

"Now then, Gerald has been running drugs in Europe, but he arrived in Negril last night because he's going to pilot a ganj run."

Rasta Philip said nothing. Rasta Hubert had said he had loaded the airplane two days early. One or the other of the Murrants had been doing business out of Negril for years. They knew the rules. This was out of form, but he'd let it slide.

Rasta Philip began to have doubts.

"Has Murrant flown that run yet?"

"No, mon."

Quint sighed and relaxed for a second as images of the interior of Miss Brown's seemed to float and drift. He forced himself to concentrate on Rasta Philip and the bomb. Quint giggled. He removed an envelope from his jacket. There was a photograph inside of Gerald Murrant and several Vrienden gathered around the bomb. The French photographer had used a good lens.

"Is that Gerald Murrant?"

"Ya, mon."

Quint removed a second envelope from his pocket. This one contained a newspaper clipping that recounted the history and disappearance of the Vrienden bomb.

Rasta Philip read the story—slowly, to be sure, but he read it.

Quint waited, trying hard not to giggle.

Philip looked up. "If we go now, mon, dere be time."

"He's going to fly it today?" Quint floated, drifted.

"Ya, mon." Rasta Philip did not want to contemplate the wrath of the Biggah Notch if Gerald Murrant used Negril to fly an atomic bomb into the United States.

24.

Rasta Philip's old boat, made of sodden, heavy wood, was pushed by a Mercury engine that must have been twenty years old. The rope pull on the starter looked a bit ragged, but the engine started on the fourth yank and they were on their way.

"If you see anything in de watah, tell me, mon." Philip slid the boat full-throttle around stumps and clumps of roots. Philip had barely gotten the job as Negril's Big Notch, and now this. Philip could hardly believe it.

Quint leaned over the bow. He held on tight, still in the grip of psilocybin. It was like being in a John Ford movie, he thought. The triumph of good coming up.

He saw the Cessna sitting at the far end of a tiny runway. The plane looked new; its startling black and yellow exterior was as yet unbleached by the tropical sun. To Quint it resembled nothing so much as a giant wasp.

The Murrants had heard the rattle of the Merc in the humid air. There was a frenzy of activity near the plane.

"Ya, mon. Look dere!" Philip aimed his old boat at the shore of the island.

Rasta Philip and Bison Jim Quint scrambled over the bow and sprinted toward the plane as hard as they could.

Quint was stunned to see Gerald Murrant emerge from a tiny hut with the Vrienden bomb cradled in his arm. The engine of the wasp popped to life and idled, the propellor going luf, luf, luf.

The engine stopped. The door to the wasp opened.

Gerald Murrant handed the bomb up to his sister and pulled himself in after her.

Quint and Philip circled to the left as Murrant settled into the cockpit beside his sister. The engine stalled, then popped to life again.

"Fuck!" Quint shouted.

Rasta Philip gestured toward the trees at the far end of the diminutive airstrip. "We weight it down, mon."

Quint understood. He aimed for the near wing, giving the quicker Rasta Philip the far wing. Murrant revved the engine. He revved it higher, higher still, his eyes on the tops of the distant trees.

Quint and Philip each had hold of a wing support.

Murrant popped the brake and the plane started forward with Jim Quint clinging, running, stumbling, from one wing and Rasta Philip from the other.

Murrant red-lined his engine and pulled back on the stick, ignoring the yanking, never taking his eye from the trees. The plane struggled, wobbled. Quint and Philip jerked and yanked from under the wings.

Quint could see the trees coming.

He winced as he caught some branches across his thighs and lost his grip. He did a slow, looping somersault into the swamp and came up vomiting. There was not a pasture in Montana that contained a pond so pissed in as to exceed the odious murk of the Great Morass.

Rasta Philip had landed not ten yards away. "Plane, it be gone," Philip said. Philip knew the only way to escape the wrath of the Bigger Notch was to help the whiteheads intercept that airplane.

Robin Murrant's speedboat was locked with a device designed to foil the most industrious Third World thief. They turned quickly to Rasta Philip's old Merc which, alas, declined to start.

"No problem, mon. Jah will provide." Philip took the handle in his fist and gave the rope a mighty yank. Nothing.

Quint looked out above the swamp in the direction the plane had disappeared. "Do it, Philip."

Philip tried once more.

"Do it." Quint had never seen such power as Rasta Philip put behind each pull.

Philip tried again. "Jah will provide."

Jah did not provide. "Shit, Philip."

Philip yanked, grunting. Nothing. Again he tried. Sweat began to slide in a lazy trickle across his ribs.

He pulled.

The rope popped, sending Philip sprawling.

Quint stared at the motor. The stump of cord had disappeared into the housing. "My God!" He sat on the ground.

Philip swabbed his forehead with the back of his arm. He looked at the motor housing. "You got Allen wrench, mon? No problem."

Quint sprinted to the hut on the far side of the diminutive strip. The door was open, there being no second-story men cruising the Great Morass. Robin Murrant had taken nothing with her. The hut was abandoned, a smuggler's leavings. There were tins of pepper, jars of salt, canned peaches, Fats Domino tapes, incense, old *Time* magazines, and a half-empty carton of tampons. There were no tools—not a hammer, not a pair of pliers, much less an Allen wrench.

Philip was smart enough to figure out the odds were slim. By the time Quint got back to the boat, Philip had used his machete to fashion a second paddle out of a board.

"Me take de front, mon. Me know where we go." He gave Quint the makeshift paddle. "Hang in back dere now, Mistah Quint."

Quint took the stern. "Philip, those people have an atomic bomb in that airplane. They'll probably go for New York. You know what Manhattan is?"

They pushed off. Philip dug into the water with powerful strokes. "Ya, mon. Times Square."

"It'll take us hours to get back to the highway."

"Jah will provide, mon."

Quint was willing to accept help from anyone who would pitch in. He tried to match Philip stroke for stroke, but that was impossible. Philip was an athlete, and had a better paddle besides. The sun glistened off a sheen of sweat on Philip's muscular back. Blisters soon began to form on Quint's hands. Pain began in his stomach muscles and worked its way up his ribs. He could not think about the pain, could not. Had to concentrate on Philip's back, had to. He never had seen a man sweat so much, work so hard, never had, never had.

"Where you gonna go to get decent lox and bagels if they blow up New York?" he asked.

"Jah will provide, mon."

Shit. Quint thought he was going to be paralyzed. "Do you think Haile Selassie..." He didn't think he could continue. New York editors had once rejected his fiction, hadn't they? Fuck the Big Apple.

"Haile de mon," Philip said.

"Do you think Haile Selassie would have a roast-beef sandwich with us in one of those Irish bars?" He dug his paddle in again. Once more.

"Haile, mon, him be direct descendant of Moses."

"How about Bogie's on West Twenty-sixth? We could go there, the three of us, Philip. You and me and old Haile. Maybe Billy Palmer'd have a waitress with big tits or something."

Rasta Philip too was wired with pain. "Brother Philip and his big bamboo." He dug and pulled, dug and pulled.

"Times Square, mon. You could take the old bamboo out and throw it over your shoulder, nobody'd care. Cosmopolitan city. Me love white pussy." Dug and pulled. Pulled.

"Billy Palmer'd pour us both cold rum and tonics. Just hold that bottle back there and let 'er rip."

"Babylon, mon."

Quint managed to smile in spite of the pain. "Ya, mon, but I love it."

"Dis be hard work, mon."

"We'll save the city, Philip. There'll be a big parade, ticker tape thrown from tall buildings. We'll ride in big convertibles."

"Big, whiteass Caddies," Philip said.

"Ya, mon. There'll be girls, Philip, white pussy. Wave that big bamboo."

"Irie, mon. Irie. Me wave dat numbah!"

"The mayor'll give us keys to a bankrupt city, Philip. Champagne."

"The blessings of Jah, mon."

"Coke, Philip. We'll toot all night and all the next day."

"Ya, mon. Much toot."

"I'm hurting some, Philip."

"Tell me bout dat bahtendah, mon. Tell me bout de girls."

It took them three hours to reach the bridge at Negril. They couldn't sit up straight at first, much less stand. The

Big Apple may have been on the line, but all Jim Quint could do was stare at his bloody hands. The public phone across the street had an out-of-order sign on it, but Quint and Philip saw a decrepit old Chevrolet taxi standing in front of Miss Brown's with its doors open to keep the heat from building up inside.

"Randy's," Philip told the taxi driver. "Be private dere, mon. You make your call dere," he said to Quint.

Quint gave the Rasta driver twenty Jamaican dollars for a paper bag of ganja and Philip rolled them each a giant spliff.

Len Meara looked at his drink with distaste: a plastic cup. Meara had spent his career in Europe. The Europeans had economies. You could buy stuff there. You got your drink in a highball glass. Bars had dishwashers. They didn't have to chip ice with an icepick. Meara guessed it was okay to talk, what with the ghetto-blaster destroying their eardrums. He leaned toward de Leeuw, who sat by the retaining wall at Randy's Café.

"Fuck, oh dear, man, I just cannot believe this place," Meara said. "What did I ever do to Tarnauer that he sends me off on a wild-goose chase? A rumor, he says."

A cat rubbed up against de Leeuw's leg. "I don't have anything for you to eat," de Leeuw said. He slipped his hand under the cat and set it to one side.

"I've yet to eat a meal here without a cat under the table begging for scraps. Cats all over the place. How do they live? I think it's probably all right to talk, Paul."

De Leeuw looked back at the bar. "They'd have to be in a submarine to scope us with a parabolic."

"They'd have to be fuckheads," Meara said. "Fuckheads don't have stuff like parabolics, yet here we are, slapping mosquitoes instead of being someplace civilized."

"I kind of like it here," de Leeuw said.

Meara shook his head. "Whatever starts your motor."

"They're friendly people."

It was Meara's turn to set the cat aside. "Another two, please." He motioned to the bartender and held up two fingers. "What's the usual wait, do you think?"

"Take it easy, Len. Life is slow here. You know that guy I talked to yesterday? I've heard that name before, I think."

"The pilot?"

"I'm sure of it."

"Where?"

"I don't know," de Leeuw said. "Somewhere. You know how it is."

"These people could be professionals. Did Quint give you the name of the company he's supposed to be working for?"

"No, but I bet Inspector Guy has it."

"If you ask for it, you'll have to tell him why you want it. Tarnauer wants us very, very low. Be shadows, he said. Real spooks. Maybe you could have another drink with Quint."

"I can do that," de Leeuw said. "What about the dead Rasta?"

"Yes, well. There's that too. Fucking cat." Meara leaned over and set the cat aside again.

"The folks here say you had to get Timothy's permission to fly ganj over Cuba. You had to ask it three days in advance."

Meara said, "Timothy's supposed to have worked through a Bigger Notch in Kingston, have I got that right? God, I love these people's lingo."

"The Bigger Notch is right."

"Okay, here it is. I want you to find out more about Jim Quint, if that's his real name. I also want you to find out who killed Brother Timothy and why."

De Leeuw sighed. "Just like that."

"Do the best you can. If this is more than a rumor, we're playing some high-stakes poker here. What we also have to do, my man, is have a little chat with the Bigger Notch."

"You want to do what?" De Leeuw looked around him.

"I want to have a chat with the Bigger Notch. You set it up; I'll do the talking."

"Oh, Christ, man. The Bigger Notch's men carry AK-47's."

"Like in the movies." Meara laughed.

"You got that right. I don't believe what you're saying."

"It's easy enough to figure out. The Bigger Notch and the Cuban government obviously get a cut out of every ganj flight over Cuba. There has to be a list of approved flights somewhere."

"You're saying if we can get our hands on the list we can check the bona fides of some flights."

"You never know," Meara said.

"Okay, I'll try. What do you have to offer the Bigger Notch?"

Meara looked surprised. "Why, the taxpayers' money. What else?" He slipped his hand under the cat's belly and tossed him gently over the retaining wall.

De Leeuw looked concerned. "What's over there?"

Meara put his feet on the wall. "I don't know. Grass maybe, dirt. A cat always lands on its feet."

"The Bigger Notch makes a Mafia Don look like a sissy."

"You make the arrangements, I'll do the talking."

De Leeuw stood up and looked over the retaining wall. There was a straight drop of fifty feet to the ocean; gorgeous turquoise water twisted and swirled at the bottom. "Oh, shit, Len."

"What's that?"

"You want to look?"

Meara looked. "I wonder if it landed on its feet?"

De Leeuw was aghast. "It wouldn't make any difference if you pitched him to the right."

"Hmmmm. Rocks," Meara said. "There's water on the left if he's a swimmer."

"You just wasted that cat." De Leeuw started laughing. He couldn't help it. Meara was so casual, it was unreal.

Len Meara said, "You know, Paul, I bet that cat never, in his screwiest nightmare, ever believed anything like that would ever happen to him."

Jim Quint was something of an apparition when he stepped onto the courtyard at Randy's Café. The brim of his soaked panama hung limply, obscuring his eyes. There were enormous yellow moons of sweat under the armpits of his filthy tee shirt. His soaked jeans hung low on his rump. His muddy boogahs squished when he walked.

Quint was still high from hallucinogenic mushrooms and working on his second spliff, but there was one fact that was directly on his mind: the fate of an American city just might hang on his ability to get a call through to Georgie Farr in Washington.

He was not so high as to miss de Leeuw and another man sitting at a table. De Leeuw looked at the other man and they rose and started in his direction.

Quint began to retreat.

The two men separated. One went right, the other left.

Quint had no idea what these men wanted. He had to phone the United States immediately. He stepped quickly behind a small service building. He couldn't see the two men. Had they gone to the main entrance to cut him off there?

Quint saw a low stone retaining wall at the far edge of the patio. He crouched low and moved swiftly across the patio, spliff in hand. Quint's solution was easy enough. He'd hide behind the retaining wall. The other man and de Leeuw would leave in a few minutes, looking for him.

Quint, watching for the two men, took a hit on his spliff and hopped backwards over the low wall. It was casually done. Athletic. Nifty.

His foot clipped the top of the wall and he wound up falling, upside down, spliff in hand, thinking of the high cliff at Painted Rock back in Montana.

It was a high dive. Quint fell upside down with ganja smoke trailing from his mouth, a French pilot going down in flames.

If there were rocks below, he was dead.

If it was water, he'd have to hold his breath.

He was half unlucky.

Quint's leg hit an outcropping of rock. His shin popped, but he remembered Marissa Stanley's advice and grabbed for his balls.

He hit the water with a dreadful whack. He plunged down, down, down into Jacques Cousteau country. Would it never end? He thought fleetingly of the girl from Lost Horse.

The way up took even longer. Quint thought he would never break the surface. When he did, he gasped for air. Pain shot through his leg. This was pain layered upon pain. He turned and floated on his back, his arms outspread.

He looked up and from the cliff above, Rasta Philip did a fabulous dive, plunging into the water a scary two yards away. Philip surfaced and began pulling Quint ashore. "Impressive, mon. Me have to hand it to you."

"My hat, Philip. I lost my hat."

"Me got it, mon. No problem."

Quint was grateful. He had his panama. "I have to phone the United States, Philip. I must."

"No problem, mon. Me find you a phone."

"Jah will provide, I suppose," Quint said.

"Ya, mon, Jah, Him be dere."

GUN LAP

25. *Gerald Murrant wasn't sure why the Soviets*

wanted him to meet Hideo Yasuda in Baltimore, but it was okay by him. Baltimore was an okay place. At least it was the U.S. Murrant was at the oyster bar in Lexington Market to swap the Vrienden bomb for Yasuda's $5 million inheritance. Murrant had no idea who had struck the bargain, and didn't care. He did as he was told. Murrant was kicked back in designer jeans and a slick leather coat. The Vrienden bomb was in a friendly old duffel bag by his knee.

Murrant looked buoyant. He gave an oyster a shot of Tabasco and slid it down his throat—that and a good slug of National Boh from a white plastic cup.

"Aahhh!" he said. He pushed some money toward the black man, who wore heavy rubber gloves. The black man shucked some fresh oysters from a tub. A sign behind him said "The oysters you eat here today spent last night in Chesapeake Bay." The oyster man wore an Orioles baseball cap. He slid a dozen Murrant's way and said over his shoulder, "Ain't no motha could field a baseball like Brooks. No motha." He shook his head furiously, sweat flying. "Don't feed me that Clete Boyer crap."

"These are good," Murrant said. He saw a young Asian with a large briefcase. "Oh, Mr. Yasuda!"

"Gerald?"

"Me bigger than hell," Murrant said.

Yasuda handed him the briefcase. "It's all here."

Murrant took a quick peek. "Okey doke." He gave Yasuda the duffel bag.

Yasuda checked his merchandise and walked out of the market without another word.

"Have a blast," Murrant said.

The money Gerald Murrant made smuggling pot into the United States was used by the Soviets to buy subsidized American wheat. Thus American pot smokers provided cheap bread for hungry Russians. The Kremlin used the rubles it saved to build ICBMs that it aimed at the pot smokers.

The money Murrant made smuggling hashish into Europe was used by the Soviets to buy subsidized butter from the European Economic Community. Thus European hash smokers provided cheap butter for hungry Russians to spread on their plentiful bread. The Kremlin used the rubles it saved to aim SS-20's at the European hash smokers.

These were just some of the benefits of the free market that the Soviets supported with enthusiasm. Murrant was one of several dozen Soviet bread-and-butter men.

After the swap was made, Murrant met Harold Woods in Woods's car parked on Eastern Avenue. It wasn't too far from where Woods had grown up. He leaned across the seat and unlocked the door for Murrant. "Well, how'd it go, pal?" he asked cheerfully. Woods was having a good time in his home town. He had chosen Baltimore so he could have some of his mom's good breakfasts.

Murrant slid onto the seat. "A piece of cake, Harold. He's a fucking madman."

"Bye-bye, Manhattan?"

"Bye-bye, baby, bye-bye," Murrant said.

"All right, my man. I've got some toot in the glove compartment there. Thought we might celebrate."

"Really?" Murrant was surprised at Woods. "Okay, Harold!" Murrant leaned forward to get the cocaine. "This it here?" He started to open a small box.

Harold Woods took a small, silenced pistol from his jacket pocket and calmly splattered Gerald Murrant's brains against the window. He got out of the car and trotted across the street to a second car. He drove off and the car containing Gerald Murrant's corpse burst into flames. The flames ruptured the gas tank, shattered the windows, twisted the metal, and toasted the bread-and-butter man.

Muhammed Bhutto had passionate brown eyes. If Bhutto wanted, they could be romantic, Kahlil Gibran eyes—soft and tender, the eyes of a poet. On the other hand, if you pushed him, he could cut your heart out without blinking. He had that look about him. His black hair, those cheekbones, and his jaw made him look a bit like the Egyptian actor Omar Sharif.

Bhutto was the chief security guard at the Karachi nuclear facility. He was new on the job. His hair was neatly combed, and shaped into a bit of a pompadour. His picture was on a plastic security badge clipped to his breast pocket. His hands were folded neatly on the table.

His eyes were sincere; they said, Trust me, Hungarian lady and American man; trust me, Frenchman. I am a humble Pakistani. I am a civil servant. I love my country and I serve it the best I can. But, praise Allah, I would never lie about something like this. Never. He turned his brown eyes on the Hungarian lady. Kahlil Gibran eyes for her.

The eyes said Bhutto liked fair-complexioned European ladies, Leonoor Lund could see that. She turned to the translator. "Can you please ask Mr. Bhutto what happened to Mr. Karn, who was chief of security at our last visit?"

Bhutto gave his answer. He looked from Harold Woods to the French inspector, Lucien Salvant, as if seeking assurance. His eyes couldn't have been more sincere.

The translator, Ali Goel, said, "Mr. Bhutto says Mr. Karn was only temporary on your last visit here. Mr. Bhutto was attending the birth of his first son, Omar, the last time."

At the mention of Omar, Muhammed Bhutto grinned broadly, the proud father.

Leonoor Lund looked at Harold Woods. Her face betrayed nothing.

Woods turned the pencil in his hand. "Can you ask Mr. Bhutto once again to explain why there are frames missing in the film for two consecutive nights?"

Goel's face turned hard, then softened. Take what they have to give, he had been told. They were Europeans sitting on Pakistani soil; it wasn't easy having to answer the same question twice. "Certainly," he said and spoke to Bhutto in Urdu.

Bhutto's eyes went savage. He turned from inspector to inspector. He repeated his answer.

"Mr. Bhutto says the same thing as before. It was camera failure, an anomaly." Goel hesitated. English was his second language and he wasn't certain he knew what anomaly meant. He'd once heard a colonel use it to placate a general.

"It does seem strange," Leonoor Lund said.

Goel stiffened. "Madame, surely you don't mean to ask him the same question three times."

Lucien Salvant leaned forward, the peacemaker. "I'm sure Mrs. Lund means no offense, Monsieur Goel. It's just that she has a grave responsibility to the international community, as we all do." He gestured to Woods.

"A grave responsibility," Woods said.

Goel looked pleased. The game was back on track. Goel's father had once told him that Europeans were like camels; you had to rap them on the snout with a stick every once in a while. "Certainly, I understand," Goel said.

Leonoor Lund looked at her companions. The physical evidence was incontrovertible. It was pointless to continue; Bhutto and Goel were obviously programmed. "Well, I'm sure this ought to be enough. We've just about got everything. Monsieur Salvant, Mr. Woods."

They rose. The inspection team followed Goel down the hallway to a waiting room where they would wait for a van to drive them back to the airport at Karachi.

When they were alone, Woods said, "Who do you suppose Bhutto is?"

"An army officer, I'd say," Salvant said.

Woods looked at Mrs. Lund.

"Yes, I agree with Lucien, an army officer. Something like that."

"What do you think happened?" Salvant asked. "Aren't they smart enough to do a better job than that of tidying up the evidence?"

"They're smart enough," Woods said.

"Then what happened?"

"Here comes the van," Woods said. "What happened was that somebody from the outside slipped in here and helped themselves. They did it in shifts, judging from the missing slides, two nights running. What's more, the Pakistanis have had more than enough time to run an accurate audit."

Just then Muhammed Bhutto, in perfect English, called Leonoor Lund's name and asked for a small word with her. The man with the Kahlil Gibran eyes had been educated in British schools. He was not a security guard. He was a Pakistani army officer who knew somebody should tell these people the truth.

"We Muslims too have our honor," Bhutto began.

26.

The phone was ringing when Jim Quint opened the door to his Chevy Chase condominium and clumped across the carpet on crutches. He dropped his valise and picked up the phone. He noticed there was a cardboard box on the floor half-filled with letters. Quint wondered what was going on.

"Hello," he said.

It was Leo Tull. "Jim! Jim! Where have you been? Where have you been? Jim! Jim!" Tull was excited.

"I went swimming," Quint said.

"I've been trying to get hold of you! I've been trying to get hold of you!"

Quint said, "You're repeating yourself. You're repeating yourself."

"Where have you been?"

"First, tell me what's going on?"

"You mean you don't know?"

"I can see the manager has collected half a cardboard box of letters. The phone was ringing when I stepped in the door."

"Jesus Christ, Quint, we got ourselves a break, a big, big break! I mean, Jim, this is it! Jim! Jim! Jim!" Tull's voice rose higher and higher, teetering on the brink of hysteria.

"What happened, Leo?"

"We really stepped into it this time. Jim! Jim!"

"Say it, Leo, you can do it."

"Oh! Oh! Jim! Remember when people found out John Kennedy was a fan of James Bond? Remember? Remember, Jim?"

My God, Quint thought. Georgie Farr must have come through. "Tell me what happened, Leo."

"President Lyle had a press conference last week. He had a lot of good stuff to report. Progress in the Middle East. The economic rebound. He and Gladys were going to Camp David for a couple of days. He said he was going to do a little reading."

"He said he reads Humper Staabs."

"Yes! I thought you didn't know."

"I didn't," Quint said. "Tell me the rest of it."

"He said he'd read all twelve Humper Staab titles twice through and a couple of them three or four times. He said you're a wonderful writer, Jim."

"Did he give any little examples?"

"Yes, yes, Jim. It was wonderful. He recited almost word for word a great sentence from *Humper Staab Tucks It Home*. Do you realize what happened to Fleming? This is movies, Jim. Bucks. Big bucks, Jim."

"Really, I'm going to be paid something?" Quint could hardly believe that.

"They print their own money in Hollywood, Jim. Listen, the calls I've been getting are unreal. The networks want to talk to you; the news magazine want to interview you. You're hot, Jim, hot. They want you on the 'Today' show, 'Good Morning America,' the 'Tonight' show, the 'Tomorrow' show, the 'Tomorrow Afternoon' show. Jim! Jim!" Tull's voice began to rise once more.

To Quint's knowledge, he hadn't accomplished a thing. Good old Georgie Farr, he thought. What a guy. It must have taken some fast talking to pull that one off. The President of the United States reading Humper Staabs!

"Jim! Jim! You can buy yourself a Greek island and drink retsina and write Humper Staabs. Think of it, Jim!"

Quint knew Leo Tull wasn't going to calm down. The prospect of money had affected his central nervous system. "How are the women there, Leo?"

"On a Greek island? Jim, I've been told Greek women are extraordinary. Succulent. Willing. Fabulous butts, you'll like that."

"You do whatever you have to do, Leo, to make us the maximum bucks. I'll ride a unicycle naked down Broadway if I have to. Anything."

"You'll have to send President Lyle autographed copies."

"Whatever," Quint said.

"We'll see you on Johnny Carson, bubbie." Tull laughed. Quint hung up.

Unknown to Jim Quint, there were two interesting letters buried in the box. The first was from Georgie Farr, who took credit for President Lyle's endorsement of Humper Staab books. The truth was, Farr had never talked to Lyle. He had never intended to. The President's mystifying endorsement was a freebie. It was like finding money on the street, and Farr couldn't resist taking credit.

Quint was squatted over the box of letters when the phone rang again. This time it was Marissa.

"Jim, my God, I thought you'd never get back. You just can't imagine what happened last week!"

"I can imagine. I just talked to Leo Tull."

"Why don't you come up for a visit now that you're a celebrity? Bring your portable."

"I've got a broken leg, Marissa."

"You've got what?"

"A broken leg, but I'm quick on crutches. I'll tell you all about it when I come up."

"Can you still fool around okay?" She sounded worried.

"Of course I can still fool around. Nothing stops a Montanan."

"Good. I'll make you chicken soup or something. I gave you my address, didn't I? West Ninety-sixth, just off the park."

"I'll take a commuter flight from National," Quint said. Quint liked New York. He'd hobble into Bogie's on West Twenty-sixth and drink a few with the mystery writers who hung out there.

"Why are you always gone when everything happens?"

"I've got a talent."

"Did you stop the bomb?" Marissa asked.

"That's something I want to talk to you about," Quint said. "We might want to think about taking a little vacation in Montana."

The steering on Hideo Yasuda's Ford Escort was about as tight as a Yokohama whore. Yasuda slowed for a tollgate on the New Jersey Turnpike. He was just past Trenton and doing fine. He fumbled for his wallet.

"Two solid weeks of rain," the gatekeeper said. "Can't believe it's stopped. My yard's a swamp." He was bored and cold.

"Humm," Yasuda said. He eased carefully away from the tollgate. He drove with extra caution so as not to break traffic laws. The bomb, still in the duffel bag, rested comfortably in a cardboard box in the Escort's luggage space.

There is a yearning people have that draws them back to familiar places—to the womb, to home, to a place and time where memories are good. So it was that Hideo Yasuda returned to his old stomping ground, so to speak, where some of those pasty-skinned round eyes had just loved taking their lumps—the area of the gay bars around Sheridan Square.

Manhattan is a long, narrow island, separated from the boroughs of Queens and Brooklyn by the East River, which runs from Long Island Sound to the Atlantic Ocean, and from the borough of the Bronx on the far north by the Harlem River.

Ellis Island and the Statue of Liberty are just off the southern tip. Wall Street, the financial district, and the Bowery are on the southern end. Just north of this is New York University and the Greenwich Village area of bohemian fame. This is all downtown.

Farther north still are Madison Square Garden, Times Square, the Empire State Building, and Grand Central Station. This is the midtown area of multinational corporations, Broadway theaters, television headquarters, and book publishing. To the visitor, midtown is awesome.

North of midtown Manhattan is Central Park, separating white money and Spanish poverty, on the east, from the ethnic melting pot on the west. North and west of the park is Columbia University, which flanks the combat zone of Harlem.

Then comes the Harlem River, the northern end of Manhattan.

Yasuda drove to Greenwich Village. He drove to Christopher Street on the west side of Sheridan Square, named after General Philip Henry Sheridan, hero of the battles of Stones River and Cedar Creek. Sheridan Square was a triangle, really, flanked by Seventh Avenue, Grove Street, and Christopher Street. Why it was called a square was one of those mysteries of the American imagination that enraged Yasuda. Learning how to pronounce r's and l's had been hard enough without having to put up with that kind of thing.

He found a place to park in front of the Lion's Head, a bar and restaurant at 59 Christopher Street. The Lion's Head, a writers' hangout since the turn of the century, was a stucco building, light blue below, beige above, with a red circular awning out front.

The base of the triangle, along West Fourth Street, was open to drug dealers and gays hanging out. The apex of the triangle, where Christopher and Grove streets met, was bounded by a high iron fence topped with spear points. This venerable fence had been painted and repainted black during the city's many well-intentioned but doomed attempts to spruce itself up. The paint was chipped and peeling, asking for yet another coat of black.

Inside this fence, General Philip H. Sheridan stood on a granite pedestal looking grand. This was the man who had led Union troops on the assault of Missionary Ridge. His troops killed the South's great cavalry leader, Jeb Stuart. His bronze exterior was green with age and streaked with pigeon shit, but he remained a dashing, flamboyant figure in a stylish slouch hat, cavalry tunic, knee-length leather boots, and spurs. He wore gloves halfway up his forearm. His left hand rested on his hip by the hilt of his sword. His head turned left, watching that flank. He was a hero of what was said to be the first modern war.

The granite pedestal of Phil's statue was surrounded by unpruned, overgrown, and ugly evergreen shrubbery. Yasuda had never paid any attention to the statue when he was a student at NYU—he had no interest whatever in the American Civil War—but the shrubbery to him was an unforgettable horror. How Americans could allow a public park to look that way was beyond his imagination. When he went back to Japan for a visit, all he could tell his friends was how Americans eat cheese on everything and don't prune their parks.

Yasuda thought it was good that this eyesore would be erased along with everything else. The overgrown shrubbery was the perfect place to stash the bomb. The gate, he knew, was locked. He assumed it was a cheap American lock, easily popped.

He was wrong. It was a real lock, made in West Germany.

Yasuda was dismayed. He could throw the bomb over the fence and then crawl over himself, but he didn't want to risk damaging the timing mechanism. Also he didn't feel like landing ankle-deep in rain-soaked muck.

He walked around Sheridan Square looking for a place where a modest little bomb could remain hidden until 5:30 p.m. the next day. A garbage can? No. It might be picked up by a truck and dumped on Long Island.

When Yasuda was a student, he had become fascinated by the large steel grids or gratings on New York sidewalks. These were the covers of freight shafts, and they varied greatly. Most were shallow, only six or seven feet deep. A few went way down, ten or twelve feet. Most of the grids were composed of small rectangles an inch or two wide and two or three inches long. Women with spiked heels had to avoid those grids. Those who walked over them saw the bottom of the shaft clearly. Other grids were tightly packed, cutting off all sunlight so that a pedestrian had to kneel to see through to the bottom.

When a grid was lifted, merchandise could be moved into the basements of the adjoining buildings. Mostly, however, the freight shafts were unused; they were receptacles for trash filtered down from pedestrians passing over the steel grid above: cigarette butts, bottle caps, broken glass—leavings of the city.

Yasuda looked at his watch. It was 3 a.m. There was a freight shaft under the sidewalk by his parked car. It was a long, narrow grill. He was about to stoop to inspect it, but was interrupted by two men strolling hand in hand. They exchanged a joint and looked at Yasuda, saying nothing.

The door to the shaft in front of the Lion's Head was about three feet long and two feet wide. It was held in place by three bronze hinges. Yasuda realized that even if he couldn't break into the door leading to the basement, the freight shaft was sufficient to hide the Vrienden bomb. It was deep, with a dense grid. A person would have to get down on his hands and knees to see the bottom.

When the gay couple was out of sight, Yasuda tried the door to the grid. It opened the first try. The lift under the door was halfway down. He moved quickly. He took the bomb under one arm and hopped down onto the lift, then to the bottom of the shaft.

He put the bomb down, and had turned to retrieve his bag of tools from the sidewalk when a light shone in his face.

"How are you doing down there, friend?" a voice asked. It was a cop. Yasuda swore in Japanese.

Two lights now shone from above. The second, belonging to a second cop, rested on the bomb.

"Howdy Doody, what's that there?" the second cop said.

Yasuda looked at the bomb. If it were possible, he would have thrown himself on the bomb and detonated it. "I was checking the door. I don't know what that is."

"Out. Now," the cop said. "Hands well above your head."

Yasuda did as he was told.

The first cop made him lie on his stomach, arms and legs outspread.

The second cop went down to check the bomb. He put his hand on the bomb and rolled it slowly to one side. "Ron, did you see that program last week about the fake bombs these kids have been leaving around lately?"

"They found one over at Union Square two nights ago. There was a junkie sitting on it sweating like a dog shitting peach pits. He'd been doing speedballs."

The cop with the bomb laughed. "I heard that from squirrel-face in records."

"Davis. He said the guy was contemplating the Second Coming."

Boyd lifted the bomb gently and weighed it in the palms of his hands. "A fake Dutch bomb. A real bomb couldn't be this light." He looked up at his partner.

"Hell, that's what it is, Boyd. Has to be. It's got all the flags and everything." Ron pointed his pistol at Yasuda, who had moved slightly. "Stay right where you are, pardner, if you don't want a new asshole."

"So what do we do with it?" Boyd ran his finger along a fin.

"Leave it there."

Boyd turned the bomb over. "That's what I say. It's not hurting anything."

Ron had wanted an electric train when he was a kid, but his parents didn't have the money for that kind of thing. "It'd be fun for a guy's den," he said.

Yasuda realized that Americans really and truly were stupid. He watched while the cop swung up to the sidewalk and replaced the metal door. They made him lean with his hands against the wall.

Boyd looked at the passport and card. "A Japanese alien. A graduate student. We wait for seven months for my brother to loan us the boat, and now, bam, just like that, no fishing tomorrow."

"Oh, boy," Ron said.

"Then after we get screwed out of a day in the middle of the Sound, we get in the courtroom and his lawyer will ask us if we actually saw him tampering with the doors. We'll say no. The lawyer will ask where the tools were. We'll say they were in a bag on the sidewalk. He'll say, Well, my client was down there under the sidewalk to contemplate Buddha. If he'd intended to break into the place he'd have had his tools with him." Boyd shook his head.

"The kid's dad is probably an industrialist or he woudn't be going to school in the U.S. His lawyer will claim we're anti-Japanese because of the cars and television sets. The judge will get uneasy because of the press."

"After all that—no fishing, the pointless hassle in the courtroom—the lieutenant will ask us what the hell we're trying to do, embarrassing the department like that."

"What do you think?" Ron asked.

"Let him go."

"I agree." Ron took the information off Yasuda's passport and student card. He took the license number of Yasuda's Escort.

Boyd gave Yasuda a hard look. "Now you listen here, friend. In the United States we don't fuck around with assholes who try to break into other people's property. Next time we catch you trying to pull a stunt like this, we'll throw you in prison and forget about you. We've got your name."

Yasuda said nothing.

Boyd said, "That's more like it."

The cop named Ron picked up Yasuda's bag of tools. "This stuff must have cost you several hundred dollars. Crime doesn't pay. You remember that."

Boyd said, "We're going to drive around the square. When we get back, you be gone."

The cops got into their squad car and began their cruise around the block, laughing at the absurdity of their work.

Yasuda got into his Ford and headed for another part of the Village. He knew some gay hangouts that stayed open all night. He decided there was time to kick at least one more yielding white butt before he got out of town. He was elated. There was no reason to worry about someone spotting the bomb underneath the grid. In that part of town people kept their eyes up, crotch level.

27.

Everything went swell for the first few weeks of President Lyle's administration. His bacon was cooked just right by the White House chefs. Leaders of the opposition party— which controlled both houses of Congress—promised their cooperation in passing the laws the country needed to get on its feet again. Members of the press were generous and properly obsequious. It was a mild winter. People felt good. Spirits soared even higher when the cherry blossoms appeared on the Potomac.

Maybe this time, people thought. Maybe it'll be different this time. Please, no more anomalies. No more Nixons. No more Carters. People wanted to believe, they really did. President Lyle was especially optimistic.

The press was the first to go bad. Reporters turned putrid by July, becoming callous sleaze artists, hateful bastards. They were bored, Lyle could see, restless for action. Come September, the statesmanlike congressmen, all bi-partisan at first, reverted to form. It turned out they were swine. Hogs. They bloated themselves at the public trough. They bullied and conned their way to the front of the line, passionate grunters. By God, they were going to get theirs.

Lyle soon tired of it all. He quietly withdrew, as had the others before him. Ike had whiled away the hours fishing and playing golf. Nixon brooded about his enemies. Gerald Ford golfed and skied.

The pattern was familiar. Every President went through the same cycle: from hope to despair, promise to reality. Still, they plugged along, their eye on the history books. They quarreled with reporters and the hogs. They tried.

After a year, Lyle decided to paint. He was at least as good a painter as Margaret Truman was a singer. Paintings by an American President would surely be worth a few bucks. He'd need something to tide him over until his memoirs were published. He could use government helicopters to ferry him to good spots. Winston Churchill had painted, hadn't he? Lyle's aides could suggest his watercolors some-how made him an intellectual, like the French President. Even this fantasy was warm poop. First of all, it was im-possible to paint with Nikons and Hasselblads peering over your shoulder. Even in the most tranquil landscape, there stood a man with a television camera.

The press balked at comparing him to the French Presi-dent, who really did have a fine mind and deserved the respect he received. Still, Lyle painted on. When an editorial cartoon in the *Washington Post* pictured him on the stern of a sinking ship, wearing a beret and serenely painting a sunset, Lyle packed his yellow ochre and Hooker's green.

One day Lyle's son-in-law, a San Franciso lawyer, left his latest Humper Staab paperback in a White House john, where the President, his bowels stirring, happened upon it.

On his next two visits, Lyle's son-in-law lost two more Humpers—the last one, he believed, was stolen from a trav-eling bag. On the fourth visit, the son-in-law casually left a Humper in the john and kept an eye on the President.

That was the beginning of an informal, unspoken arrange-ment between the two men. Whenever a new Humper Staab title appeared on the drugstore rack, the son-in-law bought it for his wife's father, an imprisoned man. It was the hu-mane, generous thing to do.

President Lyle was delighted. He enjoyed the overworked scenes of sex and mayhem. Humper was a real man. He was competent. He got things done. Humper met fabulous women who were eager to gobble his wanker like a turkey leg or hop atop it, wiggling their butts and squealing with glee.

Then came the awful day that Lyle's son-in-law stopped leaving Humper Staabs in the john. The President was ir-ritable. What had gone wrong? Finally, he took his son-in-law aside, and they had a little man-to-man.

President Lyle confessed that he'd been stealing the Hum-pers.

His son-in-law admitted that he'd known all along.

Why did you stop? Lyle asked.

The series ran out, his son-in-law replied.

My God! the President exclaimed. Find out why!

Lyle's son-in-law dutifully called the publisher, and the publisher replied that Nicholas Orr was a pseudonym for Jim Quint, a very expensive and much sought-after writer. The publisher said people who liked Humper Staabs should tell their friends so Quint-Orr would be encouraged to write more titles.

President Lyle read the stories twice through. He wanted more Humpers. He paced the floor. Finally, he did what he had to do. President Lyle endorsed Humper Staab on television.

It was, therefore, a curious constellation of unrelated events—something beyond the range of the most gifted psychic or Japanese computer—that set the scene for President Lyle's reception of some pretty grim news.

The bearer of grim news forced Lyle out of the toilet where he was closing in on an inventive Humper Staab seduction. The bearer was new on the job, and so thoughtlessly fired both barrels at once; it was bad news, bad news—boom! boom! Usually Lyle could hit the Wild Turkey between blows, but not this time.

The first bad news was that the Pakistani government had confessed to the United Nations inspection team that there had, after all, been "an anomaly contrary to Pakistan's initial assurances of normality" at its Karachi nuclear plant. "A careful reassessment suggests that five kilos of weapons-grade plutonium are in fact missing. The Pakistani government sincerely regrets any inconvenience this misinformation might have caused."

The second bad news was that newsdesks and government offices had been receiving a recorded message that a one-megaton atomic bomb was set to go off in Manhattan at 5:30 p.m. The message said the bomb, stolen from the Vrienden in Amsterdam, was packed plumb full of plutonium stolen from a Pakistani nuclear reactor.

Lyle cursed the British and checked his Seiko. It was 10:50 a.m.

"Aw, fuck!" Lyle threw *Humper Staab Flexes His* at the wall so hard that a portrait of Aaron Burr hit the floor with a thump.

28.

The President put on his spectacles and read the message through. He looked up at the other members of the National Security Council. His face betrayed nothing. He adjusted his spectacles and reread the message. He looked up again and sighed. He gave his famous Frank B. Ryan grimace.

"Mr. President?" Terry Wyland began rolling and unrolling the end of his tie like a repentant schoolboy. Was he about to get a good hiding?

"The note is from Harold Woods, a Company employee who helped reinspect the Pakistani reactor. The awful details." Lyle looked suddenly old and drawn. He didn't know what to say next.

"Would you like me to tell him, Mr. President?" Georgie Farr asked.

"Yes, Georgie, I think you've earned the privilege, if you can call it that. I want you to listen, Terry, to what this man has to say."

"Why didn't they tell us?" Wyland asked. "You said yourself the Pakistanis have an uninspected source of weapons fuel. This had to be somebody from the outside. Why didn't they tell us? Why?"

"Do you know who Abdullah Muhammed al-Zakbar is?" Farr asked.

Wyland bit his lip. "I know who he is."

"Zak the Knife. Al-Zakbar figured this for an inside job, which it was, of course. He wanted answers, so he resorted to a time-honored way of learning the truth. He systematically interrogated and tortured twenty-six people who could have conceivably stolen the plutonium. These people are now dead, every one of them."

Wyland looked at the generals, then at the President. "We asked him if anything was wrong. He should have told us. Why?"

Something snapped inside Georgie Farr. "Because you didn't tell him the whole story, you dumb son of a bitch.

You didn't tell him about our suspicions of Jones." Farr's face tightened. "Zak the Knife would have loved to have had a Western villain, would have given anything to get Pakistan off the hook. He was protecting his country's reputation. What if Pakistan asked the West for another reactor in the future? But no. You worry about spooking people with the elections a year off. And now..." Farr's voice rose. He felt a fluttering in the area of his heart.

"So it's real, then, the bomb is real?" Wyland looked dumbfounded.

"Of course, it's real, you fuckhead!" Georgie Farr didn't give a damn about his language. He was no longer impressed at being in the presence of an American President.

Lyle wondered how many pages of memoirs this scene would one day warrant. He couldn't imagine why Richard Nixon would want to tape everything. "David," he said, motioning to his press secretary, David Meyer.

"Yes, sir, Mr. President."

"We're going to have to announce the evacuation of New York City. We'll need a few minutes to discuss the matter. Mr. Tarnauer, do you have the Company's contingency plan for something like this?"

"Yes, I do, Mr. President."

"David, I want you to go out there and tell the media that I have fired Terry Wyland effective now. Please tell them we'll have an announcement in a few minutes about the bomb calls."

"Yes, Mr. President," Meyer said.

"Tell the network people I want this live on all channels. Any station showing 'Sesame Street' or a soap opera gets its license yanked. I'll see to it personally."

"Yes, sir. They'll want to know the reason for the firing, sir."

"You tell them, David, for reasons of gross incompetence, stupidity, and extreme negligence of duty. Put it in just those words. When they link the firings with the bomb, say no comment. Wyland's the first one off the sled. Does everybody know what I'm talking about?" He looked around the room. Nobody said anything. "How many more will have to go depends on what happens the rest of the day. We'll have to perform well in the next few hours."

The members of the National Security Council had heard Lyle use the image of trimming the sled on previous occasions. He was referring to the droshky, a sled used by nomads in Siberia. When they were on the move, it was said, and pursued by wolves, the nomads thought nothing of kicking a granny or senile old man off the back of the droshky. While the wolves gorged, the family escaped. Richard Nixon used the tactic during Watergate. One by one, he kicked John Mitchell, H. R. Haldeman, and John Ehrlichman off the sled, hoping that Bob Woodward and Carl Bernstein, sated, would give up.

Terry Wyland, stripped of his perks, was suddenly a pathetic figure. The pouches under his eyes looked pouchier. He was a self-important, obsequious prig. Nobody wanted anything to do with him. He smelled of failure—a disgusting odor, more foul than rotten fish. He was given extra space.

"Pay attention now, gentlemen." Lyle faced the uniformed chiefs of the armed services. "I want all our available helicopters and seacraft sent to Manhattan now, before David talks to the media people. What do we have? A sloop from the Coast Guard Academy, I suppose. Rowing sculls from West Point. Armored personnel carriers from Fort Dix. Out. Now. Go. When you're finished, get back here." Lyle watched the generals leave the room on the trot, old men with bellies and enlarged prostates. Through it all, they'd said nothing.

Lyle couldn't believe he'd been this stupid. He'd have to flay Wyland, draw and quarter him, if he expected to get reelected. The island of Manhattan was due to blow in a few hours. The man who looked like Frank B. Ryan was lip deep in warm snot. "What the hell's the name of that civil defense guy? My wife's second cousin."

"Owens, sir," Tarnauer said. Tarnauer had a firm grip on the droshky because he'd sent Meara and de Leeuw to Negril.

"Is this the guy who's been telling newspaper reporters all each person needs is a hole and a door with some dirt over it?"

"The same, Mr. President."

"Nobody has a shovel in Manhattan. Are we going to assemble everybody in Central Park? Somebody get him the hell over here. No more perks for him. Mr. Tarnauer, what does the contingency say about the President?"

"We're all supposed to be on our way to Weather Mountain, sir. That would be contingency KZY-216, sir." Tarnauer looked at the cover of the four-inch-thick summary of KZY-216 that told what everybody was supposed to do.

"No evidence of a second bomb, second city?"

"No, sir."

"We stay. No sense spreading the panic. At the same time that David makes his announcement, I want this place sealed, however. We have work to do in here. I want contact made with the New York civil defense authorities and the commanders of National Guard and army reserve units in New Jersey, New York, and Connecticut. Tell them to send out a general alert and watch television. Warren, take some notes now. I've got a lot that has to be done."

"Yes, Mr. President."

"When David tells the media, I want all airplanes waved the hell away from Kennedy and LaGuardia."

"Done."

"Lewis," he said to his Secretary of State, "I want you onto the hot line, tell the Soviets what has happened. Tell the British. Tell the French. Tell the Chinese. Do the Soviets first. Do that right now."

The Secretary of State was on his feet and moving.

The heads of the military services began returning to the room. Lyle stared at the table. "The banks!" He rubbed his eyes. "The international banks must have their records on tape. I want those tapes safely out of the city." He pointed at an army officer. "That is your responsibility. I want helicopters on the corporate rooftops of Chase Manhattan, Citibank, all the big ones. I want helicopters on the roofs within one minute following David's announcement to the press. One minute. Tapes only. Your people are to shoot people who try to get on board." This was callous, Lyle knew, but it had to be done. The dollar and the international banking system had to be protected, had to.

The army officer rose to his feet.

Lyle stopped him with a motion of his hand. "Check with the Secretary of the Treasury on this. Ask him what happens to the securities and stock exchanges if we don't have Manhattan tomorrow morning. Do they have tapes? I want the financial institutions left intact if possible."

Terry Wyland listened to the President in silence. Wyland had meant well. One small error. For that, no perks. He had always thought President Lyle was an asshole. All those years of assiduous sucking up. Wasted.

Farr glared at Wyland in undisguised fury. His heart fluttered again. He reached for his pills. They weren't there. He'd forgotten them. Farr never forgot his pills. His heart went ka-bump, ka-bump. He'd have to get his pills. The flutter was stronger. Georgie felt a slight twinge of pain. He turned to Wyland and said, "If shit were brains, mister, you wouldn't have a smell. Sorry, Mr. President, I think I'm about to have a heart attack." He looked at the others. "This is an all-American fuck-up," he said.

With that Georgie Farr hurried from the room. There was an extra bottle of pills in the glove compartment of his car. The car was parked in a garage two blocks away. Farr was scared. It didn't occur to him to have somebody else run to his car. The pain stabbed again, heavier. Farr tucked his elbow in as though that might somehow forestall the inevitable.

Georgie Farr had a pink tag pinned to his breast that identified him as a participant in the National Security Council meeting. He was supposed to turn this in to the security guard when he left, but Farr, knowing he had only minutes to live without his pills, rushed on outside.

He ran down the steps and onto the street, not realizing that more than a hundred reporters and television cameramen were assembled there to receive Meyer's scheduled statement. They stepped aside as Farr, his mouth open, his face twisted in obvious pain, lurched toward the street. Television cameramen taped everything from the moment Farr burst through the door.

The reporters watched as Farr suddenly twisted and went down. His face smacked into the concrete curb. He made a sound and turned on his side. The reporters saw blood on his face. His front teeth had popped like icicles, exposing raw nerves.

The reporters saw the pink card pinned to the breast of his jacket and were curious.

Farr was surprisingly clear-headed, even calm, despite the bolts of pain that pulsed shocks through his chest. He knew he would never get to the car. He was about to die.

He also knew that LaTrobe Blue had been right when he had whispered in Farr's ear the day of Jim Quint's debriefing. Farr had been shocked at first, then passed it off as the fantasy of an old man who refused to leave the stage, who had been told once too often that he was infallible. Blue had made an outrageous, preposterous allegation.

Now Farr knew Blue had been right. Farr knew this intuitively, in a flash, the result of his instincts and imagination—a coalescing of cause and effect, hunch and suspicion. Farr didn't trust coincidences. Why had Harold Woods asked for the New York loon list? If the Vrienden bomb wound up on Manhattan, then Yuri Andropov had his hand in there someplace. Farr was sure of it. How?

Georgie Farr knew that LaTrobe Blue—working off British videotapes—was correct in concluding that Harold Woods was an agent of the KGB.

There was a reason for the KGB blips on Gerald Murrant's Interpol record. He was KGB also, smuggling drugs for Western currency, no doubt. The Soviets must have had Murrant give the Vrienden free smoke so he could watch the bomb.

When Alistair Jones pulled his inexplicable stunt, the self-congratulating at Moscow Center must have gone on for days. The island of Manhattan had been handed to them, a gift, free, compliments of a demented British agent. Here, said fortune. Oh, yes, thank you, said the Soviets. They could score some American dollars on the side. All they had to do was find a suitable customer—somebody who couldn't be traced to the KGB.

My God, the loon list! A ragged, hard bolt of pain seized Farr's torso.

The KGB had ransacked the New York City loon list for a mad bomber.

Farr flipped over on his back. His eyes were wide. He looked at the cold and distant sun. The air on his broken teeth snapped pain through his head.

Farr wanted to scream mole!

He wanted to tell someone that it was the conniving bastards, the Soviets, who had maneuvered the bomb onto Manhattan. They were probably watching everything on television, innocents before the world. Yuri Andropov must be grinning like a lizard on a hot rock.

Pain twisted through Farr's torso. He saw a face through the haze of pain. It was a black man, a cop. He would tell the cop, tell him about the mole. The cop would get word to the Company.

"Mmmmm," Farr said. "Mmmmm." He was able to purse his lips to start the word but his jaw wouldn't move. His lips almost parted, but no. "Mmmmmooooo," he said. He was getting closer. "Mmmmooooo."

Reporters gathered around Farr and the cop.

Farr's final minutes were taped by Sonys, photographed by Nikons.

"What's that card on his lapel?" someone asked.

A woman reporter leaned close. "It says, George Farr, Op Two. It's a pass to the National Security Council."

"He's been a participant in the discussions inside," a third reporter said.

The cop knew the little man was about to croak. "Easy now, friend." An ambulance was on its way. There was nothing the cop could do.

"Mmmmmmmmoooooo."

The cop took Georgie in his arms and held him to his breast, held him close. He was a sentimental man. He believed all people deserved the reassuring touch of another as they lay dying. He did not know he was handing a Pulitzer Prize in photography to a twenty-one-year-old student intern at the *Baltimore Sun*.

Farr appreciated the warmth and strength of the embrace. "Mmmmmmooooo," he said.

"Uck!" This last sound was involuntary, caused by death spasms.

The reporters thought he had said "motherfuck." "What did he say?" one of them asked the cop. The reporters waited, pencils at the ready.

"The deceased's last word was 'mother.'" The policeman closed Farr's eyelids.

The reporters all grinned and wrote, "last word mother." What did it matter that the plump little man had been swearing like a trooper at the outrageousness of life's end? They couldn't use that one in a family newspaper. Mother was useful, good for a poignant kicker.

29.

Marty Spivak's shoelace came untied as he approached the Lion's Head. He knelt on the grid above the freight shaft on the sidewalk to tie the lace. As he jerked the knot tight, he saw the dim shape of a bomb on the bottom of the shaft. Marty cupped his hands around his eyes and put his face close to the metal grid. He grinned. It was a fake Vrienden bomb like the one he'd seen on television a week earlier. He appreciated the bizarre humor of the Village. Besides, it was fun to see the nuke lobby suffer.

Spivak decided to run the length of Manhattan, past the Bronx, to Rye, New York, on the Long Island Sound. He had a girlfriend there, Roxanne, who gave great head. Rye was twenty-five miles away, but that was no problem. Mad Marty would cruise it in five- and ten-mile spurts, resting and walking it off in between. The fashion with many runners was to train and listen to rock and roll through a headset radio. Spivak didn't do that. He had an active mind. He liked to enjoy what was going on.

When the reports started coming in over the radio, Mad Marty was tuned out, running free, running to the tonsils of sweet Roxanne.

When the unsinkable *Titanic* sank in 1912, its passengers were arranged according to class. First-class passengers, the wealthy and friends of the shipowners, occupied suites and salons on the top deck. There were restaurants with tuxedoed waiters, and quiet bars where gentlemen could discuss the affairs of Empire. One could have a whiskey or a sherry and watch the sun settle over the Atlantic. The Edwardians understood the needs of one's nether parts. The ship was barely out to sea when corseted women and cigar-smoking men arranged heady assignations. Dinner had to be shared with one's spouse, that was true. But there were compensations: real Russian caviar—hard to come by in London—roast squab, and tender spears of white asparagus marinated in a piquant vinaigrette. And the wine! Life was good.

Second-class passengers—who would assert themselves in their numbers during the coming years—occupied utilitarian cabins in the center of the vessel. They settled in as best they could, happy to be part of history. There was a small promenade on deck reserved for second-class passengers. They were allowed above on a rotating basis, as space permitted. The lucky ones got to linger for a while, got to hold hands and watch the stars, got to listen to the ship's orchestra playing in first class.

Third-class passengers stayed below. They played cribbage, listened to children cry, or groped on tiny bunks that shuddered to the rumble of enormous engines.

When the *Titanic* hit that presumptuous iceberg, Edwardian courtesies prevailed: first-class passengers went first. Second-class passengers were beginning to get their chance when the ship slipped under.

Third-class passengers stayed below. Buy cheap, get cheap. They had learned a lesson.

Question: Was a first-class gentleman worth more than a second-class child?

Of course.

Question: Was Soviet Foreign Minister Gregor Rostov worth more than the daughter of a delicatessen owner?

Well...

The problem confronting the Lyle administration was that access to the lifeboats—the bridges, subway tunnels, helicopters, and boats—was available to all New Yorkers without regard to status. An Irish bartender and the president of the Yale Club were in the same fix. Comrade Rostov, like all Soviet officials since the revolution, delighted in kicking Uncle Sam in the ass, jabbing at his eyes, and calling him a liar. He now regretted this somewhat, although he'd never had any choice in the matter. The Red Army demanded it. The Soviet people had come to expect it.

Comrade Rostov had never experienced a classless society. He was not at all sure he was comfortable with the idea.

Rostov was more equal than others; the Americans would have to evacuate him. Rostov retreated with his aide, Sergei Krimm, to the office of the Soviet ambassador to the U.N. The ambassador, Anatoly Pessin, was sent down the hall in an effort to divert officials of the nonaligned countries, who suddenly had a change of heart with regard to the Soviet bloc.

"Well, Comrade?" Rostov asked.

"They have to pick you up, Comrade."

"They don't have to do anything. I want to know if you talked to them."

Colonel Krimm frowned. "I..." he began.

"I what?"

"The Americans assure me a helicopter is on its way."

"Are they in contact with the people who have the helicopters?"

"Communications are bad, Comrade."

"Shlovock!" Rostov had brought Krimm with him from the KGB. Krimm had a good apartment, a car—enough rubles for a mistress. "Bad communications." Rostov spat the phrase out with scorn. "Of course communications are bad."

Krimm turned pale. Comrade Rostov was his ticket off the island. "They'll come and get you, Comrade. They have to." Krimm knew he sounded pathetic.

"They may *want* to," Rostov said.

"They will, Comrade."

"But what if a helicopter comes and is overwhelmed by Libyans and North Koreans? What can the Americans do, shoot them? Think of the uproar later on."

Rostov was right, Krimm knew. "What do we do?"

"Find us a place in the subway like everybody else, Comrade Krimm."

Mad Marty Spivak took a straight shot up Lexington Avenue and crossed the Harlem River at the Willis Avenue Bridge. He followed Westchester Avenue through the Bronx, his hairy legs pumping, crossed the bridge over Eastchester Bay, and headed for the seashore at Pelham Bay Park. It was then, with Marty running the firm median between water and soft sand, that word was dispatched over radio and television that folks on Manhattan had a choice of digging in deep or running a fly pattern out of the city.

Later, there would be stories about the first cabs across the bridges. Only a few were empty. Most were packed, with people clinging to fenders. Within minutes, however, panicked drivers had become snarled in an impossible traffic jam and abandoned their vehicles. This made the streets useless.

All this was happening behind Mad Marty's back. When he got to Pelham Bay Park, the Vrienden bomb was already twelve miles behind him. He heard sirens wail in the Bronx and nearby Mount Vernon, but assumed it was a fire of some kind.

When he came to a jam-packed Highway One in New Rochelle, with sirens wailing in that city as well, Mad Marty knew something frightening was happening.

People in the slow-moving cars checked their wristwatches and glanced nervously over their shoulders.

"What happened?" Marty asked of a large family mashed into a Volkswagen Rabbit. The Volkswagen edged forward. Spivak jogged alongside and talked to the wife through the open window.

"Haven't you been listening to the radio?" She looked amazed.

"I've been running," Marty said.

"There's an atomic bomb set to go off on Manhattan in another two hours."

"What?" Spivak looked incredulous.

"They're evacuating the city. Listen." She turned up the volume on their radio. A man was giving evacuation instructions and telling people how to protect themselves.

The man on the radio said, "You must be off the streets at five-thirty p.m. You must be off the streets at five-thirty p.m. Do not attempt to look at the blast; you may be blinded. If you are in Manhattan or any one of the surrounding boroughs at that time, get underground. Find a basement; go to the subway. If necessary, use the sewer. Stay put after the blast. Do not move. Radiation can be extremely hazardous to your health. Medical and evacuation teams are now being organized. Wait for instructions. You will receive instructions by radio if you have a battery-operated receiver, or by helicopter-borne loudspeaker."

"My God!" Spivak said.

"Did you see that television program last week about the Vrienden bomb?"

Oh, oh, Spivak thought. He remembered the bomb at Sheridan Square. "What happened?"

"Somebody armed that bomb with plutonium stolen from Pakistan and stashed it on Manhattan somewhere."

"The bomb covered with flags?"

"That's the one," the woman said.

"Oh, shit!" Marty Spivak was amazed.

"What's the matter?" The woman looked worried.

"I probably saw that bomb under a sidewalk when I was running in the Village this morning. I thought it was one of those fakes they were talking about on TV."

"What are you going to do?"

Marty Spivak stepped back to the edge of the road and looked toward the Manhattan skyline.

The man on the radio said, "Please do not attempt to call your local police or fire department. The lines are jammed and all personnel are helping with the evacuation. Listen to this station for instructions."

"You can't get through to the police," the woman said. "We tried when the sirens first started. We finally heard about it on the radio."

Spivak had already run fifteen miles, fueled by the promise of Roxanne. There were two hours left. He could do it. Sure he could. "I'm going to run," he said.

The husband, who had been listening to the conversation, said, "Go for it, Marty!"

Spivak gave both husband and wife a thumb-up handshake. Without a word, he turned and began to run toward the heart of the fury.

The West had been given its chance to save the queen city and show the world its men were more than drugstore cowboys. The pothead Montanan, Jim Quint, had the skills Georgie Farr wanted. Quint had a shot at it. He tried, God knows. He did his best. He was game. He was spirited. In the end, he was a dud. He wasn't worth a pinch. He was as worthless as tits on a boar.

Whatever his parentage, Marty Spivak was of the East. He had never tasted corn on the cob before the sugar changed to starch. He had rarely known crisp lettuce and never tomatoes allowed to ripen on the vine. His blood was awash with chemicals that cause cancer in mice. He trained on cole slaw and cream cheese, chicken soup and pastrami sandwiches. A lot of people had given up on the East Coast, said it was old and dispirited, sodden with acid rain. They moved to the Southwest, where the sun shines, the girls have blue eyes, and people vote Republican.

This would be the greatest race ever run by a mortal. Spivak told himself it could be done. He could do it. Pepperoni surged through the veins of his tiny body. He had a heart of garlic.

The fate of the Big Apple rode on the winged feet of a native son. Marty Spivak pumped bagels.

The gods could not have been more sweet.

30.

There on the screen was the grave face of the network anchorman, Peter Drummond. Drummond had wry wrinkles on his forehead, sincere wrinkles around his eyes. "And this is Peter Drummond, continuing with our live, commercially uninterrupted coverage of the dramatic evacuation of the city of New York. This coverage is being coordinated through the studios of our network affiliate here in Washington. We still have no details about the background to this sudden, shocking move by the government. The President continues to meet with his aides, while the evacuation of the city proceeds. We have a report from Kathy Berglund at the White House."

A pretty young woman was shown standing on the White House lawn. The lawn was crowded with reporters and cameramen. Ms. Berglund was cool and composed. She was helping report the destruction of Manhattan. Had she ever lucked out! Tapes of this would be something for her grandchildren. Maybe she would get a shot at the "Today" show. What a break! She suddenly wondered whether the blue of her scarf went with the rust checks of her skirt. Oh, my God, she thought. She looked at her wristwatch to see if there was time to get rid of her scarf. Sure, show a little breast. Too late, the red light was on and Ms. Berglund's mouth began moving.

Ms. Berglund spoke with deep, round tones. "The President has still not appeared, Peter. We're told he's still meeting with the National Security Council. The President's press secretary, David Meyer, says there will be a status report given when, quote, 'we have all the pieces in the right places.' Meyer said there is no reason for panic. The only people affected by this, he said, are the people of New York and they are being evacuated as quickly and orderly as possible."

Drummond was on the screen again. He looked concerned. "Kathy, we've been receiving rumors here for the last hour or so that Terry Wyland, the President's National Security Adviser, either resigned or was fired not long after the Council meeting began. Do you know anything about that?"

Ms. Berglund's throat was bare when she came back on screen. "Yes, Peter, we've heard the same rumors. There is a lot of confusion here right now, as you might expect. It's just impossible to know what to make of something like that. Meyer has been holding forth in the press briefing room since this started, but most of what he's had to say has been repetitious. The rumor that Terry Wyland has been fired or resigned is just that, at the moment—a rumor."

"Thank you, Kathy. This is Peter Drummond bringing you live, commercially uninterrupted coverage of the evacuation of the city of New York. Time now for station identification." Drummond hadn't realized Kathy Berglund had such a good body. The image of her breasts lingered before him as though Drummond had inadvertently looked at the sun.

Under ordinary circumstances Jim Quint and Marissa Stanley would have swum the East River and sprinted through the streets of Queens along with everybody else. They were both young and fit enough. The problem was Quint's broken leg. A hard cast was scarcely designed for swimming, and made him a candidate for the rail if he tried a bridge.

Marissa walked with Quint as he hobbled up the street on crutches and took a seat on a sidewalk bench in front of Central Park West. "Looks like it's dig-in time for me. Melvin Mole time. You go on now, you've got plenty of time for a basement in Queens." Quint got out the fixin's and rolled himself a joint. He lit up and took a hit. "You go on now, Lost Horse."

"Are you mad?"

Quint stretched out to rest his leg on the bench. "No, no. You go on."

"Asshole," she said. She plopped down beside him.

They listened to the sirens in Queens and the Bronx and across the river in New Jersey. Manhattan was strangely quiet. It was as though the police department understood that people didn't want to put up with a lot of pointless racket in their last few minutes.

Marissa said, "I'm not leaving without you, so if you care anything about me, you'll get on your God-damned feet. Now. I mean it."

"Foot," Quint said. He got to his feet.

"Whatever."

Quint glanced down Central Park West. "The Museum of Natural History's just a few blocks down the street. I like the idea of all that granite and stone. Maybe there's a basement there."

"We can join the fossils."

"Brontosauruses and pigs that sing and horses that fly."

"You think you can swing it that far, el Gimpo?"

Quint grinned. "No problem, mon. Cool runnings." He kissed the good woman who was with him and started swinging crutches.

William Derrigan's hand-held camera had a good lens. The helicopter cruised above the Hudson and East rivers, providing Derrigan's viewers with a ghastly, breathtaking close-up of the exodus. From a distance, the river looked like a smelt run: the water thrashed with people. In Derrigan's close-ups, however, they didn't look panicked; they didn't seem to be swimming furiously. In fact, most took their time, using a breast stroke or side stroke. One thing at a time; first they had to get across the river, then they had to run, and run, and run, until it was okay and they were safe. Most of them used an aid of some kind, anything that would float. Old people and babies were lashed to the jetsam of the doomed city. A piece of plywood was worth more than a roll-top desk. A man with a cheap pine table had a prize. Men and women pulled wives and husbands, mistresses, boyfriends, children. Fathers and mothers pushed babies in wicker baskets.

"These are the people of New York," William Derrigan said. He paused dramatically. "Fleeing."

Derrigan's lens turned on the streets where people inched their way to a bridge, a tunnel, a subway entrance, or to the water. Each person had to choose, had to decide, had to cast his or her lot with this or that glut of bodies. A din of sirens in the suburbs wailed above the reckoning.

Peter Drummond was back on the screen, looking solemn and haggard. "This is Peter Drummond here again at our studio central in Washington, bringing you live coverage of the evacuation of the city of New York. As you all must know by now, an atomic bomb is set to detonate on Manhattan at 5:30 p.m., Eastern Standard Time. Kathy Berglund has another report from the White House. Kathy, has there been any movement down there?" Drummond watched the monitor eagerly.

Berglund wore a new scarf, one that better, but not quite, matched the checks on her skirt. "No, Peter, there hasn't. A few minutes ago, David Meyer did say..." Berglund stopped talking and listened to instructions in her earphones. "Peter, I'm told that David Meyer, the President's press secretary, has a statement to make."

Meyer was a tall man, broad of girth, hairy of ear, disheveled, a grinning Southerner. "If y'all..." He waited for the photographers to adjust their lenses, waited for the reporters to get their notebooks out and for the commotion to settle. "If y'all will just listen up now, I'll tell you what I can about this awful business. Because of the sensitive nature of what we're up against, I'll say my piece, and that has to be it. I won't be able to answer questions. I'm doing my best to get you everything I can as soon as I'm able."

"Listen, David..." a reporter began.

"Those are the rules, Jerry. It has to be this way. Right now all the President's energies are directed at saving lives in New York. I'm sure you understand that."

The cameras had moved onto Jerry—proof to his editors in Chicago that he wasn't writing his stories off a television set.

Meyer read a statement from a single piece of yellow legal paper.

"The government has been told, presumably by the party that planted the bomb, that it is set to go off at 5:30 p.m. today. This is the time we released an hour ago, and it still stands. We are told the bomb is planted in Manhattan and is to be detonated by an automatic timing device.

"The bomb is said to be made of plutonium-239 and is of a type similar to that detonated over Nagasaki. It has a strength of one megaton, or about 20,000 tons of TNT. This again is roughly the same size as the Nagasaki bomb. The bomb itself was made by the Vrienden, an antinuclear group in Europe that you may have read about in the press. We believe the plutonium was stolen and the bomb loaded by Alistair Jones, a former British member of a United Nations nuclear inspection team, aided by a Dutch member of the Vrienden, Wim van der Elst. We believe the bomb was flown to Amsterdam by a heroin and hashish smuggler. We believe the bomb was smuggled into the Caribbean and flown to the United States from the western tip of Jamaica. We believe the person who planted the bomb is a lone indidvidual, possibly driven by psychotic impulses. We do not know his identity. There is no evidence that he is part of any organization or conspiracy. The President and the Secretary of State are in communication with the other nuclear powers. The Soviets and the Chinese know the situation.

"The President asks that you and yours join him on his knees before the Almighty in praying that some way can be found to stop this damnable outrage."

Standing at the podium, David Meyer was overcome by tears. He wadded up the piece of paper and stuffed it angrily in his pocket. Like sharks, wire service reporters went for the tears, a poignant bit. The University of Texas later paid $50,000 for the piece of yellow legal paper; oil bucks outbid Harvard's endowment.

The camera lingered on Meyer an eensie bit too long, then returned to Peter Drummond. The makeup man had added a touch of shadow under his eyes while Meyer had been on camera. Drummond looked even more solemn and grave. "A terrible, terrible day," Drummond said. Meyer's face faded on the monitor behind him. "That was the first official word from the President, relayed through his press secretary, David Meyer. Meyer said the President is working with officials coordinating the evacuation of New York and would remain with them until he is assured everything possible is being done to save human lives. Meyer confirmed the time of detonation." Drummond looked at a clock on the wall. "That's one hour from now. Kathy, isn't it unusual for the President to stay in Washington at a time like this? I'd have thought they'd have taken him to the underground headquarters at Weather Mountain, Virginia."

Kathy Berglund was back on screen again, minus her scarf. The White House was directly behind her. A breeze stirred. Kathy felt it on her breast. Oooh! "Yes, it is, Peter. Very unusual. We have always been told that it is standard operational procedure in cases like this to remove the President and his government from the capital. Sources here say the President is convinced this is an isolated incident and he does not want to cause concern or panic in other cities. Meyer said the President wishes to stress that we are in no danger of attack or anything of that sort. There is one bomb and that bomb, apparently, is in Manhattan. The Soviets have been informed of the problem." Kathy felt good about herself: the New Berglund. She turned slightly to get a better angle on the wind.

Drummond saw that the scarf was off again. Oh, yes. "Kathy, do we have word on Gregor Rostov, the Soviet foreign minister? Has he been safely evacuated from the United Nations complex?"

Damn! Berglund had completely forgotten to ask Meyer about Rostov. "Peter, David Meyer says communication with New York is very difficult. He says a helicopter has been sent to retrieve Rostov, but we don't have word back yet on the success of the mission."

Drummond wondered what Kathy Berglund would be like in bed. He had been married for thirty years. Sex with his wife had the charm of humping a tub of cold gravy. "There are fifty-five minutes left," he said. "Kathy, did you have something more to add?"

Kathy Berglund's nipples went rigid from the wind. "Peter, Meyer's assistant, Larry Tanner, tells us the President has ordered all military units in the area to assist in the evacuation. There doesn't seem much anybody can do here except wait."

"This is Peter Drummond, returning with live, commercially uninterrupted coverage of the evacuation of New York City on this terrible, terrible October afternoon. We would like to remind you that this network will stay with the story through the night. Beginning Sunday, we will bring you the first of a week-long retrospective of the city, with an emphasis on the borough of Manhattan. This has been an island of Broadway, of the book and magazine publishing industries, of writers, actors, dancers, singers, and artists; a city of bohemians, jet setters, junkies, and great sandwiches." Drummond was on a roll. He was fabulous under pressure. Everybody knew that. "We'll talk about the great ones— Boss Tweed, Robert Moses, Phil Rizzuto." For a moment, Drummond's mind went blank. He couldn't think of any more New Yorkers. "Frank Gifford, William Burroughs. A city of hookers and ward heelers, of fabulous wealth and the poverty of James Baldwin's Harlem." Had Baldwin written about Harlem? Drummond wondered. "And New York is a city of sports legends. Jackson Rainey will be showing you film clips of some of the great moments at Ebbets Field, the Polo Grounds, Yankee Stadium, and Madison Square Garden. Remember Bobby Thomson's home run, Pat Summerall's field goal? You'll see it all on this network. Right now, with fifty-three minutes left, we take you live to William Derrigan in our network helicopter above the city."

"Peter, the evacuation continues. It's impossible to describe. I don't know what to say. It hardly seems possible that so many people could live on that island. And of course, we've been talking about Manhattan. The other boroughs of the city will be hit by the blast also, but the effects shouldn't be as severe. In those boroughs, the streets leading into the Connecticut and Long Island countrysides are packed with people. Manhattan, surrounded as it is by water, has a special problem.

"The bridges appear to be downright dangerous, Peter. There are what look to be sudden, violent shifts in the crowds on the bridges. It's hard to tell what causes this. People panic and surge this way and that. Many of those on the rails aren't making it, I'm afraid. The sirens which were wailing constantly earlier on are quiet now. The city streets are blocked by abandoned vehicles. Large numbers of firemen and New York's Finest are making no effort at all to leave themselves. Manhattan is a community as it has never been before, trying to save as many lives as possible. This is William Derrigan above the city of New York."

Peter Drummond was back on screen: "There are now fifty minutes until an alleged atomic bomb is to be detonated on the island of Manhattan. We'll be going to the White House in a few minutes where our correspondent, Kathy Berglund, will have another report. But first we'll have a short talk with Dr. Arleigh Dooley, a nuclear physicist at the University of Maryland. Dr. Dooley, as succinctly as possible, just what is it these New Yorkers are facing here?"

Dr. Arleigh Dooley was a powerfully built man in his early fifties. He had a broad, square jaw, and thin, straight blond hair, which he combed to one side. He had been an athlete in his day. He looked uncomfortable in a tie and jacket. "I won't comment on how fucking stupid we've all been to let this happen to ourselves."

The engineer assigned to edit naughty words in a six-second delay before the telecast went on the air let Dooley's expletive stand. Her parents lived in Queens. If somebody wanted to can her, let them.

"I'm told this is a one-megaton bomb," Dooley said.

Drummond said, "A surface detonation."

"Well, I can give you some rough estimates of what might happen if the bomb were detonated in midtown Manhattan, say, at Times Square. I hasten to add these are only rough figures. First off, a ground-level blast produces a sudden shocking increase in air pressure—far greater, for example, than if the bomb detonated overhead, as it would in an incoming missile. About eighty-five percent of people not protected by a blast shelter will be killed in a three-mile radius; that takes in Central Park to the north and Wall Street to the south.

"There'll be a soundless flash first. The shock wave will follow.

"The level of these surface fatalities will diminish with distance. Incidentally, you're looking at a crater 175 feet deep and 700 feet wide at the point of detonation. Reinforced concrete buildings will be leveled between about Fourteenth Street and Seventy-second Street. Most small buildings will collapse between Fourth Street and Eighty-second Street, and damage will be severe from about Wall Street to Ninety-sixth Street. Your viewers in the metropolitan area should not look at the blast. They can suffer temporary blindness up to thirteen miles away."

"That's a very good point, Dr. Dooley. Those viewers in surrounding communities in Connecticut, New York, and New Jersey should watch the blast on television. Our cameras and your eyes will be protected by the same lens filters we use to photograph eclipses of the sun."

"Then there's the heat to consider. We're lucky that we're looking at a ground detonation here. An air burst would spread the heat over a far wider area. I think it's safe to say that anyone exposed in Manhattan, Brooklyn, Queens, and the Bronx, in addition to Staten Island and northern New Jersey, will be subject to first-degree burns—that's equivalent to a bad sunburn. All residents of Manhattan and some in the other boroughs can expect second-degree burns. Second-degree burns cause blisters, infections, and scars. If you're exposed from the tip of Manhattan to about One hundred twenty-fifth Street—and well into Queens and New Jersey—you risk third-degree burns. Third-degree burns destroy tissue. If you have third-degree burns over twenty-four percent of your body, or second-degree burns over thirty percent of your body, you risk shock. You'll die without medical care."

Drummond shook his head.

"Last of all, Mr. Drummond, New Yorkers will have to face the consequences of radiation. The wind, you say, is blowing to the northeast at about fifteen miles an hour."

"Off the Atlantic, over Brooklyn and Queens."

"That's good for Brooklyn and Queens, but not good for New Jersey and upstate New York. When you have a ground blast, pulverized earth, bricks, stone, and debris will be sucked up in a mushroom and pushed inland by the wind. The lighter the particles, the farther they'll travel. Anyone on the streets from Greenwich Village to about Eighty-sixth Street will suffer heavy doses of radiation. A trail of radiation will blanket a twenty-five-mile-long swath within a day. Radiation of this level—say, above 2,000 rads—affects your central nervous system. You have convulsions. You can't control your muscles. You go into shock, then a coma. You'll live two or three hours.

"At slightly lower levels of radiation—from about 500 to 2,000 rads—you'll lose the lining of your small intestines and bowels. You'll vomit. You'll have diarrhea with blood in your stool. Your bone marrow will be damaged—but that's moot, because you'll die anyway within a week to ten days."

"It is now forty-five minutes until detonation," Drummond said.

"Those levels will be spread about fifty miles inland from today's wind. In twenty-four hours from 100 to 500 rads will be pushed as far as one hundred fifty miles. We're looking at a path, say, of about eighteen miles wide. There is less effect on your gut at this level, but the bone marrow is damaged. You bruise and bleed. You're susceptible to infection. You lose your hair in about three weeks and have a year or two to live. If you're exposed to less than one hundred rads, you probably won't die right off, but you'll have nausea, vomiting, diarrhea, intestinal cramps, dehydration, apathy, and fever. The high risk here, Mr. Drummond, is cancer—cancer of the thyroid, the lungs and bones, breast cancer in women. Of one million people exposed to this lower range of radiation, about ten thousand will develop cancer. The number of childhood cancers of those exposed as a fetus would be about double that rate."

"What should people do, Dr. Dooley?"

"Obviously, people should get as far away from the city as possible in the time remaining. Be underground at blast time. Keep your eyes closed. Protect your ears. It doesn't take much to shatter eardrums. If there is any chance that you'll be in the open, wear light-colored clothing. Dark clothing absorbs light and heat."

"Thank you very much, Dr. Arleigh Dooley. Forty-four minutes until detonation. Our report now from Kathy Berglund at the White House."

"Peter, the President's press secretary, David Meyer, told us a few minutes ago that we should not lead people to believe there may be a last-minute reprieve or that the bomb might somehow be found. He reaffirmed that the government believes a one-megaton bomb is set to detonate on Manhattan island at 5:30 p.m., Eastern Standard Time."

31.

The owner of the flickering candle said, "Well, I guess it's finally going to happen. We all knew it would, sooner or later." Jim and Marissa could hardly see her at first. When they got closer, they saw she was a woman in her late fifties with silver hair and a rueful smile of resignation. "Come on in, join me please."

"We'd love to," Marissa said. She looked at Quint. "Jim?"

"Good a place as any," Quint said.

Marissa said, "I brought us some groceries in case we have a wait later on." She took Quint's crutches and helped him to the floor.

"I cleared all the furniture out of here. Mostly boxes of eyeballs. I don't know why I went to the effort, probably read it somewhere."

"Eyeballs?" Marissa asked.

"Large ones for whales, little ones for birds."

"Oh, I see. Phony eyeballs."

Quint said, "We've got the right wall if the blast comes from midtown."

Jim and Marissa introduced themselves to the woman, whose name turned out to be Roberta Hook. Hook had a tweedy, scholarly look about her. She uncapped a bottle of Irish whiskey. "Would you join me for a little toddy?" Without waiting for an answer, she slid plastic cups their way and poured liberally. "I guess most people opted for basements under glass and steel. I'm a brick and mortar woman."

"Did you get that jar of green olives?" Quint asked. He started pawing through Marissa's grocery bag.

"I stole this whiskey. First time in my life I ever stole anything. Shall we listen to the radio or wait it out?"

Quint said, "I'd just as soon wait it out."

"Same here," Marissa said.

"The folks who run the liquor shop are friends of mine. We go to the opera together and sometimes to see the Yankees. That Billy is the most damn fun. Every time he comes out of the dugout you wonder what's going to happen next." Roberta poured more whiskey for everybody.

Quint said, "You work here, don't you?"

Roberta Hook smiled. "For more than thirty years now. I started out wanting to be a sculptor. Then I got a job here helping with the reconstruction of extinct species, working from shards of bones, footprints in ancient mud, that kind of thing. I sculpt bones." Hook was obviously good at her work and was proud of it. "Species come and species go, you know, some of them rather rapidly, it seems. It's always interesting to speculate on what went wrong."

Gregor Rostov's appointment as Soviet foreign minister capped a thirty-five-year career in the Communist party. As he had risen in authority and influence, he had become more and more removed from the concerns of ordinary Muscovites. Because the people's grain programs were forever being sabotaged by bad weather, average Muscovites waited in line for their ration of meat and bread. They had to wait months or years for an apartment.

Rostov had his groceries delivered to him. If he wanted a larger apartment, he took it. Nobody argued with Gregor Rostov.

The people were told their sacrifices were necessary so that the Soviets could match the American arsenal. The Soviets were the terrible Slavs, fair game for the French and German armies. Those who were old enough to remember how it was at Leningrad suffered the deprivations with a shrug, dulling themselves with vodka.

So it was that Gregor Rostov, who had been driven everywhere for more than twenty years, found himself lining up at an entrance to the Lexington Avenue subway. A huge crowd had formed around the subway entrance. There were crowds at all the subway entrances in the city. At this entrance, as with the others, the crowd inched slowly down the stairs and into the tunnel, already glutted with people. Those well inside the tunnel—the ones who had acted quickly and bet their lives on the subway—squeezed and scrunched together, tighter and tighter, so that their fellow New Yorkers might also live.

Those still on the street, as Rostov was, listened to civil defense instructions on transistor radios. They were pressed together belly to back, belly to back, down the stairs and into the tunnel. Rostov, who had forgotten to remove his Order of Lenin medal, pressed forward along with the others. There was no traffic in the streets except for ambulances trying to get the sick and disabled uptown and into a basement. The drivers used the streets when they could, or took to the sidewalks, whenever they could move.

It took Rostov an agonizing forty-five minutes to begin the descent down the concrete stairs. He read posters for movies and Broadway plays as, at last, his head was below ground level and he would be partially protected from the direct force of the blast. In another half hour, the stairs turned to the left and he was protected from the heat. Twenty minutes later, he reached the main tunnel. The entrance was flanked by posters advertising a Broadway musical starring Mickey Rooney as a submarine commander. Ann-Margret was the navy's first female submarine executive officer.

The downtown side looked less crowded—most people believed the bomb would go off somewhere in midtown so as to gut the heart of the city and take out Wall Street at the same time. Nobody knew for certain that a midtown atomic bomb would flatten the southern tip of the island, but everybody assumed that it would.

Instinctively, the people on the platforms flanking the tracks—which were depressed four or five feet lower in the tunnel—began to inch uptown. The people collected on the tracks and track beds and made their peace. Many of these were older people or women with children. They couldn't compete on the platforms. If the bomb were planted directly above them and they were to become part of some Yankee Stadium–sized crater, then so be it. They prayed, some of them. Some listened to the radio. Others closed their eyes and remembered.

A sudden shift in the platform crowd pushed Rostov perilously close to the edge of the pit. He thought for a moment he could stop the momentum, but no. He lost his footing and fell. He was agile for a seventy-year-old, and braked his fall with the heel of his hands. He landed next to a round young woman holding two babies.

"Are you hurt?" she asked.

"Nyet," Rostov said. "I'll be fine."

"There's room here, I think," she said.

"Why, thank you," he said. He joined her in a space that was really only big enough for her alone.

"Are you sure?" he asked.

"It shouldn't be forever," she said. "At least, I hope not."

The heat from the accumulated bodies rose and hung in the tunnel. Rostov saw that he and the young woman were sitting in oil and filth. He took off his jacket and noticed the Order of Lenin. He unpinned the medal and slipped it in his pocket.

The Soviets were whooping it up in Moscow Center. Yuri Andropov had had color Sonys installed around the KGB party room so everybody could have a good view of the fun. He had tubs of vodka packed on ice. He had cases of cold Czech beer on hand. He had young girls with suntans flown up from the Crimea, and big-titted Hungarian girls as well. It had been a fabulous operation. New York! Yes!

Andropov saw the destruction of New York as compensation for the bungled attempt to kill the Pope. Andropov blamed the Pope debacle on the Bulgarians. He was undeterred. He was like a kid with a new car. He wanted to see what the Soviet Union was capable of doing.

First, the Brits had floated Alistair Jones to keep an eye on the bomb. Then the Bread-and-Butter Man reported the lovestruck Jones's bizarre agreement with the Vrienden.

Harold Woods took over from there. He was a master.

Andropov had done his bit by making sure that his old friend Gregor Rostov would be in New York to be blown up so as to distract suspicion from the Soviets.

There had been talk of secretly flying Harold Woods in to join the party. After some thought, Andropov said no. There was a risk that Woods's flight would be discovered. Woods was too big a prize to lose in a moment of foolishness. Besides, the Russians were sentimental. Kim Philby was going to be at the party. He was an old man, and must know by now that Harold Woods would one day succeed to his title as the world's greatest liar and traitor. Andropov told his friends it would be callous to fly Woods in. Why not let the old man live out his last days in glory? What did it hurt?

Both Woods and Philby were anomalies, as far as the Soviets were concerned. Austrians ski. Australians swim. Bulgarians lift weights. Russians play chess and lie. The Soviets were shocked when Bobby Fischer took the world chess championship from Boris Spassky. Then Woods emerged, a facile, fluent liar. There were those who went so far as to say he lied as well as Joseph Stalin even, and there was a man who knew how to lie.

All the top people in the KGB hierarchy were convinced that Woods was going to turn out to be an even better worm than Philby, although they went out of their way to assure the proud old man that his achievement was beyond challenge. The reason why Woods was such a good worm was that the Americans were so gullible. In Moscow, the Soviets routinely proclaim that yak manure is chocolate pudding. The Soviet on the street knows it's yak manure, and so doesn't eat any. Soviet supporters in the U.S. always wind up going yuck with a look of disgust on their faces.

Owing to his abilities as a liar, Woods had a fabulous future as a worm. He was the perfect parasite, so obnoxious as to be invisible among Americans. He would lie there in the American intestines, his presence undiagnosed, sucking the nutrients from the American intelligence establishment. The Soviets were delighted. They expected great things of Woods.

It was sweltering in the subway tunnel, and Gregor Rostov was soon awash with sweat. He stripped off his jacket and rolled his shirtsleeves above his elbows. "This will be good for us to sit on," he said.

"Are you sure? It looks like a new suit."

"I'm certain. Besides, it's hot," Rostov said.

"Were you in the army?" she asked. She found herself having to put her thighs and legs over his.

"The army?"

"Your medal there. The one you took off."

The young woman was holding two babies and Rostov had to help support her by hand. He smiled. "Oh, yes. I was in the army. I was at a meeting, you know, and we all wore our medals. I am originally from the Soviet Union."

"I was wondering about the accent. My name's Mary Frances, and these are my babies—Thomas, he's two and a half, and my daughter, Gloria, she's just about thirteen months now."

"My name is Gregor. I want to thank you again for sharing your place. Will your husband be okay? Is he in the city today?"

Mary Frances laughed. "No, Gregor, I ain't got a husband. Three months ago I had an old man, Gloria's father, but he got blown off the eighty-sixth floor of the Trade Center."

Rostov said, "He what?"

Mary Frances turned on his lap and grinned. "He got blown off the Trade Center building. He was a window washer, made big bucks. Anything above fifty or sixty floors or something like that, and he got paid hazardous-duty pay. He had this union contract, see, that said it took so many hours to do so many windows. Well, Sam—his name was Sam—he could wash those windows in an hour and a half, maybe two hours. He used the bucks and the time to put himself in the drug business. It was nice; we had a cute little apartment down in the Village."

"How did the accident happen?"

"I see what you're sayin'. The reason he got paid more for working way up there was not just because of the height.

You're just as dead from an eight-floor drop as eighty, if you see what I mean. The reason for the high bucks is the up-drafts from the heat down on the streets. Sam said the wind blows so hard up there, if you unzip your fly the wind'll rush in and pop you like a balloon. Sam always smoked pot while he worked. He probably forgot to hook his safety snaps or something. You forget things when you're high." Mary Frances was forced by the weight of her babies to lean against Rostov.

The young woman was soft on Rostov's lap. Her hair was against his face and smelled good. She was round, pliable, like a woman named Irina whom Rostov had known briefly when he was a rising young KGB officer. Irina too had had babies, like Mary Frances's little Gloria and Thomas. Irina had been a loving person, as Mary Frances seemed to be.

"Are we going to die?" she asked.

Rostov removed his rimless spectacles with his free hand. "I don't think so, unless we're right under the bomb. I should think we have a chance. If we're evacuated through these tunnels, we shouldn't get too much radiation."

Hideo Yasuda bought three television sets in Wilmington, Delaware, continued past Baltimore, and headed south down the Eastern Shore of Maryland. By 4 p.m., he was in Norfolk, Virginia, and got a room at the Dismal Swamp Motel, which advertised free cable TV. Yasuda bought himself a six-pack of Budweiser at a Seven-Eleven and returned to his room. He took a shower and tuned in his sets, one to each broadcast network and the fourth to cable news.

American television knew how to cover disasters; Yasuda had to admit that.

In the beginning, the helicopters hovered directly over the beleaguered city showing people swimming, people on the bridges, and people lined up at subway entrances. In the final half hour, they swooped low over the deserted island and recorded on videotape the startling face of Man-hattan without people. The pilots, knowing they were part of history, swooped low over the streets, making nervy runs up and down Manhattan's famous avenues, circling her museums and playgrounds—giving folks one last look at the grand city.

Steam could be seen rising from an abandoned pretzel cart. The American flag flapped listlessly above City Hall. A man on the shore of the reservoir in Central Park took a hit off a wine bottle and waved happily at the helicopter.

These shots were relayed directly to Washington, where engineers moved frantically from one camera to another in their makeshift studio central. Peter Drummond and the other network anchors provided a running commentary.

At 5:20 p.m., the helicopters suddenly rose above the skyline and the pilots, going full throttle, raced to an assigned location six miles away. There the helicopters hovered like wary butterflies. The pilots were told to expect some action when the shock wave rolled their way.

Yasuda drank some Budweiser. He wished he had a cold bottle of Sapporo. He had decided to drive south and catch a little sunshine in Florida. He wanted to go to Disney World in Orlando. A gay acquaintance in the Village had once told him about a nutty ride called the Mickey Mouse Loop-de-Doop. Yasuda wanted to try it out.

Various angles of the New York skyline were being shown on all four sets. The commentators gave summaries of Manhattan's history, and made rough estimates of how many people had made it off the island. The networks had by now filled their studios with atomic blast experts from the Pentagon. These experts were called upon to make various estimates: the number of degrees Fahrenheit at ground zero; the expected increase in mutant babies; how many days a radiation victim could expect to keep his hair.

The television cameramen in the helicopters wore special dark goggles given to them by the military. The military told them what filters they should use for their cameras.

Since Peter Drummond was the most famous of the American television anchormen, that's the network Yasuda listened to.

Drummond began a minute-by-minute countdown at 5:20 p.m. "I'm sorry to say that there are just ten minutes to go."

Yasuda loved it. It was wonderful to see the Americans suffer like this. Stupid bastards. He wondered, suddenly, if they might not close Disney World and the Mickey Mouse Loop-de-Doop out of some misguided sense of mourning. They wouldn't do that, would they? Yasuda was suddenly infuriated. He wanted to go on that ride. The Americans deserved everything they got.

Gregor Rostov and Mary Frances were listening to a transistor radio playing about fifteen yards downtown of them. "The bomb is scheduled to detonate at 5:30 p.m., that's ten minutes from now. Civil defense authorities advise all residents of all New York boroughs plus northern New Jersey to get underground immediately. Do not attempt to look at the detonation; you may be blinded. Do not remain in the open. Do not stay above ground. After the blast, stay where you are until further instructions. There is shelter enough for everyone. Please help your neighbor."

Little Gloria's pink jumpsuit was soaked with urine, so her mother stripped her out of it. The naked baby stared up at the man with the long face. It was hot in the tunnel. Gloria felt good with her jumpsuit off. Then Thomas began to fuss.

"Would you like me to take the little girl?" Rostov asked.

"Would you?"

"I've had children and grandchildren," Rostov said. He took Gloria and sat her on his bare forearm. She seemed happy there, listening to civil defense instructions on the radio. Gloria felt the urge, and peed gleefully. At her age, peeing was one of life's pleasures. She gave a warm smile to the man holding her. The urine slid down Rostov's forearm and reached his elbow before he felt the warmth.

Mary Frances saw what had happened. "Gloria!"

"Oh, it's nothing," Rostov said. He wiped his forearm on his thigh. Gloria giggled. Peeing was nice. Her bladder felt good.

When the man on the radio said there were eight minutes left, Mary Frances gave Gregor Rostov a kiss on his lips. She was a romantic, and she was about to die. "Would you hold me, please? I need to be held."

Comrade Rostov kissed her as he had once kissed Irina. Mary Frances had sweet, clean breath. She smelled delicious. He could feel the softness of her breast against his arm. He held Mary Frances tightly. He too needed someone to hold. He felt her face burrowed against his neck.

"I'm frightened," she said.

Gregor and Mary Frances clung to one another. Little Gloria and Thomas thought all the closeness was just grand. "We're underground," Rostov said. "Let us hope for the best."

32.

There was an eerie silence over the doomed city as Mad Marty Spivak turned onto Fifth Avenue for his run to the bottom of the island. Spivak thought of Pheidippides, Emil Zatopec, Frank Shorter, Alberto Salazar, great sufferers all. Spivak threw off his light shirt and let the cool air wash across his hairy, suffering little body.

The city was Spivak's family. It had nurtured him. He was a celebrity of the city, claimed by Italian, Jew, Irishman, and Puerto Rican alike. Only the New York blacks withheld judgment. The blacks went for the razzle-dazzle of the sprints. Let those stupid whites and Kenyans get out there and suffer over ten thousand meters. They could have it.

Mad Marty owed the city. He was determined to repay the debt. He didn't know what he was going to do when he got to the bomb, but there had to be something.

Pain spread to his arms and legs, but Marty ignored it. Abandoned cars made it impossible to run in the street. Spivak concentrated hard on the sidewalk ahead. Each block was a triumph, a victory over the limitations of the human body. When he reached Central Park, his body slipped into a trance-like netherworld. The pain receded. He drove himself harder yet. His body was on fire, but he coasted in warmth.

Marty Spivak and Officer Boyd Eiseley, NYPD, approached the fateful spot from opposite ends of Christopher Street. Eiseley got to the door two strides in front of Spivak and without a word yanked it open.

The shirtless Spivak hopped to the bottom like a spider monkey. He looked at the bomb, then up at the cop. "Gotta Phillips?"

"Shit," Eiseley said. "Gotta Swiss army knife."

"Give it to me."

Eiseley followed Spivak. He slapped the knife firmly into Marty's hairy hand.

Eiseley had seen Mad Marty hurtling down Madison Avenue several times. He'd seen Spivak's picture in the sports pages several times. Spivak had quick hands. "Go, Marty. Do it."

Spivak was on to the second screw. "What's your name?"

"Boyd."

"Boyd, do you believe what's happening here?" Mad Marty was on to the third screw quickly, his hand working, working, working. It was a good, solid bomb—eight screws on the back plate.

There was a lot of screwing yet to go.

At the two-minute mark, Peter Drummond's network began experimenting with split-screen images of New York landmarks. The Statue of Liberty, the Empire State Building, and the World Trade Center towers by the financial district were the favorite targets of the photographer's long-distance lenses.

The directors finally settled on the World Trade Center towers on the left—the second-highest buildings in the world—and the Empire State Building on the right.

The center of the screen was reserved for the skyline and the rising mushroom of tragedy's end.

In Paris, Jacques de Sauvetage and his wife, Emilie, turned off their television set. They had cleared a space in Emilie's painting studio, which had skylights and so was open to the early evening stars. They had opened a bottle of good Bordeaux. They had a little Brie and some Camembert. They had a wonderful collection of dancing records—sambas, rhumbas, waltzes. They were fabulous dancers. They could have taught at Arthur Murray's.

Op Premier was elegant, graceful, a simple, honest man, out of fashion. In the final minute, he danced with Emilie and wept.

Jim Quint, Marissa Stanley, and Roberta Hook watched the flickering candle and waited. Hook sipped her Irish whiskey while Jim and Marissa smoked a joint.

Hook looked at her wristwatch. "I suppose any time now," she said.

Bison Jim slipped one arm around Lost Horse Marissa and the other around Roberta Hook and held them close.

"Thank you for your company," Roberta said.

"Good luck, friends," Marissa said.

Jim Quint said, "Soon come, Jah. Cool runnings everybody."

The skyline looked exquisite, splendid, in the distance. Protestations to the contrary, the fact was that the borough of Manhattan was the center of Western civilization. The confluence of power and great wealth had made it so. There were more talented minds, talented writers, artists, musicians, scholars, on that one island than any other place on the planet.

"Thirty seconds," Drummond said.

New York waited.

"Ten seconds," Drummond said.

Drummond waited, saying nothing, then:

"So long, Manhattan."

DETONATION

33. *A flash preceded the shock wave that*

blew a huge crater in the sidewalk in front of the Lion's Head and shattered windows all along Christopher Street. There followed a Manhattan mushroom of broken glass, bottle caps, rodent droppings, used condoms, pizza crust, an unopened letter, an unpublished poem, a violin fret, a bra clasp, a McGovern for President button, a corroded money clip, and a ceramic cat's paw, in addition to the remains of Mad Marty Spivak and Officer Boyd Eiseley. The mushroom rose from the crater in the sidewalk and drifted across Sheridan Square.

It wasn't all that much in the way of booms. Nevertheless, the explosion—likened by Jimmy Breslin to the timbre of an Irish fart—caused an estimated two hundred cardiac arrests in New York subway tunnels, a fact duly recorded in the *Guinness Book of World Records* under the category: Heart attacks, group.

The folks in the subway tunnels didn't know what to think. This was not the Armageddon they had been led to expect.

There was a curious, uneasy silence in the tunnel where Comrade Gregor Rostov and Mary Frances clung together with little Gloria and Thomas. Was there another blast to follow, one that would take them under?

The man on the radio said, "There has been a nonatomic explosion in lower Manhattan. Stay where you are until further instructions. Stay where you are. Do not leave your shelter."

"Something went right! What went right?" a man shouted.

Rostov smiled. It was the same as in the Soviet Union.

"Don't worry, the city'll fix it," another man said.

Nervous laughter fluttered down the tunnel.

"An anomaly," a woman said. "No problem."

There was more laughter as New Yorkers began to think there was a chance. Something had gone right. They waited, feeling more hopeful each minute.

If things went right in Manhattan, they went slightly astray in Washington, D.C., and Norfolk, Virginia.

There were mitigating circumstances in Peter Drummond's case. If the bomb had been planted in Washington and the network had its New York facilities for studio central, there would have been no problem. The coverage of the Sheridan Square Incident, as it later became known, was accident-prone from the start. People in the field made do with borrowed equipment; the Washington studio was chaos.

Drummond later maintained the red on-camera light had never come on. He said he had peripheral vision, developed over years in the business, for an on-camera warning light. The floor people said yes, it was on, but Drummond blew it. Drummond said it made sense that if Manhattan was going to blow, the directors would keep the camera on the skyline. People were waiting for a mushroom. What if the bomb fuse was only delayed? What could he, Drummond, possibly have to say at a time like that?

Everybody in the land who owned a video recorder had it turned on to capture the historic moment. Drummond was the most trusted man in America. He had the highest Nielsens, naturally.

The camera, which had been on the Manhattan skyline, switched suddenly to Washington. Drummond was tipped back in his chair, laughing. "How do you like that, a classy adieu—so long, Manhattan—and then the place doesn't even blow up. My God, did you see the tits on Kathy Berglund? Where's she been hiding those things? Wouldn't you just love to burrow your face right in there?"

At the time, Peter Drummond was earning $1.5 million a year as network anchorman.

When the television people announced that the nonatomic explosion had in fact taken place on Christopher Street and that Sheridan Square was not contaminated by radioactivity, Yasuda turned off his Sonys. He had failed. There was only one thing he could do. He put on his ceremonial kimono and went into the kitchenette to get a knife.

The kitchenette was supplied with warped aluminum pots and pans, cups, glasses, and plates of various styles, stainless steel eating utensils, and serrated steak knives. There were no cutting knives. Yasuda took a steak knife and went outside. It was a warm, clear day; the streets were mostly deserted because people were indoors watching the story unfold from New York. He walked down the street until he spotted a McDonald's hamburger outlet. The golden arches on the red background made him think somehow of the rising sun, and home.

He knelt down on the McDonald's parking lot and thrust the steak knife into his abdomen. There would be no followers to cut off his head, but he would die honorably. He was ready to pull the knife down so as to disembowel himself, when a hand that held a bag of french fries took the knife from him and threw it away. The hand belonged to a sixteen-year-old drummer on his way to practice with his band. A half hour later, a surgeon in a nearby naval hospital saved Yasuda's life with some swift, nifty work.

When the sirens sounded all clear, folks of the Big Apple emerged, grinning, to discover that more than a hundred jewelry stores had been trashed by last-minute shoppers. They didn't care. The fresh air felt wonderful. They were alive.

There were casualties, of course. In addition to people with bad hearts, several hundred more drowned, smothered in sweltering subway tunnels, or had their plugs pulled in the rush to leave the island.

*E*PILOGUE

Mad Marty Spivak's hairy right hand, still

clutching the Swiss army knife, was found an hour after the blast. Pieces of Officer Boyd Eiseley were tentatively identified as John Doe, blood type B.

A third casualty at Sheridan Square that day was General Philip Henry Sheridan. The blast popped Sheridan's ankles and the Army of the Potomac's commander of cavalry went down, his head stuck shoulder deep in sodden goo. The old campaigner bit the mud.

Phil's ankles were eventually repaired and he was restored to his pedestal, but the witches, warlocks, and squirrelly-whirlies of the Village said he had changed somehow. Being a general wasn't what it used to be. Sheridan wasn't the lovable old Indian killer they had known. The charming, genocidal glint in his eye was replaced by a worried look, they said.

The freakos said Phil had bad karma.

At their various parties that night, New Yorkers wanted to know what had happened. Sicilians had emigrated to New York because being a gangster was more profitable there. They didn't like the idea of some nut queering the deal with a bomb. Whatsa matta heah? they wanted to know. Who fucked up? The Irish had been dumped on for generations—potato famines, the British Army, politicians of all persuasions. They gathered en masse in their bars and proceeded to get smashed, rowdy, boisterous. Who did it to us this time? they shouted. Puerto Ricans complained of stupid gringos. The blacks were enraged at whatever mothers had done this to them. And the Jews, who really did know what it was like to be dumped on and who had vowed to take it no more, asked the same question.

Who fucked up?

It was a hell of a party. One few New Yorkers would forget.

That night reporters began to work their way through the tangle of rumors, guesses, allegations, omissions, and lies. The truth—as with all the facts in the assassination of John Kennedy—would never be known. The participants involved turned on one another with different versions so that everyone might get to write a book.

The nature of Marty Spivak's mad run was made clear when a report by a family that had fled the city was matched with eyewitness accounts of Marty's sprint down Fifth Avenue as the last stragglers went underground. The statue of Gen. Philip H. Sheridan was toppled three weeks later and replaced by a splendid statue of Marty Spivak, running, grinning, fist clenched and thumb held high in triumph.

Phil Sheridan still had his partisans, even after all those years, but the history buffs were overwhelmed by public sentiment. No general could do much in those circumstances, not even Phil. The Mayor thereupon took an unadopted little girl down to the Village to smash a pitcher of draught beer over Marty's foot in the christening of Spivak Square.

But Spivak Square was a minor story compared to the nationally televised hearings of the Manhattan Special Investigation Project, an independent inquiry headed by the Chief Justice of the United States Supreme Court. Millions of Americans settled in front of their Sonys and Panasonics with stubies of beer and bowls of popcorn at the ready.

Angus Garvey, citing ill health, resigned as director of the CIA as the Manhattan Project began. He was replaced by John Tarnauer, who, as acting DCI, was second to testify, following the former National Security Adviser, Terry Wyland.

Before he took the witness stand, Wyland got old videotapes of John Dean's classic performance and studied them carefully. He decided he couldn't follow Dean's script exactly. There would have to be some adjustments of strategy.

Wyland's wife, Adrian, was excited. Hadn't they made a television movie out of Maureen Dean's life? Adrian thought about making an appointment with Vidal Sassoon, then tought no, why not give Linda Jean down the street a break? "John and Mo," Adrian said softly. "Terry and Adrian. Terry and Adrian." Mrs. Wyland was thrilled with the sound of fame.

A few minutes before he was to appear before the nationally televised hearings, Terry Wyland slipped into the toilet and put a fluid in his eyes with a small dropper. His eyes thus glistening with tears, Wyland and his wife walked dramatically into the hushed room. Wyland took his seat before the panel. His wife, in her new hairdo, sat just behind him so she'd be on television too—a loving woman supporting her husband.

Wyland carried a Bible his great-great-grandfather had brought across the country from Independence, Missouri, to Albany, Oregon, in a covered wagon. It was a handsome Bible, worn smooth by loving hands. Generations of births, marriages, and deaths were recorded in its pages. Wyland solemnly handed the Bible to the Chief Justice. He swore to tell the truth, the whole truth, and nothing but the truth. The television lights were blinding. The cameras showed every sincere pore on Wyland's nose.

To lie with his hand on that Bible would be to spit in the face of whatever it is that separates men from beasts.

Wyland almost told the whole truth. His only deviation from the original script was that he blamed everything on Georgie Farr. The inaction was Farr's fault. Farr had scoffed at reports from Amsterdam. He didn't want The Op to embarrass itself by chasing after an improbable rumor.

Wyland told the Project he considered his first duty was to his country. He said Georgie Farr couldn't face the truth— that he was single-handedly responsible for Manhattan's fate—so he had run out into the street and croaked of a heart attack. Farr had a history of heart trouble.

The reporter from the *Washington Post* the next day began his story with, "It was dark, dark, dark midst the blaze of television floodlights yesterday when former National Security Adviser Terry Wyland gave his version of the decisions leading up to the Manhattan tragedy."

John Tarnauer agreed precisely with Wyland: Georgie Farr was an incompetent who had lied and equivocated on an issue that could have cost the city of New York.

One by one, all the members of the National Security Council told the same story. The Lyle administration remained on the droshky, clinging firmly to a handrail of mendacity.

Two days before Inspector Jacques de Sauvetage was to appear on the stand, Jim Quint received a telephone call from Paris. A woman with a quiet, tired voice—speaking in slow but clear English—said, "Mr. Quint. My name is Emilie de Sauvetage. My husband, Jacques, told me recently that if he should happen to die in what in my opinion are mysterious circumstances, I should call you immediately. He left me this number." She fell silent.

Quint swallowed. "He's dead." It was a statement, not a question.

"A car ran a red light at an intersection where he goes to eat lunch every day. Jacques was crossing the street."

"Did they catch the driver?"

"No, monsieur. They are trying, they say."

"I'm very sorry about your husband, Madame de Sauvetage. He was a fine man."

"He was murdered," said Madame de Sauvetage.

"I think so," Quint said. He hung up. The cover-up had begun. He was now alone with his story. Nobody would believe him. If he tried, he too would be murdered. There was nothing he could do. Nothing. He was enraged and his leg itched inside the cast. He hobbled angrily into the kitchen for a beer.

Harold Woods, whose testimony before the Manhattan Project was considered by observers to be the most impressive of all—at once candid and filled with revealing details—corroborated the evidence of Georgie Farr's having been a pathological liar. For his poised, thoughtful performance, Woods was rewarded with a dual appointment as director of counterintelligence for the CIA, in charge of the Company's security apparatus, plus Georgie Farr's spot on The Op, with immediately expanded responsibility and authority.

There was, of course, jubilation in Moscow when Woods's promotions were announced. The Soviets had been depressed after New York survived, but this was a grand rebound. Yuri Andropov, who had kidney problems and was under doctor's orders to take it easy on the vodka, got pissed to the gills in celebration.

It turned out that Alistair Jones, in one of those moments of self-doubt rarely allowed saints and great men, had the good sense to write Jim Quint a letter. He posted this letter in Karachi before he left Pakistan, and it arrived in Chevy Chase, Maryland, along with the avalanche of Humper Staab mail. It wasn't until two weeks after the Sheridan Square incident that Jim and Marissa, opening letters as they watched the Manhattan Project on television, came across Jones's letter in the pile:

> Dear Mr. Quint,
> It was at Milan, if you recall, that you interviewed me about my duties as a UN inspector. You promised to keep my identity confidential and to use my quotes in the spirit in which I said them. I read your article in *Rolling Stone* and you kept your word. You write very well indeed.
> I have done something, Mr. Quint, that I believe is in the best interest of you, me, and all our fellow inhabitants of this planet. There are, I realize, attendant dangers. If anything happens to me before I have a chance to tell what I have done, you may use this letter to tell the public for me. I ask you only to serve the truth.
> I was sent to the Vrienden by the British government to watch the bomb. The man who sent me had no idea at the time that I was the very last person he should pick for the mission. I had become disgusted at participating in what I regarded as a sham—the charade that all's safe and well with the spread of nuclear energy. That, Mr. Quint, and I was genuinely attracted to Anita Hawkins. I love her

dearly. I will do anything for her. If you'd ever been married to a woman like Debra, you'd understand why. You should ask me about her lips sometime.

The Vrienden have an absurd notion that unilateral disarmament will work. To start the process they want to turn in their bomb, loaded, at a televised news conference. Please, I know that kind of thing is doomed. But I want it for Anita. What it will do, for a fact, is prove my point about the dangers involved in the sheer number of facilities capable of producing plutonium.

This letter is probably a foolish waste of time. You'll be watching me on television going over the same details I'm giving you here. Incidentally, I was fortunate to meet a charming young American named Gerald Murrant. After Harold Woods, I had just about given up on Americans. (You should exclude yourself from my generalizations.) Gerald is a hashish smuggler, but a fine chap. He gives the Vrienden all the hash they can smoke as his contribution to the antinuclear movement. Murrant agreed to smuggle us and the bomb to Karachi and back. There were dangers involved, but he said yes, he'd do it. He said even smugglers can help the cause.

We flew a small plane to a remote area of Pakistan where poppies are grown for heroin. We took a bus to Karachi, where we rented a car. I led the two of them through the security defenses at the Pakistani plant, splitting the operation into two nights. The first night, I explained to Wim how everything worked and the codes used to identify various grades of spent fuel and plutonium. I had Wim practice using the equipment. I want him to be a convincing witness at the press conference when Anita and the Vrienden turn in the loaded bomb.

There is something I should now tell you. The first night, when I explained the codes, I reversed everything, so that plutonium became spent fuel to Wim and Gerald and spent fuel became plutonium. The next night, Wim loaded the bomb while Gerald and I videotaped the process.

I did this, Mr. Quint, because a bomb loaded with spent fuel will still prove my point. Wim could just as well have loaded the bomb with plutonium. I'm a security man. I do hope you don't think I'm insane enough to load that bomb with plutonium. Harold Woods used to call me a worry-wart, and I guess I am. I suppose you Americans would call this a hustle or a sting. I plead guilty. It was the only way I could think of to shake people up and get them to think. I do apologize if it causes any inconveniences.

Cordially,
Alistair Jones.

Quint read the letter twice through and started giggling. Alistair Jones had bang dulued everybody. Jim Quint's kind of guy.

Quint wrote a story about the letter which was syndicated to newspapers throughout the world and was taken by the British intelligence establishment as a redemption of character. In the end, Jones hadn't let the side down. The British could tell their American cousins at Langley to shove it. They could wear their trenchcoats with pride. That sneering old owl, George Smiley, who on a BBC television series had come in from retirement to humiliate them, could bloody well shove it as well.

The *Daily Telegraph* said Alistair Jones singlehandedly laid to rest the ghosts of Guy Burgess, Anthony Blunt, and Kim Philby, traitors to King/Queen and Country. *The* (London) *Times* agreed. The *Guardian* and *The Observer* said Jones's was a perverse, awkward sort of heroism.

Jim Quint knew it had to happen. The old boys in Bison had told him blizzards follow harvest. It happens every year, they said. You carve your kid a jack-o'-lantern and drink a little cider; two weeks later the snow comes whipping down from Canada. Or maybe you drink a little bourbon and have a chance to score some poontang from a good-looking woman. But because of the whiskey you can't get it up, and in the morning you have a blinding headache and puke your guts out. Happens every time. Quint was told that if he ever dodged a neat left hook, for Christ's sake to watch out for the right cross. The old boys had endless stories. They had arrived at this truth independent of any knowledge of Oriental or other exotic philosophers. They spit Copenhagen and watched the folks in the local saloon.

This advice—not to get too cocky after good fortune— was their legacy to Jim Quint.

Quint was off his feed for a month following the incident at Sheridan Square. Manhattan had survived. Quint was nervous and irritable.

"What's wrong?" Marissa asked.

"Bounty," Quint said.

"Bounty?"

"Bullshit's next."

Sure enough, the next day the doorbell bonged, one of those cozy domestic sounds evocative of warm fireplaces et cetera. Quint answered the door.

A man with yellow hair said, "Are you James Allen Quint?"

"That's me," Quint said.

The yellow-haired man slapped an envelope into his hand, closed the door, and was gone.

He was the man with the shovel.

Quint had no sooner recognized the smell than the phone rang. He picked up the receiver. He saw that the envelope was from a lawyer. Leo Tull was on the line.

"Jim! Jim!" he said. He was excited. "Have you been served yet?"

"With a cold beer or a tennis ball? A man just shoved an envelope in my hand. I haven't opened it yet."

"Don't bother, Jim. Everything's gonna be okay. Just fine, Jim."

Quint handed Marissa the envelope and motioned with his hands for her to open it. "You want to tell me about it, Leo?"

"Just a little mix-up is all, Jim. No problem."

"What mix-up?"

"Um, we're being sued, Jim. No problem."

"We, Leo?" Are you pregnant or do you have a turd in your pocket?" Quint could see Marissa shaking her head as she read the document.

"Well, it's a long story, Jim."

"For how much money?"

"This is going to sound like a lot of money, Jim, but you have to understand it's part of the legal game. They always ask these insane sums of money but the judges and the jury know it's haw-hawing is all."

"How much, Leo?"

"Uh, six point four million dollars, Jim."

"Have you come to the how much line, Marissa?"

"Six point four million dollars," she said.

Quint said, "The rest of it, Leo."

"There's this man named Humperdinck Staab."

"Nickname of Humper, I bet."

"Yes, yes. It seems this guy Humper Staab was a CIA agent, deep covert, he says in the letter. He says almost everybody in Europe and the Middle East knew he was a secret agent. He says as an experienced thriller writer you would know that. He says ever since the President recommended your books on television that he's been subjected to the some-long-word of his family and friends."

"The word is obloquy."

"Yes, that's it, Jim. Obloquy. You know your fancy words."

"How in the hell am I supposed to know about CIA agents in the Middle East? I make stuff up. I should be able to beat that." Quint felt a little relieved.

"Yes, but then there's the other."

"What other, Leo?"

"Remember me telling you when I operated communications gear in the marines, and I was once sent on a secret mission with a take-charge CIA agent? That's my Czechoslovakian story."

"Humper Staab."

"I'd been trying to remember that guy's name ior years. But there's no problem, Jim, because I've got an ace lawyer.

Former editor of the *Harvard Law Review*. I say *editor*, Jim. He clerked under Hugo Black. I phoned him and gave him the gist of Staab's suit, and he said no sweat. He said if you want, we can burn Staab's ass in a countersuit. And you want to hear the kicker, Jim, the real kicker?"

Quint was afraid to ask. "What's that, Leo?"

"This guy just loves the arts, Jim. Has these paintings on the walls of his house and everything. He said no fee for a writer. No fee, Jim. Cinch case. No problem."

Quint said, "I'll read my summons or whatever and call you back, Leo." Editor of the *Harvard Law Review*. Clerked under a Supreme Court justice. Free? Cinch case? Quint recognized the old, familiar odor. He was suddenly frightened. He leaped up and hobbled into his study. He started pawing through folders in a metal filing cabinet.

"What are you looking for?" Marissa asked.

"There's one thing I've learned in this world, and that's to have insurance. I sat down with the best underwriter I could find and made sure I had proper insurance. It costs me a big toe and an earlobe, but it's worth it. It covers my condominium, my car; it covers me when I'm scuba diving, mountain climbing, wrestling alligators, you name it. I don't do any of those things, but it's comforting to know I can if I want. Ahh, found it." Quint adjusted his broken leg and traced the paragraph with his finger. "Here it is, love, Section F."

"What's Section F?"

"As sure as the Cubs fade in August." Quint's shoulders slumped. He stared at his expensive insurance policy. He had been told it was the best money could buy. He shook his head.

"Tell me." Lost Horse Marissa was anxious.

"Anomalies not covered," Quint said. "There's always a Section F. Don't let anybody tell you differently."

"I don't know about you," Marissa said, "but I learned that back in Montana."

The man with a face like a giant wrinkled hound was seventy-four years old and obese. LaTrobe Blue looked down at his stomach and heavy body. He was beginning to have breasts like a woman. His body hadn't seen the sun for years; the white began at the collar and his wrists. Blue pulled on his underwear and reached for his trousers. Harold Woods could not be allowed to begin his new position in the Central Intelligence Agency. Too much was at stake. If the American cousins were too stupid to make the connections, then something had to be done. Blue was surprised Georgie Farr hadn't come to the same conclusion.

Blue wheezed and picked up his socks. The socks had become a chore lately. Blue had been kept on at MI6 long after retirement age because of his fabulous skills in spotting liars and teaching others how to spot them as well. Blue was so good he really didn't need a polygraph. He regarded himself as an artist rather than a technician. Her Majesty's Government had a driver pick Blue up from his tiny London flat so that the old man wouldn't have to ride the Underground. He had gout and it was difficult for him to walk. His wife and daughter were both dead, so he sat alone at night. He listened to the BBC.

There was a radio play on BBC Radio 4. Blue liked radio plays. When he had been a British agent in occupied France, the BBC was home. He liked all the educated chit-chat and palaver.

LaTrobe Blue began the task of the shoes. They would never believe him; an old fool, they'd call him. They'd claim he was senile, embittered over Woods having beaten his students. Everybody stood to lose—the British, the French, the Germans, the Italians, everybody. It was up to Blue; there was nobody else.

Blue got out the .38 Beretta that had been given to him by a French compatriot in the underground of 1942. He got out his ancient, scarred leather suitcase with the secret pocket that had taken the Beretta across many a border and checkpoint. It would be easy. He would take Woods close up, at point-blank range. There were seventeen Nazi SS officers— if they could have been raised from the dead after forty years—who could testify as to LaTrobe Blue's nerve and skill. Woods had no reason to fear a fat old man. If Blue got away, that was fine. He'd spend his days listening to the

BBC. If he got caught, the press would really have a crazy Brit to write about. Either way, before he died, LaTrobe Blue would bring one last liar before the bar.

He knotted his tie and rang for a taxi to take him to Heathrow Airport. His trigger finger was steady and sure on the telephone dial.